D1154864

FOLKTALES OF
BRITAIN & IRELAND

BETWEEN WORLDS

FOLKTALES OF BRITAIN & IRELAND

KEVIN CROSSLEY-HOLLAND

illustrations by FRANCES CASTLE

CANDLEWICK PRESS

For Oscar and Hal and Somerset and Jago
and Danylo and Miriam with love
K. C.-H.

First published in 1987 as *British Folk Tales* by Orchard Books.
The versions of "The Green Children," "The Peddler of Swaffham," "The Wildman," "Shonks and the Dragon," "Sea Tongue," "The Dead Moon," "Yallery Brown," and "The Green Mist" reproduced in this collection were first published in 1997 as *The Old Stories* by Colt Books.

First U.S. edition 2019

Library of Congress Catalog Card Number 2019939181
ISBN 978-1-5362-0941-9

19 20 21 22 23 24 LSC 10 9 8 7 6 5 4 3 2 1

Printed in Crawfordsville, IN, U.S.A.

This book was typeset in Historical Fell Type and Wolfdance.
The illustrations were created digitally.

Candlewick Press
99 Dover Street
Somerville, Massachusetts 02144

visit us at www.candlewick.com

FOREWORD

Few things are more enjoyable than sharing a story, and it's what people have done for thousands of years.

These days, we're likely to share a story on the page or the screen. However, few people knew how to read or write until two or three centuries ago, and so they told their stories around a hearth or a campfire, to while away a long journey or to help a young child get to sleep. This is what folktales are — short, imaginative stories to be shared by families, by communities, by everyone.

It is believed that Europeans began to write folktales down when they realized these stories were in danger of being forgotten during the Industrial Revolution, when so many villagers were moving away to mill towns and cities in search of jobs.

The world portrayed in folktales is very different from our own. Technology and social norms have evolved and advanced significantly since the folktales in this book were first told. The tales' descriptions of lifestyles and relationships of a simpler time — agrarian and very basic — can sound romanticized and even idyllic. The reality would have been much harsher. None of us would wish to return to a time when intolerance, let alone outright cruelty, toward specific individuals or groups for their gender, age, physical characteristics, disability, or beliefs was regarded as acceptable.

Overall, folktales have a huge cast of characters — humans, superhumans, fairy folk, ghosts, familiar animals, and fabulous beasts. In creating this book, I have ranged widely to show not only different types of tales and different themes, but the best and worst of human nature — loving, hating, hoping, fearing, brave, cowardly, smart, dumb, patient, impetuous, and, thank goodness, able to laugh, not least at ourselves.

In most of my retellings, I've chosen to stick closely to the original written versions because they're a fine and valuable way of understanding the people who first heard and enjoyed them. This may mean that readers, in some cases teachers and librarians, have a bit more work to do. They will need to contextualize and become interpreters of these folktales themselves.

But isn't it true that the very best way to prepare for tomorrow is to better understand today — and yesterday? We forget the past at our peril.

Kevin Crossley-Holland
Chalk Hill, December 2018

PRONUNCIATION GUIDE

An acute accent over a vowel indicates that the vowel is stressed.

broch	brock
Caher	kair (to rhyme with "fair")
Caoilte	kwéel-teh
Cappagh	káppa
Carterhaugh	kaarter-hóck (-aa as in "car")
Cilgwri	kiligooree
Croagh Patrick	kró pátrick (-ro as in "grow")
Cumhail	cool
Cwm Cawlwyd	Koom kówl-wid (-ow as in "now")
Glynllifon	glinn-hlivvon (hl as in Welsh "llan")
Gruagach	gróo-gock
Gwernabwy	gwairnáb-wee
Llanddeusant	hlan-thíssant (hl as in Welsh "llan," -th as in "there," -i as in "high")
Llyn y Fan Fach	hlinn a ván vaack (hl as in Welsh "llan," -aa as in "car")
Loch Lein	loch láyne
Mellte	méhlte (-hl as in Welsh "llan")
Mochno	mock-know
Myddfai	múthi (-u as in "but," -th as in "thin," -i as in "high")
Rhedynfre	reddúnn-vre (-u as in "bun")
shillelagh	shaláylee
Sychryd	súckrud (-u as in "but")

CONTENTS

MAGIC AND WONDER

ADVENTURES AND LEGENDS

FAIRIES AND LITTLE PEOPLE

MEN AND WOMEN

Wits, Tricks, and Laughter

Ghosts

MAGIC AND
WONDER

THE DARK HORSEMAN

AS JEMMY STRODE DOWN THE ROAD TOWARD SLANE, HE BEGAN to say praises.

"Praise be and I'm Irish," he said, and he swiped at a clump of nettles with his shillelagh. "Praise be and it's the top of the summer."

Jemmy's trousers flapped at his step, and by the wayside poppies and cornflowers nodded and smoldered and beckoned.

"My cattle are sleek," said Jemmy. "They're buttery creatures! They'll sell well at the fair. And then I'll drink a whiskey, and take a turn on the whirly horses, and talk to a girl with stars in her eyes."

Jemmy Nowlan managed an estate outside Slane, and he had sent ahead his cattle early that morning. Jemmy was tall; he was very strong; he was handsome and he knew it.

"Praise be and I'm alive," he said. "Praise be and praise be and I'm Jemmy Nowlan."

While Jemmy was crossing the lonely heath just outside Slane, the clouds began to gather over his head. The summer's day that had begun with scents and sunlight and soft, dawdling wind turned beetle-browed and bellowing.

Then Jemmy heard the *clop-clop* of a horse coming up behind him. He turned 'round and saw a young dash of a man riding on a black horse: black velvet jacket, white ruffles at his wrists, starched wing collar, shiny black boots. Jemmy looked up and saw the man was swarthy, and his skin was almost dark.

"Jemmy Nowlan," said the dark horseman. "I've been looking for you all along the road."

Jemmy Nowlan looked startled. He was sure he had never seen the man before.

"Come on up!" said the man. "There's a storm in the sky. I'll take you to the fair at Slane."

Jemmy didn't want to ride with the man. Not at all. He began to feel quite nervous and gripped his shillelagh.

"Ach!" he said, looking up at the black sky and wrinkling his nose. "The weather'll be all right again soon."

And as he spoke, Jemmy could hear distant voices inside his head. He had to close his eyes to make out what they were saying: "Still such a young man and just whisked away . . . they took him into the heart of the hill . . . a prisoner, a prisoner . . . and the only times they ever saw him was along with the walking dead. . . ."

"I'm going there myself." The voice of the horseman brought Jemmy back from his reverie. "And I'd be glad of your company, Jemmy Nowlan."

"Ach!" said Jemmy. "It's not for the likes of me to ride with the likes of you."

"I insist!" said the dark horseman.

Then he stooped and just touched one of Jemmy's shoulders with his ivory whip. And the next thing Jemmy knew, he was mounted behind the dark horseman, and the horse was galloping like a storm of wind.

The horseman said nothing. He rode until the horse was sweating and foaming. He rode across wild heathland where Jemmy had never been before, and on into an oak forest, and up to a castle set in a green glade.

As they cantered over the drawbridge, Jemmy saw that dozens of servants were standing on the steps around the massive door, waiting to welcome them. They all wore the same livery—green and gold—and all of them were even smaller than the two dwarfs at Slane fair.

"Well!" they cried. "If it's not Jemmy Nowlan! Welcome, Jemmy Nowlan!" Scrambling around him and standing on each other's shoulders like a troupe of acrobats, they helped Jemmy dismount; they dusted him down; they put a drink in his fist; they asked what they could do for him.

"Very civil!" said Jemmy, and he took off his jaunting hat and ran a hand through his thick black hair. "Very civil!"

Then Jemmy saw a man waiting on the steps. He stood at least as high as Jemmy's hip, and he was wearing a sumptuous outfit of purple and gold. *So, Jemmy Nowlan,* Jemmy thought, *the lord himself has come out to greet you.*

"Take Jemmy to his room," said the lord. "Let him dress."

Several servants escorted Jemmy to his room high in the castle, where his new clothes were waiting for him: a fine suit of brown velvet, and a cap and feather. Jemmy looked at them in admiration and delight.

Far from leaving him to look after himself, the green-and-gold

servants would not allow Jemmy to lift a finger. They took off his jacket and his shirt and his trousers, untied his shoes, and washed him after his journey.

"Blessings!" exclaimed Jemmy. "There's nothing wrong with this."

When the little servants had dressed Jemmy in his resplendent new outfit, they hurried him down a flight of circular stone steps, trotted beside him along dim passageways, and led him into the castle hall.

This hall was hung with Chinese lanterns and garlands of flowers. Down at the far end, a group of musicians was playing fiddles, and the little people were dancing.

"There's a sight!" said Jemmy. "I've never seen anything so lovely."

Most lovely of all were the ladies, with their flashing smiles, and their throats and fingers all covered in jewels. Jemmy couldn't take his eyes off them.

"Will you dance with me, Jemmy Nowlan?" asked one lady.

"No, Jemmy!" said another. "You must dance with me."

And like a hundred winter sparrows and a hunk of bread, all the ladies in the hall pecked and squabbled over which of them should dance with Jemmy Nowlan in his brown velvet suit.

"Blessings!" cried Jemmy. "I'll dance with you all."

And that is what he did. He danced with every single lady in the room, until he was so tired that the only thing he wanted to do was to lie down there and then, and go to sleep.

"You can take Jemmy Nowlan to his room," said the lord, "and put him to bed. But first he must tell me a story."

"Ach!" said Jemmy. "I don't know a story. I don't know a story or I can't remember one. I was never any good at books."

"Shame on you, Jemmy!" said the lord.

"I'm very tired now, your lordship," said Jemmy. "Let me lie down and go to sleep."

"Sleep!" said the lord. "Not if I can help it." He signaled to a little redheaded man. "Throw Jemmy out!" he shouted. "He can't tell a story. I won't have anyone in this castle who can't tell me a story. Throw him out! He's not worth his supper."

So the redheaded man pushed Jemmy through the great castle door and down the steps and over the drawbridge to the edge of the oak forest.

Jemmy found a bench there, and it was long enough for him to lie on. He had just stretched himself out and put his head in the pillow of one palm when three men stepped toward him through the dim light of the wood. They were carrying a coffin.

Jemmy quickly sat up again.

"Oho!" said the men. "It's Jemmy Nowlan! He's just the man! We need a fourth man to carry this coffin."

So Jemmy fell into step with the three men and shouldered his share of the coffin. They walked through the forest. They brushed through hedges and stumbled over ditches; they tramped over firm fields and plunged through treacherous peat bogs, until at last they reached an old churchyard at the head of a valley. It was overgrown with long grasses, and the graves were green with moss and lichen. Here the procession stopped. The three men and Jemmy laid down the coffin.

"Who'll dig the grave?" asked one man.

"We must draw lots," replied their leader.

Jemmy Nowlan drew the short straw. The three men found him an old rusty spade, and he dug and he dug all night until the grave was gaping — six feet long and two feet wide and eight feet deep.

When Jemmy had all but finished, the leader of the group walked up and stood at the edge of the grave.

"This won't do," he said. "Not at all. This is never the place for a grave."

"Why not?" asked Jemmy.

"I'll have no one buried here," said the leader. "My own father's bones lie in this churchyard."

So the three men and Jemmy had to shoulder the coffin again. They tramped over firm fields and plunged through the treacherous peat bogs until they reached a second churchyard.

"Jemmy Nowlan," said the leader, "you must begin again."

"Curses!" said Jemmy. But the three men stood around him so that their shadows fell onto his in the moonlight, and he knew that he had no choice in the matter.

When Jemmy had finished digging the grave, one of the men asked, "And who shall we put in the coffin?"

"No need to draw lots!" said the leader. "Lay Jemmy Nowlan in the coffin."

The three men grabbed Jemmy and tried to throw him to the ground.

Jemmy yelled and wrestled; he landed huge punches on all three men. Had they been merely human, they would never have been able to withstand them. But after a while Jemmy felt himself weakening, and it was still three to one.

Then Jemmy saw that the leader had a forked hazel twig tucked into his belt. Jemmy bared his teeth. He shook like a dog. He jerked one arm free and grabbed the twig.

"I have it!" shouted Jemmy. He leaped up and whirled the twig 'round his head three times and then struck each of his enemies with it.

That was the end of the fight. The three men fell backward and

rolled over and lay face down in the dew. None of them even twitched a finger.

The coffin stood apart, gleaming white in the moonlight. No hand touched it, and no voice spoke.

Jemmy ran out of the churchyard. He had one thought in his mind, and that was to put as much distance as he could between himself and the three men, in case they should rise up again. Still holding the hazel twig in his right hand, he ran straight over the firm fields and zigzagged over the peat bogs; he worked his way through hedges of briar and thorn until he found himself standing in front of the castle again.

As Jemmy crossed the drawbridge, dozens of green-and-gold servants came out to meet him, as they had done before.

"Welcome!" they cried. "Welcome, Jemmy Nowlan! Come on in now! His lordship is waiting for you."

The servants led Jemmy down dim passageways and into a room where the lord of the castle was reclining on a velvet couch. "Ah, Jemmy!" he said. "You've come back. You've come back with a story after all."

"Ach!" said Jemmy.

"I allow no one in this castle to eat or drink or sleep until they've told me something — something wonderful that's happened to them."

Jemmy began to smile. "In that case," he said, "in that case, my lord, I can tell you a wonderful story: the most wonderful of all."

"You can begin now," said the lord.

"There was a man," said Jemmy, "and he was very tired. He was as tired as a dog. So he stretched out on a bench. He pillowed his head in the palm of one hand. But before he had even closed his eyes, up stepped three men through the dim light of the wood. They were carrying a coffin. . . ."

The lord listened to every word, and at the end of the tale he clapped his hands. "A long journey," he cried, "and a grim load! That's a very fine story. A story of death in life," said the lord, "and life in death. You've earned your supper." He clapped his hands for a second time, and a succession of servants carried in food on golden dishes and crystal cups filled with wine.

"Eat and drink whatever you like," said the lord. "It is all for you."

Jemmy Nowlan was ravenous. With his right hand he still held the magic hazel twig, and with his left he ate and drank. When he had finished, Jemmy felt very strange and then rather dazed. He got up from the table, but at once he reeled sideways, and he toppled over. He lay on the ground completely and utterly dead to the world.

"Where am I?" groaned Jemmy. "My head! Where am I at all?"

He was lying up against a haystack and half a dozen hens were prinking around him.

Jemmy screwed up his eyes against the morning sunlight. "Curses!" he said. "The Sun's bright this morning." Then he looked at his crumpled clothing; the brown velvet suit, the cap, and the feather — they were gone, all gone.

"Ach!" said Jemmy in disgust. "I'll get even with them. That dark horseman!"

Jemmy sat up on one elbow. "Nasty things!" he said. "Bad and shabby, stopping me from selling my cattle, and they already at the fair. Ali!" Jemmy sighed. "They could have left me that brown velvet suit."

When he stood up, Jemmy saw that he had been asleep under one of his own haystacks, no more than a hundred yards from the comfort of his own bed.

“Devil take them!” said Jemmy. “Nasty and spiteful, that’s what they are! Envious things!”

Then Jemmy saw the forked hazel twig; he was still holding it in his right hand. He looked at the shine and shimmer of the world around him. “Blessings!” he said. “Praise be and I’m alive,” he said.

THREE HEADS OF THE WELL

LESS THAN TWELVE MONTHS AFTER THE DEATH OF HIS WIFE, THE king at Colchester married for a second time. He married for money.

The king's new wife had a nature as bad as her looks (she was hook-nosed and humpbacked and had yellow skin), and her dowdy daughter was little better. From the very day they moved into the palace, they began to spread false rumors about Eleanor, the king's own daughter.

"Too pretty for her own good," the new queen said.

"And knows it," said her daughter.

"Smiles at her father," said the queen.

"And stabs him in the back," her daughter said.

"The king wants my money," said the queen. "And I want you to inherit the crown. You, not sweet Eleanor!"

So the whisperings went on — suggestions that Eleanor had

disobeyed her father in this way or that, accusations in the king's ear that his own daughter was tart and even spiteful to her new stepmother and stepsister.

Eleanor was already unhappy about her mother's death; now she suffered more as her father began to harden against her. And the princess felt quite powerless to overcome the growing distance between them. There was no place for Eleanor in her own home.

Early one morning, Eleanor found her father walking in the palace gardens. "I want to go on a journey," she said.

"Maybe," said the king. "Maybe it's for the best."

For some time, neither of them spoke. The bees hummed around them. There were long pale sleeves of cloud overhead.

"I'll go miles and miles," said Eleanor. "I'll see what I see and meet whom I meet."

"I'll give you some money," said the king. "And I'll ask your stepmother to pack some clothes and food for you."

The queen soon had a bundle ready for her stepdaughter: no money, no clothes, nothing but a canvas bag containing coarse bread, cheese, and a bottle of beer.

So Eleanor left the court and Colchester and followed a track through a beechwood. Late in the afternoon, she entered a glade, and there she saw an old man sitting on a stone at the mouth of a cave.

The track led Eleanor right up to the old man. As she approached him, he called out, "Good day, young lady!"

"Good day!" said Eleanor.

"And where are you off to?" he asked. "What's the hurry?"

"I'm going miles and miles," said the princess. "I'll see what I see and meet whom I meet."

"Ah!" said the old man. "What have you got in that bag?"

"Bread and cheese," said Eleanor. "Brown bread and hard cheese and a bottle of beer. Would you care for some?"

"Thank you, young lady," said the old man, and he gave Eleanor a toothless smile.

When the old man had eaten, he stood up and thanked the princess again for her kindness. "Just beyond this wood," he said, "you'll come to a thick and thorny hedge. There's no way 'round it, and it looks quite impassable. Take this rowan twig," said the old man. "Strike the hedge three times with it, and say, 'Hedge, hedge, let me pass through!'"

"Hedge, hedge, let me pass through!" repeated Eleanor.

"The hedge will open at once," said the old man. "Then a little farther on, you'll find a well. Sit down beside it, and almost at once three golden heads will come up out of it."

"And then?" said Eleanor.

"The heads will speak. And you must do whatever they ask of you."

Eleanor promised the old man that she would follow his instructions. When she came to the hedge, she struck it three times and spoke the right words, and the hedge opened. Then she found the well and sat down beside it, and at once a golden head came up, singing:

> *"Wash me, comb me,*
> *Lay me down softly,*
> *And lay me on a bank to dry,*
> *So that I look pretty*
> *When somebody comes by."*

"I will," said Eleanor. She took her silver comb out of her pocket and combed the head's golden hair. Then she lifted the head out of

the dark water and set it down beside the well on a bank thick with wildflowers.

At once the second and third heads came up and sang the same song. So the princess combed their hair, too, and laid them beside the first head on the bank of wildflowers. Then she sat down herself and, feeling hungry, opened her canvas bag.

Before long, one of the heads said, "What shall we do for this girl who has been so kind to us?"

"She's beautiful already," said the first head, "but I'll make her quite enchanting."

"I'll make her body and her breath more fragrant than the most sweetly scented flowers," said the second head.

"And my gift will be no less," said the third head. "This girl's a king's daughter. I'll give her a happy marriage to the best of all princes."

After this, the three heads asked Eleanor to let them down into the well again. Then the princess continued her journey. It was already late in the afternoon, and the Sun was dipping; small birds sang charms around Eleanor's head.

Now the path led through a splendid park where huge old oaks stood separate and swung at ease. Through the trees, Eleanor could see huntsmen and a pack of hounds and then, as they rode closer, a royal banner.

The princess stepped off the path; she had no wish to talk to kings.

But the king saw Eleanor. He rode up to her and, what with her great beauty and her fragrant breath, he was so bewitched that he escorted her straight back to his castle.

How the king paid court to her! For day after day, he wove fine words and teased her and wooed her. And Eleanor, she was charmed, and she fell in love with the king.

Then the king ordered white cloth and green cloth and cloth of gold for Eleanor; he set aside rooms in the castle for her use; he gave her rings and brooches and necklaces.

So the king and the princess were married. And then, and only then, did Eleanor tell her husband that she was the daughter of the king of Colchester. Her husband laughed. He ordered chariots to be made ready so that they could pay Eleanor's father a visit. And the king's own chariot was padded with purple cloth and inlaid with bloodred garnets and gold discs.

At Colchester, the king had been restless and uneasy since his daughter had left court. When Eleanor found him, just as she had left him, walking alone in the palace gardens, he was overjoyed to see her and astonished at the splendor of her clothes and jewelry.

Then the princess called for her husband, and the young king told the old king all that had happened.

The court at Colchester trembled with excitement: ladies wondered what to wear; bells rang; fine dishes were prepared; the musicians tuned their fiddles and cleared their throats. Only two people failed to join the dance: the queen and her dingy daughter.

"May she curdle!" sneered the queen.

"Let her hair fall out and her eyes jaundice," sniffed her daughter, "and her teeth turn green."

No sooner had Eleanor left court for her new home, taking a fine dowry with her, than the king's stepdaughter announced that she intended to go on a journey to seek her fortune.

"I'll see what I see and meet whom I meet," said the girl.

Her mother gave her a soft leather bag stuffed with sweetmeats and sugar cakes and almonds and, at the bottom, a large bottle of the best dry Malaga sherry.

The girl dressed herself in her best traveling clothes, complete

with a cloak with a silver clasp and strawberry satin lining. Then she left the court and Colchester and for a long time followed a track through the beechwood.

Late in the afternoon, the girl saw the old man sitting on a stone at the mouth of a cave.

"Good day, young lady!" the old man called out. "Where are you off to? And what's the hurry?"

"What's that to you?" said the girl rudely.

"What have you got in that bag, then?" asked the old man.

"Good food and good drink! All sorts of good things," the girl replied. "But they needn't trouble you."

"Won't you give me a mouthful?" the old man asked.

"No," said the girl, "you miserable beggar! Not a drop, unless you promise to choke on it!"

"Bad luck to you!" muttered the old man. "Bad luck go with you!"

The girl turned on her heel and walked on to the thick and thorny hedge. She saw a gap in it, but as she was stepping through it, the hedge closed on her. The thorns pricked her cheeks and arms and legs. By the time she had gotten through, she was scratched and bleeding.

The girl looked around to see if there was any water — a pool, even a puddle — in which to wash herself. Then she saw the well and plumped herself down beside it.

At once a golden head came up, singing:

> *"Wash me, comb me,*
> *Lay me down softly,*
> *And lay me on a bank to dry,*
> *So that I look pretty*
> *When somebody comes by."*

The girl pulled the bottle of Malaga sherry out of the sack and banged the golden head with it. "Take that!" she said. "That's for your washing."

Then the second and third heads came up, and they met with no better treatment than the first.

"What shall we do for this girl," said one head, bobbing in the dark water, "who has been so cruel to us?"

"I'll give her sores," said the first head, "all over her face."

"Her breath smells bad already," said the second head, "but I'll make it smell far worse."

"She needs a husband, and she can have a husband," said the third head. "A poor country cobbler."

The girl walked on. That night she slept under the stars, and the next morning she reached a little market town. The people in the market shrank at the sight of the girl's face.

One cobbler, though, felt sorry for the suffering girl. "You poor old creature," he said. "Where have you come from?"

"I," said the girl, "am the stepdaughter of the king of Colchester."

The cobbler raised his eyebrows; his leather face creased and wrinkled in a thinking smile.

"Well!" he said. "If I can cure your face and give you good breath, will you reward me by making me your husband?"

"I will," said the girl. "With all my heart, I will."

"This box of ointment," said the cobbler, "is for your sores, and this bottle of spirits is for your breath." (Not long before, he had mended the shoes of a penniless old hermit who had given him the box and the bottle as payment.)

"Every day," said the cobbler, "smear the ointment over your sores, and take a nip of these spirits."

The girl did just as the cobbler told her. Within a few weeks,

she was not only cured but somewhat more presentable than before. She and the cobbler got married and, after a day or two, set out on foot for the court of Colchester.

When the queen discovered that her daughter had married a poor cobbler, she was so upset that she hanged herself. So the king at Colchester inherited her vast wealth, as he had always hoped to do.

"And out of this fortune," said the king to the cobbler, "I'll give you the sum of a hundred pounds, provided you take my stepdaughter away — take her away to the farthest corner of my kingdom and stay there with her."

So this is what the cobbler did. He lived in a little village for many years, mending shoes, and his wife brought in a little extra money by weaving. She made cloth and dyed it all the colors of the rainbow and sold it at market.

THE SMALL-TOOTH DOG

THE YOUTH PUT A SCOWLING FIST IN MR. MARKHAM'S FACE. "THE cash!" he growled.

The second and third youths stood behind Mr. Markham; they said nothing.

So the poor man had no choice. On the corner of his own street, only a hundred yards from the safety of his own home, he miserably fished in his pocket. But while Mr. Markham was delving for his wallet and loose change, a big dog, brindled and shaggy, came trotting around the corner.

"Help!" shouted Mr. Markham, and he punched one youth in the stomach and elbowed another in the face.

This big brindled dog leaped into the scrum. He ripped the youths' clothes; he bit their calves and arms until they yelped and yelped and ran off. Mr. Markham was left lying on the pavement, a poor fat bundle, his head cradled in his arms.

The big brindled dog gave him a friendly look, and Mr. Markham began to unfold and put himself together again. He looked at his cuts and bruises; he looked at the dog and shook his head.

"You've saved me a paycheck," he said, clasping a hand over the inner pocket of his jacket. "I've got the week's takings in here. More than a thousand pounds."

"I know," said the dog.

"Ah!" said Mr. Markham, and he gave the big brindled dog another careful look. The dog bared its teeth in a kind of smile, and Mr. Markham saw that they were surprisingly white and neat and small for such a large, shaggy animal.

"Well!" said Mr. Markham. "I'd like to repay you for your kindness. You've saved me a fortune."

"I've saved your life," said the dog, sitting back comfortably on his haunches.

"So I'm going to give you my most precious possession," said Mr. Markham.

"What's that?" asked the dog.

"How would you like the fish?" said Mr. Markham. "It can speak Welsh and Portuguese and Bulgarian and Icelandic and . . ."

"I would not," said the dog.

"What about the goose, then?" said Mr. Markham. "Would you like the goose? It lays golden eggs."

"I would not," said the dog.

"Well then," said Mr. Markham slowly, "I'll have to offer you the mirror. . . ."

"The mirror?" said the dog.

"If you look into it," said Mr. Markham, "you can see what people are thinking."

"I've no need of that," said the big brindled dog.

"What would you like, then?" said Mr. Markham.

"Nothing like that," replied the dog. "I'll take your daughter. I'll take her back to my house."

"Corinna!" cried Mr. Markham. "Well! A man must keep his word. My most precious possession."

"Me?" cried Corinna. "Not likely!"

"He's not an ordinary dog," said Mr. Markham.

"You're daft as a brush," said Corinna.

"You'll see," said her father. "He's waiting outside the door."

"Crazy!" said Corinna.

"Go on!" said Mr. Markham.

"Never!" said Corinna.

"You'll have to go, Corinna," her father said. "I want you to humor him. Take him for a walk." Mr. Markham smiled encouragingly. "You'll be back again for tea." Then he bustled his half-laughing, half-fearful daughter into her coat and out the front door.

"Corinna!" said the big brindled dog. "On my back! I'm taking you back to my house."

As soon as Corinna had mounted, the big brindled dog galloped off down the road, leaving Mr. Markham standing and staring after them. The dog galloped over the Common and down the gray November streets. He galloped until they were right out of the city. And at last, in the middle of a beechwood on the brow of a hill, they came to the dog's house.

"Here we are!" said the big brindled dog. "You'll like it here."

Corinna didn't like it at all. She didn't like the big brindled dog. She didn't like leaving home. She didn't like the countryside. And she didn't like the dog's damp, drafty house.

The dog brought Corinna good things to eat; he promised to look after her; he sang her praises. But whatever he did seemed only to

make Corinna more miserable. And one night, when she had been at the dog's house for about a month, Corinna began to shake and sob in her sleep, and she woke up already weeping.

"What's wrong with you?" asked the dog.

"Let me go home!" sobbed Corinna. "I want to go home. My dad! He's got no one to look after him."

"I'll take you home," said the big brindled dog, "if you promise not to stay more than three days."

"Three days?" said Corinna.

"That's it," said the dog.

"You're a great, foul, small-tooth dog," said Corinna.

"All right," said the dog. "I won't take you home."

But Corinna begged and wept and wailed, and at last the dog relented. "We'll be on our way at once," he said. "What did you say you called me?"

"You?" said Corinna, and she flashed her dark eyes. "You're sweet as a honeycomb."

"On my back!" said the dog. "I'll take you home."

The big brindled dog, with Corinna on his back, trotted along for mile after mile. They crossed major roads and minor roads and fields and streams. Then they came to a stile.

"Just remind me what you call me," said the dog.

Corinna was thinking of her dad and her own room and her job and her friends. "You're a great, foul, small-tooth dog," she said.

When he heard this, the big brindled dog turned his back on the stile. Deaf to all Corinna's cries and promises, he trotted straight back to the beechwood on the brow of the hill.

Corinna had learned her lesson. And when, a week later, only just in time for Christmas, she once again persuaded the big brindled dog to take her home, she made up her mind to say nothing but loving

things — the most loving things she could think of — until she was safely home.

"Sweet as a honeycomb," she said before they set off. And "sweet as a honeycomb" again at the stile. And in the dog's pricked ears for mile after mile, "Sugar . . . sweetie . . . honey."

It was already dark as they rounded the corner where the big brindled dog had rescued Mr. Markham from the three youths. The dog quickened into a canter.

"This one," cried Corinna. "The red one!" she cried, half-joyful at getting home at last, half-angry with the dog for having taken her away for so long. She dismounted and stepped up to the front door.

"Just remind me what you call me," said the big brindled dog.

"You?" said Corinna. "You're a great . . ."

But then she saw the dog's mournful look. With her hand on the cold doorknob, Corinna thought of how, during the past weeks, the dog had always been warm and kind and patient with her, and put up with her tempers and tears. The word *foul* stuck in her throat. "Sweeter than a honeycomb," said Corinna, and she smiled.

The big brindled dog stood up on his hind legs. He put his fore-legs to the sides of his great shaggy head and pulled his head off. He pulled it off and tossed it high in the air. Then he took off his hairy coat. And there he stood, a young man, cool and smiling and just dandy. He had the smallest teeth you ever saw.

So when Corinna turned the cold doorknob and stepped into the house, the young man stepped in after her.

"Dad!" shouted Corinna.

A few months later, on the Saturday before Easter, the church bells rang, and Corinna and her dog-man got married.

"Crazy!" said Corinna.

BUTTERFLY SOUL

YOU FELL ASLEEP.

I would have fallen asleep, too, stretched out under the Sun, washed by the lullaby voices in the stream. We were so *tired,* what with scrambling and searching and shouting all day.

No need to count the missing sheep: I would have fallen asleep, too — but I saw your mouth open, and out flew a butterfly as white as first-day snow!

This butterfly flickered over your body and down your left leg, then settled on a blade of grass not near you nor far from you — just the distance of a stone's toss.

I sat up and stood up and followed the butterfly. It fluttered down a sheep run to the call of the water. It flipped across the stepping stones. It flew through a clump of reeds, in and out, in and out, like the yarn on a loom.

On it went, and still I followed it, until it nosed out something lodged in the long grass. The skull of an old horse, gleaming white, home of the winds!

The butterfly went in through one of the eye sockets. It worked its way 'round the inside wall, quivering and curious. Then out it came, out through the other socket, back through the reeds, over the stone flags, up the sheep run, along your sleeping body, and back into your open mouth.

You closed your mouth and opened your eyes. You saw me looking at you.

"It must be getting late," you said.

"It may be early and it may be late," I said. "I've just seen a wonder."

"You! You've seen a wonder?" you said. "It's I who've seen the wonder. I dreamed I was heading down a fine wide road, flanked by waving trees and a rainbow of flowers. I came down to a broad river and a great stone bridge covered with rich carvings. After I'd crossed this bridge, I entered a marvelous forest — trees like blades. On and on! I went on until I reached a palace, glorious and abandoned. I passed from room to echoing room. Then I thought I might stay there, and with that thought, I began to feel gloomy and strange and uneasy.

"So I left the palace. I came home the same way. And when I got in, I was very hungry. I was just about to settle to a meal when I woke up."

"Come with me," I said, "and I'll show you your dream kingdom."

I told you about the butterfly white as first-day snow. I showed you the sheep run and the stepping stones, the clump of reeds, the skull of the old horse.

"This poor sheep run," I said, "is your fine wide road flanked by waving trees and a rainbow of flowers. These stepping stones are

your great stone bridge covered with rich carvings. This clump of reeds is the marvelous forest—trees like blades. And this skull," I said, "this is the glorious palace you walked 'round a little while ago."

"Wonders!" you said. "You and I, we've both seen wonders."

KING OF THE CATS

I SUPPOSE I CAN THINK MYSELF LUCKY. THERE'S PLENTY IN OUR village who are drawing unemployment, and I know two more — three if you count Dan, he's taking early retirement — who reckon they'll be laid off before Christmas. At least people need me, and they always will.

It's not all laughs, mind you. The only ones who thank you are the early birds. And then you're all on your own, and you're out in every weather, too. And the old flowers, the pulpy heaps of them, they smell sickly sweet!

You get some weird experiences, I can tell you. Weird and wonderful!

One evening last summer I was out late; the vicar said they needed it for nine in the morning. I was having my break, sitting on the edge like, and swinging my legs. Well, I took a nip or two, and I was so tired that I reckon I fell asleep.

A cat woke me up. "Meow!" And when I opened my old eyes, it was almost dark, and I was down at the bottom.

I stood up and peered over the edge, and you know what I saw? Nine black cats! They all had white chests, and they were coming down the path, carrying a coffin covered with black velvet. My! Oh my! I kept very quiet, but I still had a careful look. There was a little gold crown sitting on top of the black velvet. And at every third step the cats all paused, solemn like, and cried, "Meow!"

Then the cats turned off the path and headed straight toward me. Their eyes were shining, luminous and green. Eight of them were carrying the coffin, and a big one walked in front of them, showing them the way. One step, two steps, three steps: meow!

When they got to the graveside, they stopped. They all looked straight at me. My! Oh my! I felt odd.

Then the big cat, the one at the front, stepped toward me. "Tell Dildrum," he said in a squeaky voice, "tell Dildrum that Doldrum is dead."

Then he turned his back on me and led the other cats away with the coffin. One step, two steps, three steps: meow!

As soon as they were out of the way, I scrambled out of the grave, and I was glad to get home, I can tell you. There they all were: my Mary cross-eyed with knitting, Mustard hopping around his cage, and old Sam stretched out in the corner. Everything as usual, the clock ticking on the mantelpiece.

So I told the old girl about the talking cat and the coffin and the crown. She gave me one of those looks — a sort of gleam behind her specs.

"Yes, Harry," she said.

"It's true, Mary," I said. "I couldn't have made it up. And who is Dildrum anyhow?"

"How should I know?" said Mary. "That's enough of your stories. You're upsetting old Sam."

Old Sam got up. First he prowled around, and then he looked straight at me. My! Oh my! I felt very odd again.

"That's just what the cat said," I said. "Not a word more and not a word less. He said, 'Tell Dildrum that Doldrum is dead.' But how can I? How can I tell Dildrum that Doldrum is dead if I don't know who Dildrum is?"

"Stop, Harry!" shouted Mary. "Look at old Sam! Look!"

Old Sam was sort of swelling. Swelling and staring right through me. And at last he shrieked out, "Doldrum — old Doldrum, dead? Then I'm the king of the cats!"

He leaped into the fireplace and up the chimney, and he has never been seen again.

THE BAKER'S DAUGHTER

THE BAKER WAS THIN-LIPPED; HE NEVER GAVE SO MUCH AS A CRUMB away. But his daughter was worse. Not only was she mean; she simpered and toadied to the rich, and she insulted and sniffed at the poor.

At dusk one of the good people came walking by. She picked up some old clothes that had long served their mistress and been left out for the rag-and-bone man; she slipped them on. She pressed her palms against the dusty face of the street and rubbed her cheeks.

Then the woman dragged herself into the baker's shop. The baker was out, and his daughter looked at the woman and tossed back her fair hair. "Yes?" she said.

"Can you spare me some dough?" said the woman.

"Dough?" said the girl. "Why should I? If I give dough to everyone who comes through that door, there won't be any left, will there?"

The woman hung her head. "Haven't any money," she mumbled.

"Whose fault is that?" asked the girl.

"Haven't anything to eat."

"Eh?" said the girl, pulling a small piece of dough off the floury, flabby mound that wallowed on the table behind her. "Think yourself lucky!" she said, and she shoved the piece into the oven on the rack just beneath her own trays of well-shaped loaves.

When the girl opened the oven again, she saw that the woman's dough had so risen that she had the biggest loaf in the oven.

"I'm not giving you that," said the girl, "if that's what you think."

She twisted off another piece of dough, no more than half the size of the small first piece. "You'll have to wait," said the girl, and she shoved it into the oven under another batch of her own loaves.

But this piece of dough swelled even more than the first piece, and the second loaf was larger than the first loaf.

"Or that!" exclaimed the girl. "Certainly not!"

The baker's daughter tossed back her hair in a temper and squeezed off a third piece of dough scarcely bigger than your thumb. She shoved that into the oven under a batch of fairy cakes, and slammed the door.

After a while, the girl turned around to open the oven again. Behind her, meanwhile, the woman slipped off her ragged clothing. She stood in the baker's shop, tall and white and shining.

When the girl opened the oven, she saw that the third piece of dough had so risen that it was the biggest loaf of all three.

The girl stared at the loaf. Her eyes opened, very round and very wide. "Why?" she said, turning around to face the beggar woman. "Why, who, who . . . ?"

"Whoo-whoo!" cried the good woman. "Whoo-whoo! That's all you'll ever say again."

The girl cowered on the other side of the counter.

“Whoo-whoo!” cried the woman. “This world’s put up with you for long enough — you and your sniffs and insults.” Then she raised her stick and struck the girl’s right shoulder with it.

At once the baker’s daughter turned into an owl. She flew straight out of the door, hooting, and away into the dark reaches of the night.

THE DEAD MOON

LONG AGO, THE MOON USED TO SHINE JUST AS SHE SHONE LAST night. And when she shone, she cast her light over the marshland: the great pools of black water and the creeping trickles of green water and the squishy mounds that sucked in anyone who stepped on them. She lit up the whole swamp so that people could walk about almost as safely as in broad daylight.

But when the Moon did not shine, out came the Things that live in the darkness. They wormed around, waiting for a chance to harm those people who were not safe at home beside their own hearths. Harm and mishap and evil, bogles and dead things and crawling horrors: they all appeared on the nights when the Moon did not shine.

The Moon came to hear of this. And being kind and good, as she surely is, shining for us night after night instead of going to sleep, she was upset at what was going on behind her back. She said, "I'll

see what's going on for myself. Maybe it's not as bad as people make out."

And sure enough, at the end of the month, the Moon stepped down onto Earth, wearing a black cloak and black hood over her yellow shining hair. She went straight to the edge of the bogland and looked about her.

There was water here and water there, waving grasses, trembling mounds, and great black snags of peat all twisted and bent. And in front of her, everything was dark — dark except for the pools glimmering under the stars and the light that came from the Moon's own white feet, poking out beneath her black cloak.

The Moon walked forward, right into the middle of the marsh, always looking to the left and to the right and over her shoulders. Then she saw that she had company, and strange company at that.

"Witches," whispered the Moon, and the witches grinned at her as they rode past on their huge black cats.

"The eye," she whispered, and the evil eye glowered at her from the deepest darkness.

"Will-o'-the-wisps," whispered the Moon, and the will-o'-the-wisps danced around her with their lanterns swinging on their backs.

"The dead," she whispered, and dead folk rose out of the water. Their faces were white and twisted. Hellfire blazed in their empty eye sockets, and they stared blindly around them.

"And dead hands," whispered the Moon. Slimy, dripping dead hands slithered about, beckoning and pointing, so cold and wet that they made the Moon's skin crawl.

The Moon drew her cloak more tightly around her and trembled. But she was resolved not to go back without seeing all there was to be seen. So on she went, stepping as lightly as the summer wind from tuft to tuft between the greedy, gurgling water holes.

Just as the Moon came up to a big black pool, her foot slipped. With both hands she grabbed at a snag of peat to steady herself and save herself from tumbling in. But as soon as she touched it, the snag twined itself 'round her wrists like a pair of handcuffs and gripped her so that she couldn't escape. The Moon pulled and twisted and fought, but it was no good; she was trapped, completely trapped. Then she looked about her and wondered if anyone at all would be out that night to pass by and help her. But she saw nothing except shifting, flurrying evil Things, coming and going and toing and froing, all of them busy and all of them up to no good.

After a while, as the Moon stood trembling in the dark, she heard something calling in the distance — a voice that called and called, and then died away in a sob. Then the voice was raised again in a screech of pain and fear, and called and called, until the marshes were haunted by that pitiful crying sound. Then the Moon heard the sound of steps, someone floundering along, squishing through the mud and slipping on the tufts. And through the darkness, she saw a pair of hands catching at the snags and grasses, and a white face with wide, terrified eyes.

It was a man who had strayed into the marsh. The grinning bogles and dead folk and creeping horrors crawled and crowded around him; voices mocked him; the dead hands plucked at him. And ahead of him, the will-o'-the-wisps dangled their lanterns and shook with glee as they lured him farther and farther away from the safe path over the swamp. Trembling with fear and loathing at the Things all around him, the man struggled on toward the flickering lights ahead of him that looked as if they would give him help and bring him home in safety.

"You over there!" yelled the man. "You! I'm caught in the swamp. Can you hear me?" His voice rose to a shriek. "Help! You over there! Help! God and Mary save me from these horrors!" Then the man

paused, and sobbed and moaned, and called on the saints and wise women and on God Himself to save him from the swamp.

But then the man shrieked again as the slimy, slithery Things crawled around him and reared up so that he could not even see the false lights, the will-o'-the-wisps, ahead of him.

As if matters were not bad enough already, the horrors began to take on all sorts of shapes: beautiful girls winked at him with their bright eyes and stretched out soft helping hands toward him. But when he tried to catch hold of them, they changed in his grip to slimy things and shapeless worms, and evil voices derided him and mocked him with foul laughter. Then all the bad thoughts that the man had ever had, and all the bad things that he had ever done, came and whispered in his ears and danced about and shouted out all the secrets that were buried in his own heart. The man shrieked and sobbed with pain and with shame, and the horrors crawled and gibbered around him and mocked him.

When the poor Moon saw that the man was getting nearer and nearer to the deep water holes and deadly sinking mud, and farther and farther from firm ground, she was so angry and so sorry for him that she struggled and fought and pulled harder than ever. She still couldn't break loose. But with all her twisting and tugging, her black hood fell back from her shining yellow hair. And the beautiful light that came from it drove away the darkness.

The man cried for joy to see God's own light again. And at once the evil Things, unable to stand the light, scurried and delved and dropped away into their dark corners. They left the man and fled. And the man could see where he was and where the path was and which way to take to get out of the marsh.

He was in such a hurry to get away from the sinking mud and the swamp, and all the Things that lived there, that he scarcely glanced at

the brave light that shone from the beautiful shining yellow hair streaming out over the black cloak and falling into the water at his very feet.

And the Moon herself was so taken up with saving the man, and so happy that he was back on the right path, that she completely forgot she needed help herself. For she was still trapped in the clutches of the black snag.

The man made off—gasping and stumbling and exhausted—sobbing for joy and running for his life out of the terrible swamp. Then the Moon realized how much she would have liked to go with him. She shook with terror. And she pulled and fought as if she were mad, until, worn out with tugging, she fell to her knees at the foot of the snag. As the Moon lay there, panting, the black hood fell forward over her head. And although she tried to toss it back again, it caught in her hair and would not move.

Out went that beautiful light, and back came the darkness with all its evil creatures, screeching and howling. They crowded around the Moon, mocking her and snatching at her and striking her; shrieking with rage and spite; swearing with foul mouths, spitting and snarling. They knew she was their old enemy, the brave bright Moon, who drove them back into their corners and stopped them from doing all their wicked deeds. They swarmed all around her and made a ghastly clapperdatch. The poor Moon crouched in the mud, trembling and sick at heart, and wondered when they would make an end of their caterwauling and an end of her.

"Damn you!" yelled the witches. "You've spoiled our spells all this last year."

"And you keep us in our narrow coffins at night," moaned the dead folk.

"And you send us off to skulk in the corners," howled the bogles.

Then all the Things shouted in one voice, "Ho, ho! Ho, ho!"

The grasses shook and the water gurgled and the Things raised their voices again.

"We'll poison her — poison her!" shrieked the witches.

"Ho, ho!" howled the Things again.

"We'll smother her — smother her!" whispered the crawling horrors, and they twined themselves around her knees.

"Ho, ho!" shouted all the rest of them.

"We'll strangle her — strangle her!" screeched the dead hands, and they plucked at her throat with cold fingers.

"Ho, ho!" they all yelled again.

And the dead folk writhed and grinned all around her, and chuckled to themselves. "We'll bury you — bury you down with us in the black earth!"

Once more they all shouted, full of spite and ill will. The poor Moon crouched low and wished she were dead and done for.

The Things of the darkness fought and squabbled over what should be done with the Moon until the sky in the east paled and turned gray; it drew near to dawn. When they saw that, they were all worried that they would not have time to do their worst. They caught hold of the Moon with horrid bony fingers and laid her deep in the water at the foot of the snag.

The dead folk held her down while the bogles found a strange big stone. They rolled it right on top of her to stop her from getting up again.

Then the Things told two will-o'-the-wisps to take turns at standing on the black snag to watch over the Moon and make sure she lay safe and still. They didn't want her to get away and spoil their sport with her light, or help the poor marshmen at night to avoid the sinking mud and the water holes.

Then, as the gray light began to brighten, the shapeless Things fled into their dark corners, the dead folk crept back into the water or

crammed themselves into their coffins, and the witches went home to work their spells and curses. And the green, slimy water shone in the light of dawn as if nothing, no wicked or evil creature, had ever gone near it.

There lay the poor Moon, dead and buried in the marsh, until someone would set her free. And who knew even where to look for her?

Days passed, nights passed, and it was time for the birth of the new Moon. People put pennies in their pockets and straw in their caps so as to be ready for it. They looked up at the sky uneasily, for the Moon was a good friend to the marsh folk, and they were only too happy when she began to wax, and the pathways were safe again, and the evil Things were driven back by her blessed light into the darkness and the water holes.

But day followed day, and the new Moon never rose. The nights were always dark, and the evil Things were worse than ever. It was not safe at all to travel alone, and the boggarts crept and wailed 'round the houses of the marsh folk. They peeped through the windows and tipped the latches until the poor people had to burn candles and lamps all night to stop the horrors from crossing their thresholds and forcing their way in.

The bogles and other creatures seemed to have lost all their fear. They howled and laughed and screeched around the hamlet, as if they were trying to wake the dead themselves. The marsh folk listened, and sat trembling and shaking by their fires. They couldn't sleep or rest or put a foot out of doors, and one dark and dreary night followed another.

When days turned into weeks and the new Moon still did not rise, the villagers were upset and afraid. A group of them went to the wise woman who lived in the old mill and asked her if she could find out where the Moon had gone.

The wise woman looked in the cauldron, and in the mirror, and in the Book. "Well," she said, "it's odd. I can't tell you for sure what has happened to her."

She shook her head, and the marsh folk shook their heads.

"It's only dark and dead," said the wise woman. "You must wait a while and let me think about it, and then maybe I'll be able to help you. If you hear of anything, any clue, come by and tell me. And," said the wise woman, "be sure to put a pinch of salt, a straw, and a button on the doorstep each night. The horrors will never cross it then, light or no light."

Then the marsh folk left the wise woman and the mill and went their separate ways. As the days went by, and the new Moon never rose, they talked and talked. They wondered and pondered and worried and guessed, at home and in the inn and in the fields around the marshland.

One day, sitting on the great bench in the inn, a group of men was discussing the whereabouts of the Moon, and another customer, a man from the far end of the marshland, smoked and listened to the talk. Suddenly this stranger sat up and slapped his knee. "My Lord!" he said. "I'd clean forgotten, but I reckon I know where the Moon is."

All the men sitting on the bench turned 'round to look at him. Then the stranger told them about how he had got lost in the marsh and how, when he was almost dead with fright, the light had shone out, and all the evil Things fled from it, and he had found the marsh path and gotten home safely.

"And I was so terrified," said the stranger, "that I didn't really look to see where the light had come from. But I do remember it was white and soft like the Moon herself.

"And this light came from something dark," said the stranger, "and was standing near a black snag in the water." He paused and puffed at his pipe. "I didn't really look," he said again, "but I think I remember

a shining face and yellow hair in the middle of the dazzle. It had a sort of kind look, like the old Moon herself above the marshland at night."

At once all the men got up from the bench and went back to the wise woman. They told her everything the stranger had said. She listened and then looked once more into the cauldron and into the Book. Then she nodded. "It's still dark," she said, "and I can't see anything for sure. But do as I tell you, and you can find out for yourselves. All of you must meet just before night falls. Put stones in your mouths," said the wise woman, "and take hazel twigs in your hands, and say never a word until you're safe home again. Then step out and fear nothing! Make your way into the middle of the marsh until you find a coffin, a candle, and a cross." The wise woman stared at the circle of anxious faces around her. "Then you won't be far from your Moon," she said. "Search, and maybe you'll find her."

The men looked at each other and scratched their heads.

"But where will we find her, mother?" asked one.

"And which of us must go?" asked another.

"And the bogles, won't they come for us?" said a third.

"Houts!" exclaimed the wise woman impatiently. "You parcel of fools! I can tell you no more. Do as I've told you, and fear nothing." She glared at the men. "And if you don't like my advice, stay at home. Do without your Moon if that's what you want."

The next day at dusk, all the men in the hamlet came out of their houses. Each had a stone in his mouth and a hazel twig in his hand, and each was feeling nervous and frightened.

Then the men stumbled and stuttered along the paths out into the middle of the marsh. It was so dark that they could see almost nothing. But they heard sighings and flusterings, and they could feel wet fingers touching them. On they went, peering about for the coffin, the candle, and the cross, until they came near the pool next to the great snag where the Moon lay buried.

All at once they stopped in their tracks, quaking and shaking and scared. For there they saw the great stone, half in and half out of the water, looking for all the world like a strange big coffin. And at its head stood the black snag, stretching out its arms to make a dark, gruesome cross. A little light flickered on it, like a dying candle.

The men knelt down in the mud, crossed themselves, and said the Lord's Prayer to themselves. First they said it forward because of the cross, and then they said it backward, to keep the bogles away. But they mouthed it all without so much as a whisper, for they knew the evil Things would catch them if they did not do as the wise woman had told them.

Then the men shuffled to the edge of the water. They took hold of the big stone and levered it up, and for one moment, just one moment, they saw a strange and beautiful face looking up at them, and looking so grateful, out of the black water.

But then the light came so quickly and was so white and shining that the men stepped back, stunned by it, and by the great angry wail raised by the fleeing horrors. And the very next minute, when they came to their senses, the men saw the full Moon in the sky. She was as bright and beautiful and kind as ever, shining and smiling down at them; she showed the marsh and the marsh paths as clearly as daylight and stole into every nook and cranny, as though she would have liked to drive the darkness and the bogles away forever.

Then the marsh folk went home happy and with light hearts. And ever since, the Moon has shone more brightly and clearly over the marshland than anywhere else.

ADVENTURES AND LEGENDS

THE SLUMBER KING

"OWEN," SAID A VOICE.

Owen spun around and looked into the bright eyes of a small, boyish-faced, middle-aged man. "Who are you?" he demanded.

"Don't you worry about me," said the man pleasantly. "Loomis. Loomis is the name."

"I mean, how did you know my name?"

"I've been watching you," said the man. "You can tell most things by watching. You've been standing here on London Bridge, and your mind has been on a long journey back to your parents, back home to Wales."

"How do you know that?" said Owen, startled.

"And I can tell you this," said the man. "You should value that stick of yours."

Owen looked at his hazel walking stick; he had cut it from a bush

under the Rock of the Fortress and seldom went anywhere without it.

"Under the place where that stick grew," said Loomis, "there's gold in the ground."

"There's gold all over the mountains," said Owen. "Red gold."

"No," said the man. "Right under the place where that stick grew. Do you remember it?"

Owen nodded.

"Take me to it, and the gold is yours."

Owen took Loomis with him back to Wales. He led him to his own valley, in the mountains north of Swansea, and they walked past the pool where the rivers Mellte and Sychryd meet, through a rising wood of oak and ash and up to an old hazel bush.

Directly above it reared the mighty Rock of the Fortress.

"You're sure?" said Loomis.

"This is it," said Owen.

The little man sat down on the carpet of twigs and puzzled with the straps of his canvas bag, and at length he pulled out two spades.

Owen laughed. "You're full of surprises," he said.

"Now," said Loomis. "We've got to dig up this bush."

Under the roots, under all the dark webbing, lay a large flat stone, a little bigger than the cover of a manhole. Owen had to dig wide and deep before he was able to pry it out of the ground. And as it came up, he saw it hid the entrance to a rock passageway.

"Ah!" said Loomis, raising his eyebrows and smiling at Owen agreeably. "Well, shall I lead the way?"

Owen nodded and stepped back.

"Don't you worry!" said Loomis. "I'll tell you what to do and what not to do." He groped in one pocket, then another, then a third, and

fished out two boxes of matches. "You'll need these," he said, handing one box to Owen, "unless you're able to see in the dark."

"Can you?" Owen asked.

"Of course not," said Loomis.

Feet first, Loomis and Owen lowered themselves through the entrance. Then each lit a match, and Owen saw rough, dank walls and a narrow passageway. Starting forward in Loomis's footsteps, he felt the ground gently falling away under his feet. They were going in under the mountain.

"Watch out for the bell," said Loomis, and now his voice sounded eerie and hollow. "Don't touch it, whatever you do."

Owen saw a large bell standing in the middle of the passageway and ducked low under it. Now the passage began to widen and lighten, and suddenly it opened on to a vast cavern. Owen realized that he was standing at the top of a flight of roughly hewn steps, halfway between the cavern roof and floor, and he gazed, breathless, at the wonders below him.

Thousands of warriors lay there, sleeping. They lay in a huge circle, their feet pointing inward and their heads outward. Each warrior was clad in bright armor and by the side of each lay his sword, his lance, and his shield.

The whole cavern was brightly lit, as if ten thousand candles were burning in it, and all this light came from the warriors' weapons and war gear. Chain mail and plated helmets, the blades of battle-axes, spear tips, shield bosses: they all shone with a steady bright light.

Owen stared. He saw that one of the warriors was distinguished by the most magnificent war gear. His massive sword was damascened with a wavy serpent pattern. His shield was inlaid with the wild beasts of battle. And at his side lay a flashing crown.

"You see?" said Loomis.

"Yes," breathed Owen. "King Arthur! Arthur's warriors!" He saw two great heaps in the middle of the circle — one heap of gold coins, one of silver.

"You can take that away," said Loomis. "As much as you can carry."

"The gold and silver?" said Owen.

"Not both," said Loomis. "One or the other. They won't wake." Owen picked his way down the steps and softly past the sleeping heads and into the circle. He filled his pockets with gold, his shoes with gold; he opened his shirt and stuffed gold into it.

"And you?" said Owen, when he had gotten back to the steps.

Loomis shook his head.

"Why not?" asked Owen.

"What's the use of it?" said Loomis.

With that, he led the way out of the cavern. Clinking and clanking, Owen followed him.

"Watch the bell!" said Loomis. "If you touch it, one of the warriors will wake. He'll lift his head," said Loomis, "and ask, 'Is it the day?' And you must call out at once, 'No! Not yet! Sleep on!'"

"And then?" Owen whispered.

"And then he'll lay down his head again and go back to sleep." Owen was so heavy with gold that while he was trying to edge 'round the bell, he staggered and banged into it. The clapper swung: the bell rang. At once a sleeping warrior raised his head and called out, "Is it the day?"

"No!" shouted Owen. "Not yet! Sleep on!"

So Owen and Loomis got out of the cave and levered the flat stone back over the entrance and replanted the hazel tree.

"You'll be going up the road now to your parents," said Loomis. "And I'm going to walk down out of the mountains."

Owen looked at Loomis — his kind and curiously blank face, his bright blue eyes.

"No point in asking," said Loomis. "Just learn to look."

"Yes," said Owen.

"You've enough gold there to last for years."

"Yes," said Owen again.

"And you can always go back down. You know the way down and you can take some more: gold or silver, one or the other. But be careful of that bell."

"No!" said Owen quickly. "Not yet! Sleep on!"

"That's it," said Loomis.

"And King Arthur?" asked Owen. "And his sleeping warriors?"

"Sleeping and ready," Loomis replied, "ready for the day when the Black Eagle and the Golden Eagle go to war. When they fight, the ground will tremble; then the bell will ring and the warriors will wake. Those warriors, they'll fight all the enemies of Wales and conquer the whole island of Britain."

"I know a song about that," said Owen.

"The Welsh will rise: they will give battle
War bands 'round the ale and soldiers in swarms
Every Welshman's son will shout for joy"

Loomis looked rather pleased. "The Welsh," he said, drawing himself up to his full height, such as it was, and raising one hand, "will have their king and government at Caerleon, as they used to do. Wales will be a country of justice and peace for as long as this world lasts."

Owen did not use the gold wisely or well. True, he did set up his parents in a new house, but that was all he had to show for it. He left his job

in stinking London; he never did another day's work; he gambled; and within five years he had very little gold left.

Owen returned alone to the cavern. He entered it and gazed on sleeping Arthur and his warriors, and once again reeled out under the weight of a great load of gold. On his way back down the passage, Owen bumped into the bell. The bell rang and a warrior lifted his head.

"Is it the day?" he called, and his voice echoed 'round and 'round the cavern.

Owen was out of breath. And he was scared — so scared that the words froze in his head. He knew they were in there, and he couldn't remember them.

Several warriors woke now. They came out from the cavern into the gloomy passageway. They took hold of Owen and shook him until the ground around him was carpeted in gold.

Then the warriors turned their lances and beat squealing Owen with the wooden shafts. They thrashed him and broke his arms and ribs and legs. Then they threw him out of the passageway onto the soft soil above and drew the flat stone back over the entrance.

Owen crawled through the wood, past the pool where the rivers Mellte and Sychryd meet, and down to the little road. There his own parents found him. And in the high village where he had been born, he lived poor and crippled for the rest of his life.

Quite often Owen returned with friends to the oak and ash and hazel wood under the soaring dark rock. They looked for the entrance to the cavern. They dug for it. How they dug for it. It was there, and it was not there.

THE GREEN CHILDREN

CLAC STRAIGHTENED HIS BACK, BRACED HIS ACHING SHOULDERS, and grunted. Sweat trickled down his face and dripped from the end of his nose. He licked his lips; they tasted of salt. Clac glanced down the long, straight rows of corn; then, rubbing the back of his neck between his shoulder blades, he considered the position of the Sun. But his stomach was his best clock. He filled his lungs, cupped a huge hand to his mouth, and bellowed, "FOOD."

The other villagers heard him. One by one they stopped work and mopped their brows; one by one they left their own strips of land and began to walk slowly toward him.

Their scythes gleamed in the midday Sun; a very small wind moved over the land and whispered warnings to the ears of uncut corn.

"Come on," called Clac. He sat on the ridge dividing his strip

from the next, waiting impatiently. "This Sun. I've had enough of it."

"So have I," sighed Swein, collapsing in a heap like a sack of potatoes.

"Come on," cried Clac. "You and you and all the rest of you." He picked up a side of ham with one hand and with the other a gourd of cider. "I'm for the shade. Shade first, then food. Who'll carry the apples?"

"I will," said Grim.

So the villagers, nine of them in all, set off across the common land on which their cattle grazed. They walked toward the wolf pits — where, in winter, wild creatures roamed — and toward the high, waving elms.

Clac led the way. He always did; he liked leading. And the lord of the manor, Sir Richard de Calne, who had recognized this quality in him, had put him over the other villagers and serfs. As the tired, hungry men approached the elms, Clac stopped in his tracks. "Look!"

"What?" said Grim.

"Where?" said Swein.

"Look!" Clac exclaimed again. "Look! There!" He pointed toward the trees. "Follow me." And throwing down the side of ham and the gourd, he started to run. He ran, and at last he came to the old wolf pits just beyond the elms.

"Look!" insisted Clac, pointing again. "Look!"

And there, huddling in the hollow of the largest pit, the villagers saw what Clac had seen: two green children. Their skin was green, their hair was green; they wore green clothes. And one was a boy, the other a girl.

For a moment, nobody moved; nobody spoke. The villagers

looked down at the green children, and the green children looked up at the villagers.

"Blessed Edmund preserve us!" exclaimed Clac. And he made the sign of the cross.

"Indeed!" muttered Grim. And he crossed himself too.

"Who can they be?" said Swein helplessly.

"Ask them," said Clac.

Swein laughed nervously.

"All right, then," said Clac. "I will. I'll ask them."

The villagers bunched together anxiously.

"They might be little folk," Swein warned him.

"Let's leave them alone," said Thurketil.

"Look at them," Clac replied. "Do they look as if they mean harm?"

The villagers crowded 'round the edge of the pit, watching breathlessly. If one man had moved, the rest would have toppled headlong down. The boy and the girl were clutching each other, looking up at the nine men fearfully. And then the green girl buried her face in her hands and began to sob.

"You see?" said Clac. He stepped forward, slipped down the grassy bank, and walked toward the children.

The closer he drew, the more astonished he became — so much so that he completely forgot his nervousness. In all his thirty years, he had never seen or even heard of anything like it before: green children . . . a boy and a girl with green cheeks, green fingers, and, poking out of their green sandals, green toes.

"Hello!" said Clac in his gruff, friendly voice. "Who are you?" And he smiled encouragingly.

The children huddled still closer together. They gazed at Clac, bewildered, and said nothing.

Clac looked at the children closely and guessed the girl was about

nine and the boy about seven. He saw that they resembled each other not only because they were green, but also in their features. "You must be brother and sister," he said. "Who are you? Where do you come from?"

The children continued to gaze at him silently.

Well, thought Clac. *It's clear enough: either they're dumb or they don't understand me.*

At this moment the boy turned to the girl and spoke several strange words.

"That settles it," said Clac. "You don't understand me. And I can't pretend to understand you."

The green girl looked at Clac; suddenly, she flashed a smile at him, opened her mouth, and pointed at it.

"Blessed Edmund preserve me!" exclaimed Clac. "She's got a green tongue." He nodded and grinned. "I see," he said. "You're hungry."

He turned around, waved reassuringly to the other villagers, and called, "What are you doing up there, you idlers? Get the side of ham and bring it down. And bring the cider too."

In no time, the villagers were pouring down into the pit, bringing the food with them. They swarmed around the children, their superstition at last overcome by curiosity.

"Here! Give me the side of ham," said Clac. Swein passed it to him.

Clac sniffed at it, then showed it to the two children.

They looked at it blankly, then turned to each other and shook their heads. Then the girl sniffed it and wrinkled up her nose.

"Look at that!" marveled Clac. "They've never seen a side of ham before."

Now it was his turn to shake his head. "What about the apples, then?" he said. "Give me two red apples."

"Here," said Grim, and passed them over.

The two children looked at them, turned to each other again, and shook their heads a second time.

Clac was dumbfounded. He didn't know what to do, but he didn't like to admit it. "How about that?" he asked. "How about that? They've never seen apples before."

Despite their behavior, it was clear that the two children were famished. Again and again they pointed to their mouths. And once more the green girl began to weep.

"I think we should take them to Sir Richard," said Clac. The other villagers nodded in agreement.

"Sir Richard's a traveler," Clac continued. "He's traveled far and wide, almost as far as the edges of Earth. Perhaps he's heard of green children."

So the villagers escorted the green children to the manor of Sir Richard de Calne. And as they walked, they sang, for they were not altogether sorry to miss an afternoon's work under the blazing Sun. But the children were dazzled by the bright light. They kept their heads down and shielded their eyes with their arms.

The fortified manor was surrounded by a moat. Clac strode to the brink and shouted to the guards on the other side. For a while the guards conferred, then they let the drawbridge down. The little group, with the children in their midst, walked across and on into the great hall.

"Wait here!" said a guard, his eyes bulging out of his head as he looked at the two children. "Until Sir Richard comes."

Inside the hall, out of the sunlight, the children looked about them with great curiosity. They ran to and fro, exclaiming in wonder at the huge stone fireplace, the narrow window slits, the yellow rushes on the floor. They chattered excitedly and for a moment even forgot their hunger.

⁕

"Green children," boomed a voice at the entrance of the hall. "What's all this?"

The villagers swung around.

And there, hands on hips, stood Sir Richard de Calne, an enormous, potbellied man.

The villagers liked him well. He was a just lord, and a generous one, though his moods were as variable as the weather: one day he was laughing and smiling, the next thundering commands to his frightened servants.

But now he was completely silent. He was staring at the green children openmouthed.

"Please, my lord," said Clac, stepping forward. And he explained to Sir Richard how he had discovered the green children at the wolf pits. "And they don't speak English," he said, "and they won't eat our food."

From his great height, Sir Richard looked down at the shrinking children. He frowned and stroked his beard.

Sir Richard liked problems; he enjoyed solving them. But green children, green as grass, who couldn't speak English, who wouldn't eat apples . . . that was another thing altogether.

"So they don't speak English," echoed Sir Richard after a long pause. "Ah well! I don't blame them. Perhaps they speak Norman." He stooped, smiled warmly at the green girl, and began, "*D'où venez-vous?*"

The green girl gazed at him blankly. Then she looked to her brother; he shrugged and repeated the strange words that Clac had heard in the wolf pits. Whereupon the girl looked up at Sir Richard, pointed at his potbelly, and opened her mouth.

Sir Richard bellowed with laughter. "I understand you," he cried.

"Food's a common language. All right. Sit them down." Then walking to the entrance of the hall, he shouted at the top of his voice, "FOOD! FOOD!"

Clac led the two children over to the trestle table and sat them at the wooden bench. In no time, a servant bustled in, bearing part of a chicken on a platter; a second followed, carrying a bunch of succulent, black grapes; and the third brought a pitcher of red wine. "Give them each a wing," said Sir Richard. "That'll tempt them. You see if it doesn't."

But the children pushed the chicken away, indicating that they would not eat it.

"What about the grapes, then?" suggested Sir Richard.

The black, succulent grapes were set before them. The girl fingered one and said something to her brother. Then they refused them too.

Sir Richard strode up and down the hall, disconcerted. "Bring them some cheese, then," he instructed.

A servant hurried out of the hall, reappeared with a bowl of cream cheese, and placed it on the table. The two children took one look at it and pushed that away too.

"Well!" exclaimed Sir Richard. "I don't know. What *will* they eat?"

At this moment, it so happened that an old servant was crossing the far end of the hall. In his arms, he carried a pile of freshly cut beans, still attached to their stalks.

Seeing the beans, the green children cried out with delight. They leaped up from the bench and ran toward the old man, who was so startled at the sight of them that he threw down the beans on the spot and ran out of the hall as fast as his old legs could carry him.

The children fell upon the pile and immediately began to tear

open the stalks, thinking the beans were in the hollows of them. Finding none, they were utterly dismayed and began to weep dismally once more.

"Look!" said Clac. "Like this." He quickly opened a pod and showed them the naked beans.

And so at last the green children began to eat.

The villagers stood watching them.

"I see," said Sir Richard eventually. "I see. Green children, green food."

After they had eaten their fill, the green children smiled gratefully at Sir Richard de Calne and the villagers.

"Well! Now what?" said Sir Richard. "What are we going to do with them now?"

This was a question no one could answer. And as the two children showed no inclination to leave the hall, Sir Richard instructed that they should be allowed to remain at the manor for as long as they desired. He asked his priest, Father John, to teach them to speak English.

And for many, many months the green children ate nothing but beans.

The great fair at Stourbridge came and went. Sir Richard de Calne journeyed there, laden with packs of wool, and returned with Baltic furs, French cloth and lace, and salts and spices from the East. And all this time the green children stayed at the manor. Father John took his duties seriously; each day the children had English lessons with him. They both worked hard and made good progress.

And the old priest, a lean, angular man who often declared he loved no one but God, began to love the green boy and the green girl as if they were his own children.

"They must be baptized," he told Sir Richard one day. "They may be green, but they still have souls."

And so the children were baptized. The ceremony was attended by Sir Richard de Calne and by all his household, and by his villagers and serfs.

August grew old; September was born. High winds wrestled with the Sun. Leaves fell, carpeting Earth in copper and bronze and gold. The elms by the wolf pits looked like skeletons.

Clac and his fellow villagers brought the harvest home and began to prepare for winter. They killed pigs and cattle and fowl, and gave them to their wives, who cut them up, salted them, and stored them away for harder days.

During the cold days of November, the green boy became listless. He would eat no more beans; he made little progress in his work; he lost interest in playing checkers and spinning tops; and nothing his sister said could cheer him.

Nobody could say what was wrong with him; he ran no fever, sported no spots. And his sister could speak so little English that she was unable to explain.

Father John was anxious. He made the green boy eat mugwort and mayweed, crab apple, thyme, and fennel; he sent to Bury for water from the Well of Our Lady; he offered prayers.

It was all to no avail. One dark day, when the ground was like iron underfoot and the shifting skies were gray, the green boy threw up his hands and died.

Throughout the long hard winter his sister could not be consoled. Often she wept; it was so cold the tears froze on her cheeks. But at last, as spring threw off winter, she too threw off her grief. The crocuses flowered.

One evening, Sir Richard de Calne and his family, his servants and guards, and all the villagers and serfs who worked on his land gathered in the great hall.

First the company ate. The food was drawn from the ground and air and sea. There was crane and swan, peacock and snipe; there was suckling pig and, out of season, venison; there were lampreys, sea trout, and sturgeon. And to wash down this sumptuous fare, there was spiced wine.

After the meal it was customary for the minstrel to sing. The company turned from the tables to face the minstrel and the fire.

"Not tonight," called Sir Richard. "We'll not have songs tonight. I've asked you all for a special reason." He paused and looked around the hall. "Our guest," he continued, and smiling, turned to the green girl, "can speak English at last. She has told me who she is and where she comes from. And now I have asked her to tell her story to you."

There was a rustle of excitement.

The green girl stood up and walked over to the minstrel's place beside the flickering fire. Her shadow danced on the wall behind her. All at once she smiled, the same alluring smile she had first flashed at Clac in the wolf pits. Then she began in a strong, clear voice, "I come from a green country. The people are green, the animals are green, the ground and sky are green. There is nothing that is not green.

"The Sun never shines in my country. The light there is a constant green glow, as if the Sun were always just below the horizon."

A puff of wood smoke filled the room. The listeners coughed and rubbed their smarting eyes, then settled again. They had never heard such a thing in their lives.

"From the hills of our country," said the girl, "you can see

another, much brighter land — though I have never been there — divided from ours by a broad river."

"But tell us where your land is," said Sir Richard, "and how you got here."

"Well! One day my brother and I . . . my poor brother, who died of homesickness . . . we were tending sheep on the hills, and they began to stray. We followed them and came to the mouth of a cave, a great cave we'd never seen before. The sheep entered the cave, and we walked in after them. And there, ahead of us, we heard the sound of bells: a most beautiful sound, loud bells and soft bells, treble bells and bass bells, ringing, ringing.

"It seemed," said the green girl, "that the sound came from the far end of the cave. The bells were so beautiful they pulled us toward them. We *had* to find them. So we walked through the cave, on and on. At first it was flat; then we began to climb. And the bells rang and rang, tugging us toward them.

"The cave was gloomy but not dark; then, suddenly, we saw a bright light some way ahead of us. 'That's where the bells are coming from,' my brother said. So we hurried toward it. It grew and grew, dazzling us. And all at once we climbed up and out, out of the cave," said the girl. "The ringing stopped. The sunlight blinded us." She clapped her hands to her eyes. "We were knocked senseless by the Sun. We lay in a swoon for a long time."

Everyone in the hall was leaning forward. The fire roared.

"When we recovered our senses, we saw we were in some deep pit. And although we looked for the entrance to the cave, it had completely gone; we couldn't find it again. 'What shall we do?' my brother asked me. 'I don't know,' I said. I felt rather afraid. 'But as we can't go back, we'd better go forward.' So, very cautiously, we climbed out of the wolf pit."

"That's it," exclaimed Clac excitedly. "I remember. That's when I saw you."

The green girl smiled.

"'Blessed Edmund preserve us!' I said," continued Clac. "Two green children!"

"If you were surprised to see green children," the girl replied, "think how astonished we were to see pink men!"

Everyone laughed. "Not only astonished," continued the green girl, "but frightened too. My brother and I backed down into the pit again. But we couldn't find the entrance to the cave, and so you caught us."

The assembled company sighed and nodded.

"That's my story," said the green girl. "The rest you know. Thank you all for your great kindness to me. I've been very happy here, but if ever I can find the entrance to the cave, I must return home."

With that, she sat down.

But that was only the beginning. Many were the questions asked of her that night; many were the answers given.

But the years passed, and the green girl did not return home. She remained at the manor, for she was unable to find the entrance to the cave.

In time she learned to eat meat, and the fruits of Earth, and even to enjoy them. And slowly her skin lost its green tinge; her hair became fair.

She always said that she was very happy in this world. But often Clac and the villagers saw her wandering down by the wolf pits, alone. At such times, they never went near her. For they knew that she must be lonely for her own people and looking for the entrance to the cave.

One spring the green girl married. She left the manor of Sir

Richard de Calne and went to live with her husband near the port of Lynn. But even then she used to return to the wolf pits from time to time. Her feet were anchored to this ground, but her heart and mind sailed on to another far-off land.

How, then, did it end? What became of the girl who climbed up from the green land? All this happened years and years ago. Eight hundred years ago. Some things live longer than centuries; others do not. We know much about the green girl, but there is much we do not know.

And nobody knows — unless you do — whether the green girl lived on Earth to the end of her days or whether, one day, near the wolf pits, she simply disappeared.

THE LAST OF THE PICTS

LONG AGO, THERE WERE PEOPLE CALLED PICTS LIVING IN THIS corner of the world. They were very short, with red hair and long arms and feet so broad that when it rained they put them up over their heads and used them as umbrellas. The Picts were great builders; they built all the old drystone brochs in the country. And this they did by standing in a long line stretching from the quarry to the building site, and passing stones from man to man until they had as many as they needed.

The Picts were also great drinkers, and they brewed their ale from heather. For this reason, it was an extraordinarily cheap drink, because heather was just as plentiful then as it is today.

Their skill as brewers was much envied by the other people living in the country, but the Picts never gave away their secret recipe. They handed it down from father to son with strict orders that no one should ever reveal it.

In time, the Picts were caught up in great wars against the Scots. Most of them were killed, and soon no more than a mere handful of them was left. It seemed likely that they would die out altogether.

But the Picts still hung on to their secret recipe; they were determined that their enemies should never wring it from them.

Well, the Picts and the Scots fought one last great battle, and the Picts lost the day. They lost it completely. All but two of them — an old man and his son — were wiped out.

The king of the Scots had these men brought before him, to see whether he could frighten them into telling him how to brew heather ale. He warned them bluntly that if they would not disclose the recipe of their own free will, he would have them tortured until they revealed it.

"Since you are going to have to tell it to me anyhow," said the king, "you'd do better to tell it to me now."

"Well," said the old father, "I see we can no longer resist you. But before I tell you the recipe, you must agree to one condition."

"What is that?" asked the king.

"Will you promise to carry it out, if it's not anything against your own interests?" said the old Pict.

"Yes," said the king. "I will, and I promise you I will."

"All right!" said the Pict. "This is the condition. I want my son to be put to death, and I'd rather not take his life myself."

The king was astonished at the old man's words. Nevertheless, he kept his promise and at once had the boy put to death.

When the old man saw that his son was dead, he leaped up with a great leap and cried, "Now do with me as you will! You might have forced my son to talk, for he was only young. But you'll never force me."

Now the king was even more amazed than before — because he had been completely outwitted by a wild Pict. He saw, however, that there was no need to kill the old man, and that his greatest punishment would lie in being allowed to live.

So the old Pict was taken away as a prisoner. He lived for many years after that until he was freed as a very, very old man, bedridden and blind.

Most people had forgotten there was one Pict still alive. But one evening, when a group of young men in the house where he lived was boasting about their strength and their great feats, the old Pict said that he would like to feel one of their wrists.

"Let me compare it," he said, "with the arms of men long dead — the strong men who used to live in this world."

Then one of the young men covered a piece of iron piping with a cloth and held it out, pretending that it was his wrist.

The old Pict took it between his fingers and snapped it, as if it were a twig. "That's a good bit of gristle," he said. "But no! It's nothing compared to the wrists I knew when I was a young man!"

And that was the last of the Picts.

THE OLDEST OF THEM ALL

HOW LONG HAD THE EAGLE OF GWERNABWY BEEN MARRIED TO his wife?

Snow fleeced the hills; cowslips buttered the valley; the sky's rose opened, and the eagle's roost was robed in gold. The high winds argued, and then it was the fleece again. . . . So many years he could no longer remember.

And how many children had he fathered? The eagle started counting. When he had counted up to a thousand, he began to feel drowsy. Before he had finished, he fell asleep.

When his wife died, the Eagle of Gwernabwy lived on his own for a while. He was not unhappy, but he was not happy, either, and so, after a number of years, he thought he would marry for a second time. He chose for his bride the Owl of Cwm Cawlwyd.

"I'll marry her," he screeched, "if she's old enough. I'll marry

her if she doesn't want children. More than one thousand is quite enough."

The eagle soared over the hill and the valley and found the Stag of Rhedynfre lying up against the fallen trunk of an ancient oak tree.

"Stag," said the eagle, "how old is the Owl of Cwm Cawlwyd?"

"I knew this oak when it was an acorn," bellowed the stag.

"Go on," said the eagle.

"All its life was calm and untroubled. No one ever bothered it or hurt it. Once each day I rubbed myself against it, and that's as much strain as it ever knew. It lived to a great age: it lost its bark; it lost its leaves."

"Go on," said the eagle.

"I knew it when it was an acorn, and I never remember seeing the Owl of Cwm Cawlwyd look a day younger than she does today."

"Good!" said the eagle.

"But there is one," said the stag, "who is older than I, and that is the Salmon of Glynllifon."

The eagle soared over the hill and the valley and found the salmon in the glassy stream.

"Salmon," said the eagle, "how old is the Owl of Cwm Cawlwyd?"

"I'm as many years old as the sum of my scales," mouthed the salmon, "and the thousands of spawn still growing inside me."

"Go on," said the eagle.

"And I've never seen the Owl of Cwm Cawlwyd look a day younger than she does today."

"Good!" said the eagle.

"But there is one," said the salmon, "who is older than I, and that is the Blackbird of Cilgwri."

The eagle soared over the hill and the valley and found the blackbird sitting on a stone.

"Blackbird," said the eagle, "how old is the Owl of Cwm Cawlwyd?"

"You see this stone?" piped the blackbird. "It's so small now that a man could pick it up and carry it in his hand."

"Go on," said the eagle.

"I saw this stone when it was so huge that a hundred oxen would have had trouble moving it. Nothing has touched it; nothing has disturbed it . . ."

"Go on," said the eagle.

". . . except that each evening I rub my yellow bill against it, and each morning I spread my wings and touch the stone with the tips of them. That is how it has worn down, and I've never seen the Owl of Cwm Cawlwyd look a day younger than she does today."

"Good!" said the eagle.

"But there is one," said the blackbird, "who is older than I, and that is the Frog of Mochno Bog. If he doesn't know the age of the owl, no creature does."

The eagle soared over the hill and the valley and found the frog climbing up onto a glob of mud.

"Frog," said the eagle, "how old is the Owl of Cwm Cawlwyd?"

"I've never eaten anything but the earth you see around us," croaked the frog, "the earth and whatever creeps and crawls through it."

"Go on," said the eagle.

"And I've a poor appetite," said the frog. "A little earth is enough."

"Go on," said the eagle.

"You see those great hills?" said the frog. "The green slopes that overshadow Mochno Bog?"

"I do," said the eagle.

"They're all formed of my own excrement," said the frog, "and

nothing but that. The land was flat when I came to live here. And I've never seen the Owl of Cwm Cawlwyd look a day younger than she does today. She's always looked like a horrible old hag and always made that hideous noise — *too, hoo, hoo!* — scaring all the children for miles and miles around."

"Enough!" said the eagle.

"Does that satisfy you?" said the frog, and he slipped back into the brown water.

So the Eagle of Gwernabwy and the Stag of Rhedynfre and the Salmon of Glynllifon and the Blackbird of Cilgwri and the Frog of Mochno Bog are old, and older than old; and the Owl of Cwm Cawlwyd, she is the oldest of them all.

FAIR GRUAGACH

WHEN GRUAGACH, THE FAIR LEADER, THE SON OF THE KING OF Ireland, was on his way to court with many of his followers, he was stopped by a woman whom people called the Lady of the Green Gown.

"Come and sit with me for a while and play a game of cards," said the Lady.

So Gruagach sat down to play cards, and he played a winning hand.

"What stakes are we playing for?" said the Lady.

"I don't think you own anything you can stake," Gruagach said. "Or if you do, I've never heard of it."

"Come here tomorrow," said the Lady, "and I will meet you."

"I will be here," said Gruagach.

On the next day, they met and began to play cards again, and this time the Lady of the Green Gown won the game.

"What stakes are we playing for?" said the fair leader.

"Never mind about stakes," said the Lady. "I am going to put you under spells. I lay you under crosses and under the oaths of holy herdsmen of quiet traveling women. I command the little calf, feeble as he is, to take away your head and strip you of your life if you stop and rest by day or by night. Where you eat breakfast, you shall not eat dinner; and where you eat dinner, you shall not eat supper; not until you find out where I live in the four brown quarters of the world."

Then the Lady of the Green Gown took a handkerchief from her pocket. She shook it and disappeared, and there was no telling where she had come from or where she had gone.

Gruagach, the son of the king of Ireland, went home heavy-hearted and black sorrowful. He put one elbow on the table, and one hand under his cheek, and he gave a great sigh.

"What's wrong with you?" asked his father. "Are you under spells? Forget them! I'll have them lifted from you. I own a blacksmith workshop down by the shore, and I own ships crossing the sea. I'll give you all the profits from them, for as long as I have gold and silver, until such time as I have these spells lifted from you."

"Father," said Gruagach, "you will not! You're so generous that you'll end up without anything yourself. You will not be able to lift these spells. Your kingdom will go to rack and ruin, and even then the spells will not be lifted."

"I'll have them lifted from you," said the king.

"And then you'll lose your company of followers," said Gruagach. "Father, look after all your own men! If I go to find the Lady, and do not stop or rest by day or by night, I'll have only myself to lose."

The next morning, Gruagach left his father's court. He went without dog, without servant, without calf, without child.

Gruagach walked and walked, and crossed the country. His soles

darkened, and there were holes in his shoes. The black clouds of night swarmed 'round him, and the bright, quiet clouds of day went west, and he found nowhere to rest or lay his head.

For a week, Gruagach walked without seeing a house or a castle or any building at all. He grew ill for want of sleep or rest or meat or drink, and from walking for a whole week.

In despair the fair leader looked around him, and what should he see but a castle. Gruagach walked toward it and then right around it, but there was not so much as a door or a window in its walls.

Gruagach's shoulders fell. He turned away, heavyhearted and black sorrowful, and set off again. And at that moment, he heard a shout behind him.

"Fair Leader!" said the voice, and the voice was that of a beautiful girl. "Son of the king of Ireland! Come back! There's a feast for you here — a feast such as you'll not see again in a year."

Gruagach turned back, and now, to his astonishment, he found the castle walls had a door for every day of the year and a window for every day of the year. Then the son of the king of Ireland entered the castle. The feasting table was spread with meat and drink such as he had never dreamed of, and at once the musicians struck up to entertain him and the girl who had summoned him.

Servants made up a bed with down pillows for the prince. They washed his feet with warm water, and he went to lie down. And when he got up the next morning, he found the feasting table covered once more with sumptuous foods. Gruagach was so royally entertained that he was scarcely aware that time was passing.

One day the beautiful girl leaned against the lintel of Gruagach's door. "Fair Leader!" she said. "Son of the king of Ireland! How do you feel now?"

"I'm well," said Gruagach.

"Do you know how long ago you came here?" she asked.

"If I stay here until this evening, I'll have been here for a week," said Gruagach.

"You've been here for twelve weeks," said the girl. "And until you want to go back home, you're welcome to meat and drink and bed just as fine as they are now."

Time passed, and it seemed to Gruagach that he had stayed at the castle for a full month.

One day the beautiful girl leaned against the lintel of Gruagach's door. "So!" she said. "Son of the king of Ireland! How do you feel today?"

"Very well!" said Gruagach.

"And strong in mind and body?"

"I'd like to pick up that peak over there," said the son of the king of Ireland, "and set it down on that tabletop of a hill."

"Do you know how long ago you came here?"

"I've been here for just one month, I think," he said.

"You've been here two years today," she said.

"And now I'm so well," said Gruagach, "that I don't think there's ever been a man on the face of Earth who could get the better of me in tests of strength and speed."

"You're stupid," said the girl. "Near here lives a warrior band called the Feen, and they'll get the better of you. There's never been a man who could better them."

"I won't eat a morsel or drink a drop or sleep a wink until I have seen them and found out who they are," said Gruagach.

"Fair Leader!" said the beautiful girl. "Don't be so stupid! You're light-headed — let it pass!"

"I will not rest by day or night," said Gruagach, "until I've seen them."

"It's soft and misty today," said the girl, "and you'll find the Feen netting trout. You'll see the Feen on one side of the river and Finn, their leader, alone on the other side. Go straight over to Finn and bless him."

"I will," said Gruagach.

"And he'll bless you in return. Then ask Finn if he'll take you into his service. He'll tell you he can offer you nothing, and that the Feen are strong enough already. He'll say he will not throw a man out of his band to make room for you."

"And then?" asked Gruagach.

"He'll ask you your name. And you will say, 'Gruagach, the son of the king of Ireland.' And then Finn will reply, 'Though I've no need of another man, how can I refuse the son of your father? But listen to me: don't start ordering the Feen around!'"

Gruagach, the fair leader, the son of the king of Ireland, left the castle. He reached the place where the Feen were living and found them fishing for trout, Finn on one side and all his companions on the other side of the river. Gruagach went straight over to Finn and blessed him, and Finn blessed him in return.

"I've heard of your feats," said Gruagach, "and come to ask you to take me into your service."

"Well!" said Finn. "I've no need of another man at the moment. What's your name?"

"I've never hidden my name. Fair Gruagach, son of the king of Ireland."

"I spent my childhood at his court," said Finn, "and that is where I will live in my old age. Who can I take into service if I refuse your father's son? But listen to me," said Finn. "Don't start ordering the Feen around! Come here and hold the end of this net, and drag it along with me!"

Gruagach began to drag the net with Finn and his companions. Then he glanced up at the crag above him, and what should he see but a deer.

"Wouldn't you do better—you strong, lithe, young men," said Gruagach, "to be hunting that deer than trawling the river for a pert trout? A morsel of fish and a mouthful of juice are never going to satisfy you. One bite of venison and one mouthful of broth would nourish you."

"You may be right," said Finn, "but we're seven times tired of that deer. We know enough about him already."

"Well," Gruagach persisted, "I've heard that one of your companions is called Speed. I've heard he can catch the swift March wind, and the swift March wind can't catch him."

"Since this is your first suggestion, we'll send out a man to follow the deer," said Finn.

Finn summoned Caoilte, and Gruagach said to him, "This is what I want you to do: run after the deer I saw up on that crag."

"The fair leader has joined our company today," said Finn, "and we should take his advice on his first day with us. You, Caoilte, go and follow that deer."

"Many is the day I've chased him," said Caoilte, "and I've nothing to show for it—nothing but frustration at being unable to catch him."

Then Caoilte left the band and ran up to the crag.

"How fast can Caoilte run?" asked Gruagach.

"He can cover three fathoms in one stride," Finn said.

"And how many fathoms can the deer cover?"

"He can cover seven fathoms in a stride," said Finn, "when he is running as fast as he can."

"How far has the deer to run before he reaches safety?" asked Gruagach.

"He has to cross seven valleys and climb seven hills and pass seven summer lodges before he reaches a place of safety," Finn replied.

"Shall we drag the net again?" said Gruagach.

So Finn and Gruagach and the band of Feen fished for trout again, and then the fair leader looked around him and said, "Finn, son of Cumhail, put your finger on your wisdom tooth, and find out how far Caoilte is behind the deer."

Finn put his finger on his wisdom tooth. "Caoilte is covering two fathoms in one stride, and for the moment, the deer is doing the same."

"How far have they run?" asked Gruagach.

"Two valleys and two hills," said Finn. "They still have five to run."

"Let's drag the net again and fish for trout," said Gruagach.

After they'd been working for a while, the fair leader turned around and said, "Finn, son of Cumhail, put your finger on your wisdom tooth, and find out how far Caoilte is behind the deer."

"Caoilte is covering three fathoms in one stride, and the deer is covering four, and Caoilte is running as fast as he can," said Finn.

"How many valleys and hills and summer lodges have they still to run?" asked Gruagach.

"There are four behind them," said Finn, "and three in front of them."

"Let's drag the net again," said the fair leader. And for a while the band fished for trout.

"Finn, son of Cumhail," said Gruagach, "how far has the deer to run?"

"One valley and one hill and one summer house," replied Finn.

Gruagach threw down the net and ran up to the crag. He was

able to catch the swift March wind, and the swift March wind could not catch him. Gruagach came up behind Caoilte, blessed him, and passed him.

The deer kicked its legs in the air and leaped over the ford of the Red Stream. Gruagach was right behind him, and he leaped, too, and caught one of the deer's back legs before he landed.

The deer gave a roar, and the old woman at the ford cried, "Who has seized the beast I so love?"

"I have," said the fair leader, "the son of the king of Ireland."

"Gruagach, son of the king of Ireland!" said the old woman. "Let him go!"

"I will not," said Gruagach. "I've caught the deer, and he's my beast now."

"Give me a fistful of his bristles," beseeched the old woman, "or a mouthful of broth, or a morsel of venison."

"You," said Gruagach, "will have no share in it."

"The Feen are on their way here," the old woman said, "and Finn is at their head. Not one of them will escape. I'll bind them all back-to-back."

"You do that," said Gruagach. "I am going on my way."

Gruagach left the ford, taking the deer with him, and he kept walking until he met the Feen.

"Finn, son of Cumhail," said Gruagach. "Take this deer!"

Finn sat down with the deer tethered beside him, and Gruagach went down into the valley. He made straight for the workshop of the twenty-seven blacksmiths and had them forge three small iron hoops for each member of the Feen. Gruagach took a hammer from the workshop and carried the hoops back to the band. There, he put three hoops over the head of each of the Feen and tapped them down with a hammer.

Then the old woman appeared, screeching, "Finn, son of Cumhail, give me back the beast I so love!"

The old woman's screech was so piercing that the top hoop on each of the Feen's heads shivered and shattered.

Then the old woman yelled for a second time, and the middle hoop burst. For a while there was silence. Then the old woman screamed for the third time, and the third hoop burst.

The old woman left the Feen and walked into a wood. There she cut and twisted a branch. Then she came back, and now that they were no longer protected from her by iron, she bound the whole warrior band back-to-back — every man except for Finn.

Gruagach killed the deer and flayed it. He took out the heart and all the offal and buried them under the turf. Then he hung a cauldron over the fire, cut up the deer and put it into the cauldron, and threw more wood on to the re.

"Finn, son of Cumhail," said Gruagach, "would you rather go and dispose of that witch or stay here and watch the cauldron?"

"Well!" said Finn. "It's no easy job, this cauldron! If one morsel of venison is not properly cooked, the deer will stand up unharmed; and if one drop of the broth spills into the fire, he'll rise up unharmed. I'd rather stay and watch over the cauldron."

Once more the witch appeared. "Finn, son of Cumhail," she said, "give me a fistful of his bristles or a clenched fist of his heart; give me a gulp of broth or a morsel of venison."

"I did not catch this deer or kill him, and I'm not free to give any away," said Finn.

Then Gruagach and the old woman began a contest. They challenged each other to make bog out of rock and rock out of bog. On stony ground, they challenged each other to sink up to the knees; on muddy ground, they challenged each other to sink up to the eyes.

"Finn, son of Cumhail," said Gruagach, "have you seen enough of this witch?"

"I'd seen enough of her long ago," Finn replied.

Gruagach seized the old hag and kicked her on the back of one knee — right in the crook of the bough — and felled her.

"Finn," said Gruagach, "shall I cut her head off?"

"I don't know," said Finn.

"Finn, son of Cumhail," said the witch, "I lay you under crosses and under spells, under holy herdsmen of quiet traveling women. I command the little calf, feeble as he is, to take away your head and strip you of your life unless, three hours before daybreak, you make love to the wife of the griffin."

"I," said Gruagach, "lay you under crosses and under spells, under holy herdsmen of quiet traveling women. I command the little calf, feeble as he is, to take away your head and strip you of your life unless you stand with one foot on either side of the ford of the Red Stream and have every drop of its water flow through you."

Gruagach forced the old woman to stand up.

"Lift your spells from me," said the witch, "and I'll lift mine from Finn."

The fair leader walked over to the fire and unhooked the cauldron. He picked up a fork and knife and prodded the meat with the fork. Then he carved a morsel of venison and ate it. After this, Gruagach cut a shaving of turf and stopped the mouth of the cauldron with it.

Then Gruagach and Finn let the old woman go, and she did not return. She went straight to the ford and put one foot down on either side.

"Finn, son of Cumhail," said Gruagach, "it's time we were on our way. Are you a good horseman?"

"I can learn," said Finn.

Gruagach picked up a switch and handed it to Finn. "Strike me with this," he said.

Finn struck Gruagach and turned him into a brown mare.

"Mount me!" said Gruagach. "And be careful now!"

The mare Gruagach sprang forward and leaped over nine ridges, and Finn was not thrown. Then the mare sprang forward again and leaped over nine more ridges, and again Finn was not thrown. Then the mare began to gallop. She was able to catch the swift March wind and the swift March wind was not able to catch her.

"There's a little town down in that valley," said the mare. "You must go down there and get three flasks of wine and three wheat loaves, and give me one of the flasks and one of the loaves. And then you must comb me — first against the nap, then with the nap."

Finn secured the wine and the loaves, and soon they came to the towering wall beyond which the griffin lived.

"Finn, son of Cumhail," said the mare. "Dismount and give me a flask of wine and a wheat loaf."

Finn dismounted and did as the mare asked.

"And now comb me against the nap, then with the nap."

Finn did that too.

"Be careful now!" said the mare.

Then the mare ran at the wall and leaped, but she was only able to jump one-third as high as the wall.

"Give me another flask of wine and another loaf, and comb me against the nap, then with the nap," said the mare.

Finn did as the mare asked.

"Be careful now!" said the mare.

The mare ran at the wall and leaped, and she was able to jump two-thirds as high as the wall.

"Give me that last flask of wine and the last loaf, and comb me against the nap, then with the nap," said the mare.

Finn did as the mare asked.

The mare leaped and landed right on top of the towering wall.

"Finn, son of Cumhail," said the mare, "all is well! The griffin is away from home!"

Then the mare carried Finn over the wall, and Finn walked alone to the lair of the griffin. Meat and drink were set before him. He lay down to sleep — and three hours before daybreak he made love to the wife of the griffin.

Finn rose before daybreak. He left the lair and rejoined the mare Gruagach, and they galloped away from that place.

"The griffin is away from home," said Gruagach, "but when he comes back, his wife will not hide anything from him. He'll come after us, but come in such haste that he forgets his book of spells. Without it," said Gruagach, "I'll be able to get the better of him. With his book, the griffin is the most powerful beast in the world."

"What are his powers?" asked Finn. "And how will you counter them?"

"He'll charge at me as a bull, and I'll rear up as a bull in front of him. I'll jolt his head to one side with the first blow I give him and make him roar in pain."

"And then?" asked Finn.

"He'll spring at me as a donkey, and I'll spring up as a donkey in front of him. And the first butt I give him, I'll take a mouthful out of him."

"And then?" asked Finn.

"Then he'll take the shape of a hawk of the heavens," said Gruagach, "and I'll fly up in front of him as a hawk of the wood. And the first stoop I make, I'll rip out his heart and his liver. Then I'll swoop down, and you must wrap me up in this cloth. Cut away some turf and put me under it, replace the turf, and stand on it."

"And then?" asked Finn.

"While you're standing on the turf and I'm under the soles of your feet, the griffin's wife will come. She'll have the book of spells concealed in a bale of hay strapped to her back."

"And then?" asked Finn.

"And then she'll say: 'Finn, son of Cumhail, you're a man who has never told a lie. Tell me who in the world killed my husband.' And you will reply: 'I do not know who above Earth killed your husband.' Then the griffin's wife will run off, weeping and wailing."

Finn and the mare Gruagach walked on a little way, and who should they see coming but the griffin.

The griffin turned into a bull, and Gruagach turned into a bull in front of him, and jolted his head to one side with the first blow he gave him, so that the griffin roared in pain.

Then the griffin sprang at Gruagach as a donkey and Gruagach sprang up as a donkey in front of him; with the first butt Gruagach gave him, he took a mouthful out of the griffin. Then the griffin took the shape of a hawk of the heavens and Gruagach flew up in front of him as a hawk of the wood. Then Gruagach swooped down and Finn seized him and wrapped him up in the cloth. Finn cut away some turf, put Gruagach under it, replaced the turf, and stood on it. And then the griffin's wife came, with the book of spells concealed in a bale of hay strapped onto her back.

"Finn, son of Cumhail, you're a man who has never told a lie. Who killed my husband?"

"I do not know who above Earth killed your husband."

Then the griffin's wife ran off, weeping and wailing, and went far, far away.

Then Finn took the hawk in the cloth and lifted him into the

air and carried him to the castle where the Lady of the Green Gown lived. He gave the cloth bundle to the Lady. "You may find something in there," he said.

The Lady of the Green Gown retired to her own room, and when she opened the bundle, Gruagach turned himself back into a man again.

"Where is Finn?" asked Gruagach.

"Finn, son of Cumhail," said the Lady of the Green Gown, "Gruagach, son of the king of Ireland, is asking for you."

"Of all the things I've ever heard," said Finn, "I like this best: that Gruagach is asking for me."

The Lady of the Green Gown put meat and drink in front of Finn and Gruagach, but they wouldn't eat a morsel or drink a drop until such time as they were able to share the deer with the rest of the Feen.

Finn and Gruagach reached the place where the warriors were still bound and loosed each and every one of them. They were all ravenous, and Gruagach spread out the deer in front of them. But much as they ate, they still left three-quarters of the deer uneaten.

"I will go and tell this tale to the old woman," said Gruagach. He got up and went to the ford of the Red Stream and found the witch there. Every time Gruagach started another episode of his and Finn's adventures, the old woman started to bristle and rise up; and each time she started to rise up, Gruagach seized her and crushed her bones and broke them and went on telling his tale.

Then Gruagach returned to the band of the Feen, and he and Finn proceeded to the castle of the Lady of the Green Gown.

"Blessings be with you, Finn," said Gruagach, son of the king of Ireland. "I've found everything I was looking for—each person and place and marvel—and now I'll return home to my own father's palace."

"So you're going to leave me," said Finn, "after everything I've

done for you. You're going to tie yourself to someone else and leave me on my own."

"Is that what you think?" said Gruagach. "If that were the choice, I'd prefer your service and your company to that of any woman I've ever met. Finn, come to my father's palace with me."

Gruagach and the Lady of the Green Gown and Finn went to the palace of Gruagach's father. And there a priest married Gruagach and the Lady of the Green Gown.

A great feast was held for them, full of laughter and joy. Music was raised and misery cast down. Dishes were piled high with meat; cups were replenished with gleaming wine; instruments kept their owners busy. The wedding feast lasted for a year and a day, and it was as happy on the last day as the first.

THE PEDDLER OF SWAFFHAM

ONE NIGHT, JOHN CHAPMAN HAD A DREAM. A MAN STOOD BY him, dressed in a coat as red as blood, and the man said, "Go to London Bridge. Go and be quick. Go; good will come of it."

John the peddler woke with a start. "Cateryne," he whispered, "Cateryne, wake up! I've had a dream."

Cateryne, his wife, groaned and tossed and turned. "What?" she said.

"I've had a dream."

"Go to sleep, John," she said, and she fell asleep again.

John lay and wondered at his dream, and while he lay wondering, he, too, fell asleep. But the man in scarlet came a second time, and said, "Go to London Bridge. Go and be quick. Go; good will come of it."

The peddler sat up in the dark. "Cateryne!" he growled. "Wake up! Wake up! I've had the same dream again."

Cateryne groaned and tossed and turned. "What?" she said. Then John told her his dream.

"You," she said. "You would believe anything."

The moment he woke the next morning, the peddler of Swaffham remembered his dream. He told it to his children, Margaret and Hue and Dominic. He told it to his wife again.

"Forget it!" said Cateryne.

So John went about his business as usual, and as usual, his mastiff went with him. He fed his pig and hens in the backyard. He hoisted his pack on his broad shoulders and went to the marketplace; he set up his stall of pots and pans, household goods of one kind and another, vials and potions, and special trimmings for ladies' gowns. He gossiped with his friends — the butcher, the baker, the blacksmith, the shoemaker, the weaver, the dyer, and many others. But no

matter what he did, the peddler could not escape his dream. He shook his lion head, he rubbed his blue eyes, but the dream seemed real, and everything else seemed dreamlike. "What am I to do?" he said.

And his mastiff opened his jaws and yawned. That evening John Chapman walked across the marketplace to the tumbledown church. And there he found the thin priest, Master Fuller; his holy cheekbones shone in the half-light. "Well, what is it?" Master Fuller said. Then John told him about his strange dream.

"I dream, you dream, everyone dreams," said the priest impatiently, swatting dust from his black gown. "Dream of how we can get gold to rebuild our church! This ramshackle place is an insult to God."

The two of them stood and stared sadly about them: all the walls of stone were rickety and uneven; the roof of the north aisle had fallen in, and through it they could see the crooked spire.

John Chapman gave a long sigh. "Gold," he said. "I wish I could."

Then the peddler left the church and went back to his small cottage. But he was still uneasy. Nothing he did, and nothing anyone had said, seemed to make any difference; he could not forget his dream.

That night Cateryne said, "You've talked and talked of the man with the coat as red as blood. You've been more dreaming than awake. Perhaps, after all, you must go to London Bridge."

"I'll go," said John. "I'll go and be quick."

The next day, John Chapman got up at first light. At once he began to make ready for his journey. He hurried about; he banged his head against a beam; his face turned red. "I must take five gold pieces," he said. "I must take my cudgel."

"You must take your hood," said Cateryne.

Then John looked at his mastiff. "I must take you," he said. And the mastiff thumped the ground with his tail; dust and chaff flew through the air.

"Tell no one where I've gone," said John Chapman. "I don't want to be the laughingstock of Swaffham."

Then, while the peddler ate his fill of meat and curds, Cateryne put more food into his pack—cheese, two loaves made of beans and bran, and a gourd full of ale.

So everything was ready. And just as the June Sun rose behind a light cloud, a great coin of gold, John kissed his wife and his children goodbye.

"Come back!" called little Dominic.

They stood by the door, the four of them, waving and waving until the peddler with his pack, his cudgel, and his mastiff had walked out of Swaffham, out of sight.

John Chapman strode past the archery range just outside the town; he hurried between fields white with sheep. At first he knew the way well, but then the rough highway that men called the Gold Road left the open fields behind and passed through sandy heathland where there were no people, no sheep, no villages.

Soon the rain came, heavy, blurring everything. John pulled his hood over his head, but the water seeped through it. It soaked through his clothes and dripped from his nose.

By midday, he was tired and steaming. So he stopped to eat food and give a bone to his mastiff. And while they ate, some lord's messenger, decked out in red and blue, galloped by and spattered them with mud.

"The devil take him!" the peddler said.

During the afternoon, the rain eased, and the peddler and his dog were able to quicken their pace. One by one, the milestones dropped away; they made good progress.

But that evening it grew dark before the peddler could find any shelter, even a peasant's shack or some deserted hovel. John had no

choice but to sleep in the open, under an oak tree. "God help us," he said, "if there are wolves."

But there were no wolves, only strange night sounds: the tree groaning and creaking, wind in the moaning leaves and wind in the rustling grass, and the barking of fox and vixen. When first light came, John could barely get to his feet for the ache in his cold bones and the cramp in his empty stomach.

And his mastiff bobbled about as if he were a hundred.

So for four days they walked. Each hour contained its own surprise; John talked to a friendly priest who had been to Jerusalem; he kept company with a couple of vagabonds who wanted him to go to a fair at Waltham; he shook off a rascally pardoner who tried to sell him a ticket to heaven; he saw rabbits and hares and deer; he gazed down from hill crests at tapestries of fields; he followed the way through dark forests where only silence lived. Never in his life had John seen so many strangers nor set eyes on so many strange things. "I'll tell you what," he said to his mastiff. "You and I are foreigners in our own country."

Sometimes the peddler's pack chafed at his shoulders; often he envied the many travelers with horses — pilgrims and merchants, scholars and monks — but not for one moment did he forget his purpose. For as long as it was light, John Chapman made haste, following the Gold Road south toward London. And each night after the first, he stayed at a wayside inn.

On the morning of the fifth day, the peddler and his dog came at last to the city of London: at the sight of the high walls, John's heart quickened, and so did his step.

And his mastiff leaped about, barking in excitement.

They hurried through the great gate, and there before them were crowds of people coming and going, toing and froing — men shouting their wares, women jostling and gossiping, small children begging,

and many, many others sitting in rags in the filthy street. And there were houses to left and right, and after that, more houses, more streets, and always more people. John had never seen such a sight nor smelled such a stink nor heard such a hubbub.

A tide of people swept him along until he came to a place where four ways met. There, John stopped a man and asked him the way to London Bridge.

"Straight on," said the man. "Straight as an arrow's flight, all the way."

The broad river gleamed under the Sun, silver and green, ruckled by wind; gulls swooped and climbed again, shrieking. The great bridge spanned the water, the long bridge with its houses overhanging the river. It was a sight to gladden any man. And when he saw it, John Chapman got to his knees. He thanked God that his journey had been safe, and that he had come at last to London Bridge.

But the moment the peddler stepped onto the bridge itself, he felt strangely foolish. All his hope and excitement seemed long ago. People were passing this way and that, but no one so much as looked at him. No one took the least notice of him. Having at last found London Bridge, the poor peddler of Swaffham felt utterly lost.

He walked up and down; he stared about him; he watched boats shoot the bridge; he added up his money. Hour after hour after hour went by; the peddler waited.

Late that afternoon, a group of pilgrims on horseback gathered on the bridge. And they began to sing: "*As you came from the holy land of Walsingham . . .*"

"Walsingham!" cried John. "I know it well. I've taken my wares there a hundred times. Will this song explain my dream?"

As if to answer him, the group of pilgrims broke up and rode off, still singing, even as he hurried toward them.

"Wait!" bawled John. "Wait!"

But the hooves of the horses clattered, and the poor peddler was left, in the fading light, looking after them. John felt heavyhearted. He wearily asked a passerby where he might stay and was directed to the Three Cranes, a hostelry on the riverbank, a stopping place for passengers coming down the river, a sleeping place for travelers in all weather.

There John Chapman and his mastiff shared a bed of straw; they were both dog tired.

Early on the morning of the second day, the peddler and his dog returned to the bridge. Once again, hour after hour went by. But late that day, John saw a man with matted red hair lead a loping black bear across the bridge. "Look!" he exclaimed delightedly.

And his mastiff looked carefully.

"A rare sight!" said John. "A sight worth traveling miles to see. Perhaps here I shall find the meaning of my dream." So the peddler greeted the man, and he thought he had never seen anyone so ugly in all his life. "Does the bear dance?" he asked.

"He does," said the man. He squinted at John. "Give me gold and I'll show you."

"Another time," said the peddler. And he stepped forward to pat the bear's gleaming fur.

"Hands off!" snapped the man.

"Why?" asked John.

"He'll have your hand off, that's why."

The peddler stepped back hastily and called his mastiff to heel.

"He had a hand off at Cambridge," said the man.

"Not the best companion," said John.

"He'll bite your head off!" growled the man, and he squinted more fiercely than ever.

So the second day turned out no better than the first. And on the

third day, the poor peddler waited and waited; he walked up and down and he walked to and fro, and no good came of it. "Now we have only one piece of gold left," he said to his mastiff. "Tomorrow we'll have to go home; I'm a great fool to have come at all."

At that moment a man shaped like an egg waddled up to John. "For three days," he said, "you've been loitering on this bridge."

"How do you know?" asked John, surprised.

"From my shop I've seen you come and go, come and go from dawn to dusk. What are you up to? Who are you waiting for?"

"That's exactly what I was asking myself," said the peddler sadly. "To tell you the truth, I've walked to London Bridge because I dreamed that good would come of it."

"Lord preserve me!" exclaimed the shopkeeper. "What a waste of time!"

John Chapman shrugged his shoulders and sighed; he didn't know what to say.

"Only fools follow dreams," said the shopkeeper. "Why, last night I had a dream myself. I dreamed a pot of gold lay buried by a hawthorn tree in a garden, and the garden belonged to some peddler in a place called Swaffham."

"A pot of gold?" said John. "A peddler?"

"You see?" said the egg-shaped man. "Nonsense!"

"Yes," said John.

"Dreams are just dreams," said the shopkeeper with a wave of his pudgy hand. "You're wasting your time. Take my advice and go back home."

"I will!" said John Chapman.

So it was that, on the evening of the twelfth day after his departure, John Chapman and his dog — spattered with mud, aching and

blistered, weary but excited — returned home. They saw the leaning church spire; they passed the archery range; they came at last to John's small cottage of twigs and clay.

Cateryne had never in her life been so glad to see her husband.

Margaret and Hue leaped about, and their ashen hair danced on their heads.

"Come back!" cried little Dominic.

"So," asked Cateryne, "what of the dream, John?"

Then John told them in his own unhurried way. He told them of his journey; he told them of the long days on London Bridge; and, at last, he told them of the shopkeeper's words.

"A man follows one dream and returns with another," said Cateryne. "How can it all be true?"

"I've asked myself that a thousand times," the peddler said, "and there's only one way to find out."

The gnarled hawthorn tree stood at the end of the yard; it had lived long, perhaps hundreds of years. And now its leaves seemed to whisper secrets.

The hens clucked in the dusk, and the pig lay still, one eye open, watching John.

"I'll start here," said the peddler quietly. Then he gripped his round-edged spade and began to dig, making a mound of the loose soil.

"Can I?" asked Margaret.

"Let me!" said Hue.

"Wait!" said John. And again he dug. The spade bit into the packed soil.

At once they heard it, the grind of metal against metal, muted by soil. The peddler took one look at his family and began to dig as fast as he could. Earth flew through the air. "Look!" he gasped. "Look! Look!" He had partly uncovered a great metal pot.

John tossed away his spade. He bent down and tugged. He worked his fingers farther under the pot and tugged again. Then suddenly the dark ground gave up its secret. John staggered backward, grasping the pot, and as he fell, the lid flew off. The ground was carpeted with gold!

At first they were all utterly silent. Only the tree, the tree in the gloom, went on whispering.

"Well! Gather it up," said the peddler, slapping dirt and straw from his coat with his great hands. "Take it inside."

They picked up the gold coins and put them back into the pot. Then they carried the pot into their cottage and placed it on the floor in front of the fire.

"Look! What's this?" said Hue, rubbing the lid of the pot. "It's writing."

John frowned and shook his head. "It's words," he said. "I know; I'll hide the gold here and take the empty pot with the rest of my wares to the marketplace. Someone is sure to come along and read it for us."

The next morning the peddler was in the marketplace early, and before long Master Fuller came picking his way toward him through the higgledy-piggledy stalls — a dark figure amid bright colors, a silent man in a sea of noise. "John Chapman," he exclaimed. "Where have you been?"

"To and fro," said the peddler.

"And where were you last Sunday?" asked the priest. "I missed you at mass."

"Well, I . . ."

"Excuses! Always excuses!" said the priest sharply. "Who shall be saved? Men are empty vessels." And he rapped the great metal pot with his knuckles; it rang with a deep note. "Now that's a fine vessel!" said Master Fuller.

"It is," agreed John Chapman.

"There are words on it," said the priest. He raised the lid and narrowed his eyes. "It's in Latin. It says, 'Under me'... yes... 'Under me there lies another richer than I.'" The priest frowned. "What does that mean?"

John Chapman scratched the back of his head.

"Where did you get it?"

"Out of a backyard," said the peddler, shrugging his broad shoulders.

"I must go," said the priest suddenly. "All this idle chatter. Men would do better to give time to God." And with that, the priest walked off toward the rickety church.

At once, the peddler packed up his wares and hurried home.

"This time you shall dig," he told his children.

Then Hue grasped the spade and began to dig; the rounded edge sheared through the darkness. His face soon flushed; he began to pant.

"Now let Margaret have it," the peddler said.

Hue scowled and handed the spade to his sister.

Margaret threw back her hair, stepped into the pit, and dug yet deeper. Deeper and deeper. Then, once again, metal grated against metal — the same unmistakable sound. Margaret shivered with excitement. "You," she said, and handed the spade back to her father.

Once more John dug as fast as he could; once more he tugged and tugged; and once more the reluctant Earth yielded its secret — a second great pot, an enormous pot twice as large as the first. The peddler could barely heave it out of the hole and onto the level ground. When he levered off the lid, they all saw that this pot, too, was heaped to the brim with glowing gold. "It's like a dream," said John, "and because of a dream. But we're awake, and rich."

Cateryne stared into the gaping black hole. "Who hid it there?" she said. "And why?"

"Someone who lived here before us?" said the peddler. "Or travelers on the Gold Road? How shall we ever know? People always say the hawthorn tree is a magic tree."

"What are we going to do with it?" asked Cateryne.

For a moment John did not reply. His blue eyes closed; his face wrinkled. "I know," he said at last. "I know. A little we'll keep—enough to pay for our own small needs, enough to buy ourselves a strip of land. But all the rest, every coin, we must give to Master Fuller to build the new church."

Cateryne drew in her breath and smiled and clapped her hands. "Amen!" she said.

"Amen!" chimed the children.

"In this way," said John, "everyone in Swaffham will share in the treasure."

"Now," said Cateryne, "and in time to come."

That afternoon, John Chapman found the priest skulking in the gloom of the tumbledown church. "Master Fuller," he said, "I can give gold for the new church."

"You?" said the priest. "Gold?"

"Wait here," said the peddler. He hurried out of the church and back to his cottage. There, he counted one hundred pieces of gold for his own needs and the needs of his family and hid them in the inner room, under the bed of straw.

Then the peddler and his wife, and Margaret and Hue, followed by Dominic and their loyal mastiff, carried the two pots to Swaffham Church. As they crossed the marketplace, they shouted to their friends, "Come with us! Come to the church!"

So the butcher, the baker, the blacksmith, the shoemaker, the

weaver, the dyer, and many others left their work. In no time, a great procession, curious and chattering, was filing into the silent church.

In the nave, John and Cateryne turned one pot upside down. Then Margaret and Hue emptied the other. A great mound of coins glowed mysteriously in the half-light.

The townspeople gasped, and Master Fuller's eyes gleamed.

"Explain!" he said.

So John Chapman told them the whole story from beginning to end. And no storyteller, before or since, has ever had such an audience.

"There's enough gold here," said Master Fuller, "to rebuild the north aisle and the steeple." Then he raised his right hand. "Let us pray," he said, "and after that . . . let us sing and dance the night away."

"Sing in the churchyard? Dance in the churchyard?" everyone cried.

"Even until this old church falls down," said Master Fuller. And for the first time that anyone could remember, he laughed. He threw back his head and laughed.

So, that same evening, a man with a bugle, a man with a hum-strum, and a man with cymbals and clappers played as if they meant to raise the roof off every house in Swaffham. The townsfolk sang and danced until midnight. And John the dreamer was tossed by the dancers into the air, higher and higher, toward the stars.

And his mastiff sat on his haunches and laughed.

THE WILDMAN

DON'T ASK ME MY NAME. I'VE HEARD YOU HAVE NAMES. I HAVE no name.

They say this is how I was born. A great wave bored down a river, and at the mouth of the river it ran up against a great wave of the sea. The coupled waves kicked like legs and whirled like arms and swayed like hips, sticks in the water snapped like bones, and the seaweed bulged like gristle and muscle. In this way the waves rose. When they fell, I was there.

My home is water as your home is land. I rise to the surface to breathe air; I glide down through the darkening rainbow. The water sleeks my hair as I swim. And when I stand on the seabed, the currents comb my waving hair; my whole body seems to ripple.

Each day I go to the land for food. I swim to the shore; I'm careful not to be seen. Small things, mice, shrews, moles — I like

them to eat. I snuffle and grub through the growth and undergrowth and grab them, squeeze the warm blood out of them, and chew them.

Always before sunset I'm back in the tugging, chuckling, sobbing water. Then the blue darkness that comes down over the sea comes inside me too. I feel heavy until morning. If I stayed too long on the land I might be found, lying there, heavy, unable even to drag myself back to the water.

My friends are seals. They dive as I do and swim as I do. Their hair is like my hair. I sing songs with their little ones. They've shown me their secret place, a dark grotto so deep that I howled for the pain of the water pressing around me there and rose to the surface, gasping for air. My friends are the skimming flatfish and the flickering eel and the ticklish trout. My friends are all the fishes.

As I swam near the river mouth, something caught my legs and tugged at them. I tried to push it away with my hands, and it caught my hands and my arms too. I kicked; I flailed; I couldn't escape. I was dragged through the water, up out of the darkness into the indigo, the purple, and the pale blue. I was lifted into the air, the sunlight, and down into a floating thing.

Others. There were others in it, others, others as I am. But their faces were not covered with hair. They had very little hair that I could see except on their heads, but they were covered with animal skins and furs. When they saw me, they were afraid and trembled and backed away, and one fell into the water.

I struggled and bit, but I was caught in the web they had made. They took me to land, and a great shoal gathered 'round me there. Then they carried me in that web to a great high place of stone and tipped me out into a gloomy grotto.

One of them stayed by me and kept making noises; I couldn't

understand him. I could tell he was asking me things. I would have liked to ask him things. How were you born? Why do you have so little hair? Why do you live on land? I looked at him, I kept looking at him, and when the others came back, I looked at them: their hairless hands, their legs, their shining eyes. There were so many of them almost like me, and I've never once seen anyone in the sea like me.

They brought me two crossed sticks. Why? What are they? They pushed them into my face; they howled at me. One of them smacked my face with his hand. Why was that? It hurt. Then another with long pale hair came and wept tears over me. I licked my lips; the tears tasted like the sea. Was this one like me? Did this one come from the sea? I put my arms around its waist, but it shrieked and pushed me away.

They brought me fish to eat. I wouldn't eat fish. Later they brought me meat; I squeezed it until it was dry, and then I ate it.

I was taken out into sunlight, down to the river mouth. The rippling, rippling water. It was pink and lilac and gray; I shivered with longing at the sight of it. I could see three rows of webs spread across the river from bank to bank. Then they let me go; they let me dive into the water. It coursed through my long hair. I laughed and passed under the first web and the second web and the third web. I was free. But why am I only free away from those who are like me, with those who are not like me? Why is the sea my home?

They were all shouting and waving their arms, and jumping up and down at the edge of the water. They were all calling out across the gray wavelets. Why? Did they want me to go back after all? Did they want me to be their friend?

I wanted to go back; I wanted them as friends. So I stroked back under the webs again and swam to the sandy shore. They fell on me

then, and twisted my arms, and hurt me. I howled. I screamed. They tied long webs around me and more tightly around me, and carried me back to the place of stone, and threw me into the gloomy grotto.

I bit through the webs. I slipped through the window bars. It was almost night, and the blue heaviness was coming into me. I staggered away, back to the water, the waiting dark water.

CHILDE LAMBTON NEVER WENT TO MASS ON SUNDAY MORNINGS.

"Think of your position," said his father.

"You go your way," said the childe, "and I'll go mine."

"Think of your soul," said Lord Lambton.

But the next Sunday was no different. While Lord Lambton and all the servants at the hall and the workers on the estate crossed the bridge over the Wear, and made their way into the Lambton chapel, the childe went fishing.

The young man whistled and pulled on his waders. He sidestepped down the steep riverbank. He stood in a pool of golden light and cast his line into the laughing water.

"Hell!" swore the childe when his hook snagged a lump of sodden weed, and "Hell!" when an hour had passed, dark and swift, and he had still caught nothing, not even a minnow.

The water glittered. The young man screwed up his eyes and cast his line once more, and then at once he saw the float disappear and felt a great tug at his line. He played his catch and began to haul it in.

The childe was astonished at the sight of his catch. The creature on the hook looked more like a lizard or a small snake than a fish. It was at least one foot long, with nine holes on either side of its mouth, and dry skinned and scaly.

"Hell!" shouted the childe. "Hell and damnation! What in God's name is this?"

"What's wrong?" said a voice.

The childe spun 'round, and up above him was an old man, his face acorn brown and his clothes in tatters.

"What have you caught?" the old man called. "Swearing like that! And on a Sunday!"

"Look!" said the childe. "I think I've caught the devil himself."

The old man levered himself down the bank and stared at the creature. "You have and all," he said.

"Do you recognize him, then?" asked the childe, grinning.

"It's wicked," said the old man, "whatever it is. And it won't do you no good, that's for sure."

"Finished?" said the childe, and he looked at the creature that was lashing its tail and trying to get off the hook.

"Don't you throw him back," said the old man. "You caught him, and you keep him." And with that, he turned his back on the childe, hauled himself up the bank, and went on his way.

Childe Lambton stared at the wriggling creature, and with its cold, glassy eyes, the creature stared at him.

"Gruesome," said the childe. "That's what you are. And I know what I can do with you."

Still holding his rod with the creature attached to it, the childe climbed up the riverbank and strode to the nearby well.

"Gruesome!" said the childe. "And I never want to see you again." Then he grasped the creature's dry skin, unhooked it, and tossed it into the well.

Time passed, and the creature grew too large to live in the well. One spring morning it stuck out its head and blinked its lidless eyes. It opened its mouth and roared!

A half-grown worm, it thrust up and out and shrithed down to the river. It coiled itself around a rock out in the quick water.

But that night the worm left the river and went visiting. It wrapped itself around a cow and sucked her dry. It chased five skipping lambs and ate them. It snarled and hissed in the darkness and terrified the workers on the estate and the servants in the hall.

In the early hours, the worm sidled and slid to a nearby hill and wound itself three times around it. There it rested until daybreak. But then it made its way back to the river, and the whole dreadful cycle began again.

Childe Lambton went to mass; every day he went, and on his knees prayed that they should all be delivered from the worm. The young man did penance. But now the worm attacked calves and sheep and lashed its tail, and every night the darkness was filled with terrible noises.

"If I leave this district," said the childe, "will the worm leave it too? I'll go on a pilgrimage to the Holy Land; then God may forgive me and spare us all this terrible scourge."

The childe was as good as his word. Only a few days later, he said a sad farewell to his father and set off from the hall. Then at once the worm's behavior changed, but far from leaving old Lord Lambton in peace, it grew even more dangerous and daring. In the evening it crossed the

fields between the River Wear and Lambton Hall and slowly shrithed up toward the hall itself. Inside the hall, the servants were terrified. The men picked up kitchen knives and cudgels, the dogs barked and barked, and in the stables the horses neighed and whinnied in terror.

One old steward kept his head. "Milk!" he said. "I've heard that worms drink milk." He hurried across to the dairy and found the two dairymaids there. "Bring out the milk!" he ordered. "Every pail! As quick as you can!"

Lifting two pails himself, the steward led the way to the stone trough in front of the hall. He poured the frothing milk straight into it, and the dairymaids followed him. In all, they poured the milk from nine cattle into the trough.

The worm crossed the herb garden and the rose garden and nosed its way up to the trough. It sniffed at the milk and at once began to lap it up. Splashing and slurping, it drank until it had drained the trough dry, and then it shot out its forked tongue and licked the stone. After this, the worm turned away from the hall; it lumbered away to the hill, wrapped itself around it, and settled down for the night.

From that day on, the steward made sure that the trough was filled each evening with the milk of nine cattle. When once several of the cattle fell sick and did not produce much milk, the worm hissed and snarled. It shrithed around the park, lashing its tail in fury, and uprooted two huge oaks and a fir tree.

The seasons turned and the years passed, and one knight and then another and then a third came to the aid of Lord Lambton. Each was sure he could kill the worm and win fame and a name forever. But all three knights came to the same end. The worm coiled itself around them, one by one, and squeezed them to death.

For seven years Childe Lambton did penance in the Holy Land, and at the end of the seventh year he came home.

The young man saw that the fields around the hall had not been plowed, and in the corner of one field stood a plowshare, rusty. The paddocks once full of bullocks and lambs were deserted. No brazen pheasants paraded on the lawns. Many of the park trees had been uprooted. The childe looked about him in utter dismay.

Inside the hall, the childe found his old father, grown white with time and frail with worry. The hall itself was webbed and dusty. For fear of the worm, every single servant except the faithful steward had fled from the place.

The childe took his father into his arms.

"I forgive you," said his old father, trembling.

"Oh! Father!" said the childe.

"Will you go and see the wise woman at Brugeford?" said his father. "Will you ask her if there is anything at all you can do to save us from this worm?"

When Childe Lambton had found the wise woman, she told him at once, "You brought this on our heads, and only you can release us."

"I'd lay down my life to spare my father more suffering," the young man said.

"Maybe you will," said the wise woman. "But you, and only you, can kill this worm."

"How?" asked the childe.

"Take your suit of armor to the blacksmith. Have him spike it. Ask him to inlay it with sharp spear points. Then, before dawn, go down to the river. Wait for the worm there."

"I will," said the childe.

"There's one thing more," added the wise woman. "You must swear

an oath that, if you kill the worm, you'll put to death the first living thing you meet on your way back to the hall. Do this, and all will be well. Fail, and the Lambtons will be cursed. No Lambton will die in peace, in his own bed, for nine generations."

"I swear," said the childe.

Childe Lambton went straight back to the hall to report what the wise woman had said.

"If I kill this worm," the childe said, "I'll blow my bugle three times. If you hear three blasts, open the doors and let Tempest run out to me."

Tempest wagged his tail at the sound of his name.

"Whatever you do," said the childe, "be sure not to come out before the dog does. There's no other way to do it," he muttered.

Then Childe Lambton went to the forge, and when the blacksmith had inlaid his armor with vicious spikes, he withdrew to the chapel at Brugeford. He prayed and renewed his vow, and before dawn he donned his armor and went down to the river.

As soon as darkness paled, the worm shrithed from the hill toward the water, and swam up the river toward the weeping rock. At once it saw the childe. It rapped the water with its tail and raised a sheet of flying spray. Then the worm snarled and surged forward; it seized the young man and wound its coils around him and tried to crush him to death.

But the tighter the worm squeezed, the more fiercely the spear points dug into its flesh. The worm hissed; the river darkened.

Then the worm eased its grip; it unwound its coils. As soon as his right arm was free, the childe raised his sword. He crashed it down: with one savage blow, he cut the creature in half.

The tail end of the worm was at once swept away in the dark waters. But its head and body renewed the attack, and again coiled 'round the

childe in his armor. Once more the spear points did their worst. Poisonous blood spurted into the river, and when it unwound itself for a second time, the worm was too weak to fight any longer. Its eyes were bleary. It slumped into the water, coughing foam and blood, and as the hurrying current took it, it rolled over onto its back and died.

The childe raised his visor and staggered up the riverbank. In his armor he walked across the wrecked park and into the rose garden. There he raised his bugle to his lips and blew three resounding blasts.

The old lord and the steward stared at each other. They grasped each other's arms. In their excitement, they forgot what they were meant to do and swung open the hall doors and hurried out first themselves.

Childe Lambton grasped his sword, still dripping with the worm's blood. He stared at his father, horrified. "The oath! The oath!" he shouted. And he raised his bugle and blew another blast.

The old lord and his steward stopped in their tracks. For a moment they stood there, and then they turned away. They stumbled back through the doors and untied Tempest.

The young man's loyal hound came bounding out to meet him. Then the childe pursed his lips; he swung his sword and lopped off Tempest's head.

Childe Lambton had killed the worm, and seven years of terror were at an end; but he had broken his vow, and one curse was replaced by another. No Lambton died in peace, in his own bed, for nine generations.

SHONKS AND THE DRAGON

"ME?" ASKED THE LORD OF THE MANOR OF PELHAM.

"You," said his daughter, namely Miss Eleanor. "You've no choice."

The lord of the manor, alias Sir Piers Shonks, crossed the huge trunk of his left leg over the huge trunk of his right leg and sighed terribly. He stared into the fire until his eyeballs were burning.

"Mmm!" he said.

"Think of Sigurd and Beowulf and Carantoc!" exclaimed Eleanor.

"Tittle-tattle!" said Shonks.

"Assipattle, you mean," said Eleanor.

"Prittle-prattle," muttered her father.

"And now," exclaimed Eleanor, "Sir Piers Shonks!"

"Shonks, conks, honks," said the lord of the manor of Pelham. "Does it sound as if I'm a dragon slayer?"

“Brave men need dragons,” Eleanor said, and there were dragons dancing in her eyes.

“I don’t need a dragon,” said Shonks. “No, thank you.”

“You do,” said Eleanor. “To prove yourself. Anyhow, you’ve got no choice.”

“I have!” said Shonks.

“You’ve no choice in the matter,” Eleanor repeated. “You’re the lord of the manor, and he’s the dragon of Brent Pelham. You’ve got to fight him.”

The lord of the manor had a difficult dream. He had decided once and for all not to fight the dragon. “Dragons be blowed!” he could hear himself saying. “Dragons be blowed, be blasted, be brummagemmed . . .”

But then the dragon of Brent Pelham came visiting. It shrithed into the manor and, most mysteriously, seemed to turn into his daughter, so that whenever Shonks looked at Eleanor, he seemed to be looking at the dragon.

And then, even more strangely, Shonks dreamed he was turning into the dragon himself. He was becoming a wrongdoer, an evil flamethrower, and the very people who depended on him now began to avoid him.

So when Shonks woke up, sweating and cold, after a horrible argument with his sheets and blankets, he knew his daughter was right. He had no choice! In the name of every man, woman, and child living in Brent Pelham — why, in his own name, modest as it was — he had to fight the dragon.

“Brute!” said Shonks, most miserably. “Biggonet, bastion, blabber, bodily, bone-white . . .” On and on he went, as if he were a walking lexicon. But quite what he was talking about was impossible to tell.

If anything, Sir Piers Shonks' armor was even more reluctant than its owner. It had long since gone into retirement; its shoulders and elbows and knees and ankles creaked and cracked, and for year after year armies of clothes moths had picnicked in the woolen padding inside the helmet.

"Darn!" grumbled Shonks. And then, "Drat! Devil's teeth!"

"Courage!" said Eleanor, helping her father secure his sword belt.

"That's what you're going to need, my girl," said Shonks.

"Me?" said Eleanor.

"I'm taking you with me."

Eleanor's eyes opened sky wide.

"You're the best man I've got," said her father. "Anyhow, I'm between squires."

So while the armorer oiled Shonks's groaning joints and the blacksmith sharpened his sword and spear, Eleanor stepped upstairs and changed into the best dress in her wardrobe.

"And now for my snood," she said. "Snood! I hate that word."

The dragon had made a mess of Brent Pelham. He had set fire to two of the embattled old oaks, guardians of the village green since the days of King Alfred. He had flattened whole hedgerows. And worst of all, he had knocked down seven little cruck cottages, eaten three harvest-heavy pigs and dozens of chickens, and blown out the new nativity window at the east end of the church.

"Blessed Virgin, preserve me!" said Shonks.

"She's nothing but glass splinters," Eleanor said. "All over the churchyard. You'll have to make do with the saints. Saint Martha and Saints George, Philip, and Pol."

Father and daughter galloped along on the ride between Great

Pepsells and Little Pepsells, and Shonks's three best hounds galloped beside them — and all three were so fleet and light of foot that one old man, rather the worse for wear, was quite certain they had wings.

In both fields, the poor corn looked as if it had run this way and run that way and pressed its ears to the ground.

And underground, in its lair beneath the roots of the great yew tree, the dragon heard them coming. It rose to the light.

"Dear God!" said Shonks. And then "BACK! BACK!" he shouted at Eleanor. "My beautiful! Brightest! Best! My everything else beginning with *B*!"

Then Shonks dismounted, and he and the dragon joined in battle. Shonks raised his ashen spear, and the dragon raised its head. It bellowed and blew out vile, sulfurous smoke.

Many is the battle won by mistake. When the dragon threw fire at him, Shonks stepped sideways to avoid the jet stream; he stepped and tripped and fell forward; and falling, he thrust his spear right down the dragon's throat.

"Aargh!" said the dragon.

Gargle and spit! Humans, horses, hounds, and all the birds in heaven itself were coated with flecks of pink foam. It made the three hounds grin and sneeze.

"Listen to the birds!" shouted Shonks. "Life! That's what they're singing. Life, life, life!"

"Father," called Eleanor. Quickly she dismounted, then she picked up her skirts, ran toward Shonks over the bumpy ground, and threw herself into his metal embrace.

When Sir Piers and Miss Eleanor had disentangled themselves, they saw a man leaning quite nonchalantly against one side of the dead dragon.

"Good morning!" he said, and he smiled and blew on his long white fingers. He was very slight, and his hair and eyes were both dark. "Good morning to you both!"

"Where have you come from?" asked Shonks.

"Immediately," said the man, "from Cambridge. Or do you mean, how did I get here?"

"Well," said Shonks, "I haven't seen you around here before."

"No," said the man, still smiling, and he flexed his fingers. "I live in your hereafter."

"My hereafter?"

"So we should be seeing plenty of one another before too long."

"What do you mean?" asked Eleanor, and she took her father's arm. "What's your name?"

"I have many names," said the little man quite affably. "Some say, 'the great dragon.'"

"I know my book of Revelation," said Shonks quickly. "I know who you are."

"Then you know why I'm here," said the man.

"Saint Matthew and Saint Mark and Saint Luke and Saint John," murmured Shonks. "May they trample the dragon under their feet!"

"I see you've killed my servant," said the little man. "Well! A life for a life! You've killed the dragon of Brent Pelham, so when you die, Piers Shonks, I'll have you."

"No!" cried Shonks. "Not! Never! *Numquam!*"

"Oh yes, Shonks. I'll have you, body and soul."

"Not if I'm buried inside the church. I'll have them bury me inside the church."

"Inside the church, outside the church, it doesn't matter to me; I'll have you either way."

"Never!" shouted Shonks again.

The man winked at Miss Eleanor. "And you, my pretty," he said, "you're my witness."

Piers Shonks shook off one of his gauntlets and bowed his head and crossed himself. "I commend my soul to God," he said. "And when I die, my body will lie — lie undisturbed and asleep — exactly where I choose."

The man arched his black eyebrows and smiled at Shonks. There were flames in his freezing eyes. Then he simply stamped one foot and disappeared.

Years passed, and Sir Piers Shonks became old. He became very old and his mouth grew dry.

"Dreary, devil, dragon, dropsical, Dunstable," muttered Shonks as he lay on his deathbed. "And everything else beginning with *D*." And then, rallying himself considerably: "Carry me outside! Bring me my longbow!"

Six manor servants lifted the lord of the manor of Pelham, still lying on his bed. They carried him down to the moat, and there Miss Eleanor put his longbow in his speckled hands.

"Cut from the great yew — the one between Great Pepsells and Little Pepsells," said Eleanor. "Do you remember, Father?"

"Oh, do shut up!" said Shonks. "Give me an arrow!"

Shonks screwed up his eyes and drew in his lips and notched an arrow.

"Now listen to me!" he said. "I'll shoot this one arrow and then I'll die."

The manor servants began to get down on their knees in the wet grass.

"Bury me wherever this arrow falls! Wherever it falls. Do you understand me?"

The six servants nodded.

"As you choose, Father," said Miss Eleanor.

"Inside or outside, indeed!" grumbled Shonks. "Inside the church, outside the church, I'll show him."

Then the lord of the manor of Pelham summoned up all the remaining strength in his body. He drew back the bowstring as far as he could, and then even a little farther, and released it.

The string hummed and shuddered and fell still, but the arrow flew singing through the bright air. It rose and sped and dipped, dipped and stuck into the north wall of Brent Pelham Church.

So Shonks died smiling. Not inside the church, not outside the church: he was buried deep within the church wall. The devil reached out his long white fingers, and he still could not touch him.

SEA TONGUE

I AM THE BELL. I'M THE TONGUE OF THE BELL. I WAS CAST BEFORE your grandmother was a girl. Before your grandmother's grandmother. So long ago.

Listen now! I'm like to last. I'm gold and green, cast in bronze. I weigh two tons. Up here, in the belfry of this closed church, I'm surrounded by sounds. Mouthfuls of air. Words ring me.

High on this crumbling cliff, I can see the fields of spring and summer corn; they're green and gold, as I am. I can see the shining water, silver and black, and the far fisherman on it. And look! Here comes the bellringer — the old bellwoman.

I am the bellwoman. For as long as I live I'll ring this old bell for those who will listen.

Not the church people: they have all gone. Not the seabirds, not the lugworms, not the inside-out crabs nor the shining mackerel. Whenever storms shatter the glass or fogs take me by the throat, I ring for the sailor and the fisherman. I warn them off the quicksands and away from the crumbling cliff. I ring and save them from the sea god.

I am the sea god. My body is dark; it's so bright you can scarcely look at me, so deep you cannot fathom me.

My clothing is salt-fret raised by the four winds, twisting shreds of mist, shining gloom. And fog, fog, proofed and damp and cold. I'll wrap them around the fisherman. I'll wreck his boat.

I remember the days when I ruled Earth. I ruled her all — every grain and granule — and I'll rule her again. I'll gnaw at this crumbling cliff tonight. I'll undermine the church and its graveyard. I'll chew on the bones of the dead.

We are the dead. We died in bed; we died on the sword; we fell out of the sky; we swallowed the ocean.

To come to this: this green graveyard with its rows of narrow beds. Each of us separate and all of us one.

We lived in time and we're still wrapped in sound and movement — gull glide, gull swoop. We live time out, long bundles of bone bedded in the cliff.

I am the cliff. Keep away from me. I'm jumpy and shrinking, unsure of myself. I may let you down badly.

Layers and bands, boulders and gravel and grit and little shining

stones: these are Earth's bones. But the sea god keeps laughing and crying and digging and tugging. I scarcely know where I am, and I know time is ending. Fences. Red flags. Keep away from me. I'm not fit for the living.

We are the living. One night half of a cottage—Peter's cottage—bucketed down into the boiling water, and he was left standing on the cliff edge in his nightshirt.

After that, everyone wanted to move inland. We had no choice. You've only to look at the cracks. To listen to the sea god's hollow voice!

Every year he comes closer. Gordon's cottage went down. And Martha's. And Ellen's. The back of the village became the front. And now what's left? Only the bellwoman's cottage and the empty shell of the church.

I am the church. I remember the days when the bellows wheezed for the organ to play. I remember when people got down on their knees and prayed.

I've weathered such storms. Winds tearing at the walls, flint and brick, salt winds howling.

And now, tonight, this storm. So fierce, old Earth herself is shaking and shuddering. Ah! Here comes the old bellwoman.

I am the bellwoman. There! Those lights, stuttering and bouncing. There's a boat out there, and maybe ten.

Up, up these saucer steps as fast as I can. Up!

Here in this moldy room, I'll ring and ring and ring, and set heaven itself singing, until my palms are raw. I'll drown the sea god.

I am the sea god. And I keep clapping my luminous hands.

Come this way, fisherman, over the seal's bath and here along the cockle path. Here are the slick quicksands, and they will have you.

Fisherman, come this way over the gulls' road and the herring haunt! Here, up against this crumbling cliff. Give me your boat.

I am the boat. To keep afloat, to go where my master tells me: I've always obeyed the two commandments.

Now my master says forward, but the sea god says back; my master says anchor, but the night storm says drag. My deck is a tangle of lines and nets and ropes; my old heart's heavy with sluicing dark water. I'm drowning; I'm torn apart.

Groan and creak: I quiver; I weep salt. Shouts of the fishermen. Laughter of the sea god. Scream of the night storm.

I am the night storm. I AM THE STORM.

Down with the bell and down with the belfry. Down on the white head of the bellwoman. Down with the whole church and the tilting graveyard. Down with the cliff itself, cracking and opening and sliding and collapsing. Down with them all into the foam and snarl of the sea.

I'm the night storm, and there will be no morning.

I am the morning. I am good morning.

My hands are white as doves, and healing. Let me lay them on this purple fever. Let them settle on the boat.

Nothing lasts forever. Let me give you back your eyes, fisherman.

I am the fisherman. I heard the bell last night. Joe and Grimus and Pug—yes, we all did! I heard the bell and dropped anchor. But there is no bell. There's no church; there's no belfry along this coast. Where am I? Am I dreaming?

Well! God blessed this old boat and our haul of shiners. He saw fit to spare us sinners. We'll take our bearings now and head for home.

But I heard the bell. And now! I can hear it! Down, down under the boat's keel. I can hear the bell.

I am the bell. I am the tongue of the bell, gold and green, far under the swinging water.

I ring and ring, in fog and storm, to save boats from the quicksands and the rocky shore; I'm likely to last; I'm cast in bronze. I weigh two tons.

Listen now! Can you hear me? Can you hear the changes of the sea?

FAIRIES
AND LITTLE
PEOPLE

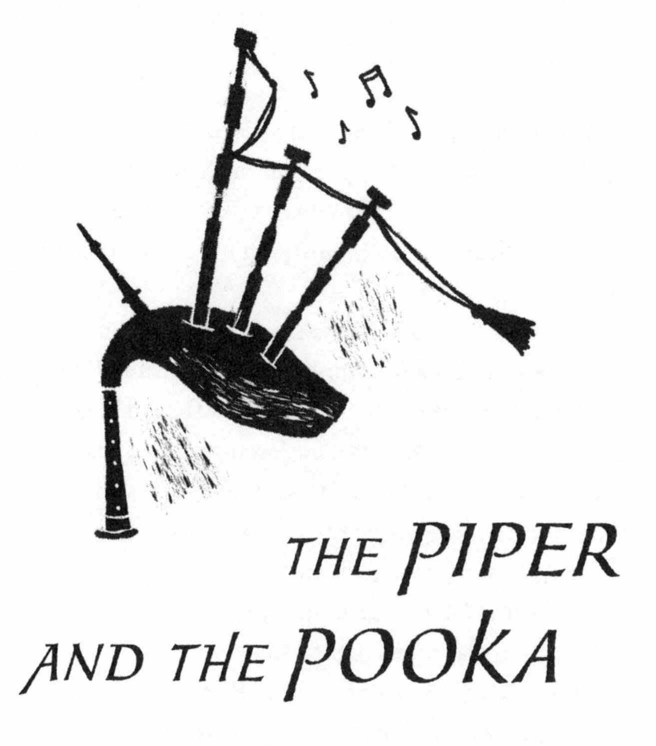

THE PIPER AND THE POOKA

THE ONLY TUNE THAT PATSY COULD PLAY WAS "BLACK ROGUE." He put a pillow of wind in his bagpipe, and he played it loud and played it soft; he played it for all he was worth and on every occasion.

The trouble was that Patsy was as dim as a donkey. Much as he loved music and dancing, he was unable to learn more than one tune. When at a dance some strutting cockerel or eye-bright hen called on him to play another tune, he'd smile and strike it up only to frown and break off after a few snatches, shaking his head and muttering to himself, "It's gone. Where's it gone?"

Late one night, Patsy was walking home after playing at a dance in a neighboring village. It wasn't too friendly a way, what with hanging rocks on either side of the road, and it wasn't too friendly at night — dungeon dark and the November wind whistling sharp and out of tune.

Weaving down the tiddly road and warbling to himself, Patsy felt a little lonely, and when he reached the humpbacked bridge, he was still two miles out from the village of Dunmore and the warmth of his mother's cottage. So he unstrung his pipes and put wind in the bag and began to play.

Up behind the piper crept a shape. The shape had horns. First it was two-legged, now it was four-legged. It grinned and lowered its head.

"Wowk!" shouted Patsy as first he felt the horns jammed against his buttocks, and then he lost his footing and was tossed into the air.

Patsy did a backward somersault and landed on the creature's back. He got a good grip on its horns and yelled, "The devil take you, you nasty beast! Let me go home!"

"Never mind home," said the creature.

"I've been playing all night," shouted Patsy. "I've got a sixpenny piece for my pains, and it's for my mother."

"Never mind your mother!" said the creature.

"She needs it to buy stuff," cried Patsy.

"Stuff!" replied the creature. "You just keep a hold on my horns. If you fall off, you'll break your pipes — and you'll break your neck too."

So Patsy gripped the creature's shaggy back with his knees, and before long, as they trotted along, it said, "Play up, Patsy! Play 'Poor Old Woman' for me."

"How can I do that?" said Patsy. "I've never heard of it."

"Never mind whether you have or you haven't," said the creature. "You play up and I'll see you know it."

So the piper put wind in his bag and began to play. Oh! The darkness lightened, and clouds danced in front of the Moon; the sharp-tongued wind stood back. Patsy played high and low, simple and intricate. The listening cows and rabbits and sheep pawed at the ground and stamped, all of them longing to be part of the dance.

At last Patsy came to the end of the tune. The pipes wheezed and fell silent, and Patsy took a deep breath. "My!" he said. "You're a fine music master."

The creature said nothing. It kept trotting forward at a steady pace, untroubled by the dark or the piper on its back.

"Where are we going?" asked Patsy. "Will you tell me that?"

"There's a great feast tonight," said the creature, "in the house of the weeping women."

"Where's that, then?" asked Patsy.

"Up on top of the holy mountain," said the creature. "Croagh Patrick."

"Is that right?" said Patsy. "You're saving me a journey, then. I stole Father William's white gander at Martinmas. And when he found out, he told me my penance was to go to Croagh Patrick."

Now the creature increased the length of his step and broke into a canter. Around rugged outcrops and over squelching peat bogs, into tapering valleys and up steep slopes — on they went until at last they came to the top of Croagh Patrick.

The creature stopped. He struck the ground three times with one hoof. Then in the half-light Patsy saw a great rock door slowly open, and at once the creature passed through it with the piper still on his back. They entered a great shining hall.

Patsy let go of the creature's horns and slipped off its back and looked about him. In the middle of the room stood a huge table, the largest Patsy had ever seen in his life, and it looked as if it were made from gold.

Around the table sat a crowd of old women — there must have been hundreds of them — and all of them had long hair, and eyes red as embers from waiting and weeping. They wore green dresses and gray cloaks.

Now there was a great scraping and rustling. The women stood up and called out, "A thousand thousand welcomes to you, Pooka of November! Who is this you've brought with you?"

"The best piper in Ireland," said the pooka.

One of the old women stepped toward Patsy and struck the ground with her stick. At once a little door in the rock wall opened, and out stepped a white gander, the same that Patsy had stolen from Father William.

"My!" said Patsy. "By my conscience, I ate this gander!" The piper eyed the bird and the bird eyed Patsy. "My mother and I, we ate every piece of him — all except one wing, and I gave that to Red Mary. The devil take her, it's she who told Father William."

But now the gander seemed to have lost interest in Patsy. It waddled away and started to clear the plates and goblets from the table.

"Now, Patsy," said the pooka, "you must play up! Play a tune for these ladies."

So Patsy played "Black Rogue," the only tune he knew, and the old women began to dance — backward and forward and 'round and 'round, their gray hair and white hair streaming out behind them. But then Patsy struck up a second tune and a third, a whole succession of tunes that, like "Poor Old Woman," he'd never even heard of before. The old women danced until they were too tired to dance any longer.

"Pay the piper, ladies!" shouted the pooka, grinning from ear to ear. "Pay the piper!" The old women stumbled and fumbled as each and every one of them found a gold coin in a purse or hidden pocket and gave it to Patsy.

"Bags of it!" brayed Patsy. "By the tooth of Saint Patrick, I'm as rich as the son of a lord."

"Come with me," said the pooka. "I'll take you home."

Patsy and the pooka turned toward the door, and just as the piper was about to mount the creature's back once more, the white gander prinked up to Patsy and presented him with a brand new set of pipes.

"That's very handsome," said Patsy. "Very civil! I wish I hadn't eaten you."

It wasn't long before the pooka brought Patsy back to the little humpbacked bridge only two miles outside the village of Dunmore.

"Go home, Patsy!" said the creature, and its black eyes gleamed in the light of dawn. "You've got two things now you didn't have before."

"What's that?" asked Patsy.

"Some wits between your two ears," said the pooka, "and a memory for music."

So Patsy strode home to his mother's cottage and, in the first pale-green light, banged on the door. And when his sleeping mother took more than a moment to rouse herself, Patsy banged again and bawled, "Let me in! Let me in! I'm as rich as a lord and the best piper in Ireland."

"I'll tell you what you are," said Patsy's mother. "You're as drunk as a lord, and a rogue into the bargain."

"Not at all," said Patsy. "I haven't drunk a drop. Not a drop since midnight."

Patsy's mother opened the door and let her son in. Then she crossed the little room and knelt down in front of the dozy fire and cupped her hands and began to blow at the peats.

"Look!" said Patsy, emptying his pockets. "There!" he shouted, as the gold pieces ran all over the floor.

"Patsy!" cried his mother. "Where in heaven's name . . . ?" The old

woman scrambled to left and to right, gathering up all the pieces of gold so they lay in one shining pool in her lap.

"And these new pipes!" said Patsy proudly. "Wait till you hear the music I play."

Patsy buckled on the pipes and filled the bag with wind. But what music! Instead of responding to his quick fingers, the pipes made a hideous cackling, as if all the ganders and geese in Ireland were tucked inside them and cackling together.

"Stop!" shouted Patsy's mother. "Stop!"

Patsy needed no encouragement. He unstrapped the pipes and put them in the corner of the little room. But the terrible racket had already woken up all the neighbors in the surrounding cottages. Tipsy with sleep and tousled, they came stumbling through the door one after another, first indignant, then curious, then mocking.

"I'll put on my old pipes then," said Patsy stubbornly.

"And play 'Black Rogue'!" said several voices, none too kindly. "'Black Rogue,' Patsy! Is that what you'll do?"

But Patsy did not play "Black Rogue." He closed his eyes and opened his eyes, and his fingers remembered all the dances and every note that he played for the weeping women on the top of Croagh Patrick.

"And then there's this," said Patsy's mother slyly, untying the shawl in which she had secreted all the gold and laying it out in front of her friends and neighbors.

Then Patsy himself sat down in front of the laughing fire and told them everything that had happened since he'd left the dance the previous night. "All of it," he said, "while you were asleep. All of it between midnight and first light."

After they had eaten later that morning, Patsy's mother had a peep into

the shawl for the second time. It was full of crackling leaves, nothing but November leaves, russet and gold and brown.

"Ah! Patsy!" said his mother sadly, and with one clump of a fist she covered her eyes.

Then Patsy went to find Father William and told him everything that had happened the previous night.

Father William shook his head. He kept shaking his head and he smiled. "Cock and bull!" he said. "Claptrap, Patsy! And you know it."

"It's true," said Patsy, indignantly. "I'll show you. I'll put these pipes on me." He buckled on the new pipes and filled the bag till it was bursting. Once more the pipes made a horrible honking and screeching.

"Get out, you thief!" shouted Father William.

"And now these," said Patsy, as soon as the caterwauling had died away.

"Out!" shouted Father William. "Away with you! And off to Croagh Patrick!"

But Patsy stood his ground and fastened on his old pipes. And then what music he played! First he played well-known tunes, and then the unfamiliar tunes he had played for the weeping women at the top of the mountain — and all with neat fingering and fine phrasing, true to the circle of the dance.

The old priest clicked his fingers, and inside his shiny black shoes his toe began to tingle. Little birds looked in at his window.

And from that day until the day he died, Patsy was hailed as prince of pipers in the county of Galway.

TOM TIT TOT

THERE WAS ONCE A LITTLE OLD VILLAGE WHERE A WOMAN LIVED with her giddy daughter. The daughter was just sixteen and sweet as honeysuckle.

One fine morning, the woman made five meat pies and put them in the oven. But then a neighbor called 'round, and they were soon so busy gossiping that the woman forgot about the pies. By the time she took them out of the oven, their crusts were as hard as the bark of her old oak tree.

"Daughter," she says, "you put them there pies in the larder."

"My! I'm that hungry," says the girl.

"Leave them there and they'll come again," says the woman. And what she meant, you know, was that the crusts would get soft.

"Well!" the girl says to herself, "if they'll come again, I'll eat these ones now." And so she set to work and ate them all, first and last.

When it was suppertime, the woman felt very hungry. "I could just do with one of them there pies," she says. "Go and get one off the shelf. They'll have come again by now."

The girl went and looked, but there was nothing on the shelf except an empty dish. "No!" she calls. "They haven't."

"Not none of them?" says the woman.

"No!" calls the girl. "No! Not none."

"Well!" says the woman. "Come again or not, I'll have one for my supper."

"You can't if they haven't come," says the girl.

"I can, though," says the woman. "Go and get the best one."

"Best or worst," says the girl, "I've eaten the lot, so you can't have one until it's come again."

The woman was furious. "Eaten the lot? You dardle-dumdue!"

The woman carried her spinning wheel over to the door, and to calm herself, she began to spin. As she spun she sang:

"My daughter's ate five, five pies today.
My daughter's ate five, five pies today."

The king came walking down the street and heard the woman.

"What were those words, woman?" he says. "What were you singing?"

The woman felt ashamed of her daughter's greed. "Well," she says, beginning to spin again:

"My daughter's spun five, five skeins today.
My daughter's spun five, five skeins today."

"Stars of mine!" exclaims the king. "I've never heard of anyone

who could do that." The king raised his eyebrows and looked at the girl, so sweet and giddy and sixteen.

"Five today," says the woman.

"Look here!" says the king. "I want a wife, and I'll marry your daughter. For eleven months of the year," he says, "she can eat as much food as she likes and buy all the dresses she wants; she can keep whatever company she wishes. But during the last month of the year, she'll have to spin five skeins every day, and if she doesn't, I'll cut off her head."

"All right!" says the woman. "That's all right, isn't it, daughter?"

The woman was delighted at the thought that her daughter was going to marry the king himself. She wasn't worried about the five skeins. "When it comes to that," she said to her daughter later, "we'll find a way out of it. More likely, though, he'll have clean forgotten about it."

So the king and the girl were married. And for eleven months the girl ate as much food as she liked, bought all the dresses she wanted, and kept whatever company she wished.

As the days of the eleventh month passed, the girl began to think about those skeins and wondered whether the king was thinking about them too. But the king said not a word, and the girl was quite sure he had forgotten them.

On the very last day of the month, though, the king led her up to a room in the palace she had never set eyes on before. There was nothing in it but a spinning wheel and a stool.

"Now, my dear," says the king, "you'll be shut in here tomorrow with some food and some flax. And if you haven't spun five skeins before dark, your head will be cut off."

Then away went the king to do everything a king has to do.

Well, the girl was that frightened. She had always been such a giddy

girl, and she didn't know how to spin. She didn't know what to do next morning, with no one beside her and no one to help her. She sat down on a stool in the palace kitchen and heavens, how she did cry!

All of a sudden, however, she heard a sort of knocking low down on the door. So she stood up and opened it, and what did she see but a small little black thing with a long tail. That looked up at her, all curious, and that said, "What are you crying for?"

"What's that to you?" says the girl.

"Never you mind," that says. "You tell me what you're crying for."

"That won't do me no good if I do," the girl replies.

"You don't know that," that said, and twirled its tail around.

"Well!" she says. "That won't do me no harm if that don't do me no good." So she told him about the pies and the skeins and everything.

"This is what I'll do," says the little black thing. "I'll come to your window every morning and take the flax, and I'll bring it back all spun before dark."

"What will that cost?" she asks.

The thing looked out of the corners of its eyes and said, "Every night, I'll give you three guesses at my name. And if you haven't guessed it before the month's up, you shall be mine."

The girl thought she was bound to guess its name before the month was out. "All right!" she says. "I agree to that."

"All right!" that says, and lork! how that twirled that's tail.

Well, next morning, the king led the girl up to the room, and the flax and the day's food were all ready for her.

"Now there's the flax," he says. "And if it isn't spun before dark, off goes your head!" Then he went out and locked the door.

The king had scarcely gone out when there was a knocking at the window.

The girl stood up and opened it, and sure enough, there was the little old thing sitting on the window ledge.

"Where's the flax?" it says.

"Here you are!" she says. And she gave it the flax.

When it was early evening, there was a knocking again at the window. The girl stood up and opened it, and there was the little old thing, with five skeins over its arm.

"Here you are!" that says, and it gave the flax to her. "And now," it says, "what's my name?"

"Is that Bill?" she says.

"No!" it says. "That ain't." And that twirled that's tail.

"Is it Ned?" she says.

"No!" it says. "That ain't." And that twirled that's tail.

"Well, is that Mark?" says she.

"No!" it says. "That ain't." And that twirled that's tail faster, and away it flew.

When the girl's husband came in, the five skeins were ready for him. "I see I shan't have to kill you tonight, my dear," he says. "You'll have your food and your flax in the morning," he says, and away he went to do everything a king has to do.

Well, the flax and the food were made ready for the girl each day, and each day the little black impet used to come in the morning and return in the early evening. And each day and all day the girl sat thinking of names to try out on the impet when it came back in the evening. But she never hit on the right one! As time went on toward the end of the month, the impet looked wickeder and wickeder, and that twirled that's tail faster and faster each time she made a guess.

So they came to the last day of the month but one. The impet returned in the early evening with the five skeins, and it said, "What, hain't you guessed my name yet?"

"Is that Nicodemus?" she says.

"No! 'T'ain't," that says.

"Is that Samuel?" she says.

"No! 'T'ain't," that says.

"Ah well! Is that Methusalem?" says she.

"No! 'T'ain't that either," it says. And then that looks at the girl with eyes like burning coals.

"Woman," that says, "there's only tomorrow evening, and then you'll be mine!" And away it flew!

Well, the girl felt terrible. Soon, though, she heard the king coming along the passage, and when he had walked into the room and seen the five skeins, he says, "Well, my dear! So far as I can see, you'll have your skeins ready tomorrow evening too. I reckon I won't have to kill you, so I'll have my supper in here tonight." Then the king's servants brought up his supper, and another stool for him, and the two of them sat down together.

The king had scarcely eaten a mouthful before he pushed back his stool, waved his knife and fork, and began to laugh.

"What is it?" asks the girl.

"I'll tell you," says the king. "I was out hunting today, and I got lost and came to a clearing in the forest I'd never seen before. There was an old chalk pit there. And I heard a kind of humming. So I got off my horse and crept up to the edge of the pit and looked down. And do you know what I saw? The funniest little black thing you ever set eyes on! And what did that have but a little spinning wheel! That was spinning and spinning, wonderfully fast, spinning and twirling that's tail. And as it spun, it sang:

'Nimmy nimmy not,
My name's Tom Tit Tot.'"

Well, when the girl heard this, she felt as if she could have jumped out of her skin for joy, but she didn't say a word.

Next morning, the small little black thing looked wicked as wicked when it came for the flax. And just before it grew dark, she heard it knocking again at the windowpane. She opened the window and that came right in onto the sill. It was grinning from ear to ear, and ooh, that's tail was twirling 'round so fast!

"What's my name?" that says, as it gave her the skeins.

"Is that Solomon?" she says, pretending to be afraid.

"No! 'T'ain't," that says, and it came farther into the room.

"Well, is that Zebedee?" she says again.

"No! 'T'ain't," says the impet. And then that laughed and twirled that's tail until you could scarcely see it.

"Take time, woman," that says. "Next guess, and you're mine." And that stretched out its black hands toward her.

The girl backed away a step or two. She looked at it, and then she laughed and pointed a finger at it and sang out:

"Nimmy nimmy not,
Your name's Tom Tit Tot."

Well! When the impet heard her, that gave an awful shriek, and away it flew into the dark. She never saw it again.

MONDAY, TUESDAY

POOR LUSMORE! HE WAS ALL MISSHAPEN. HIS LEGS WERE BOWED, and the hump on his back was as big as a football. When he stood up, he seemed almost to be squatting, and when he sat down, he rested his chin on his knees for support.

Lusmore's arms, though, were strong and tanned, and his fingers were nimble. Almost every day he sat on his low stool outside the cottage where he lived with his old parents — he was almost thirty himself — and braided rushes and straw into baskets and hats. And he always got a good price for his work because everyone felt so sorry for him.

Everyone talked about him too, of course! Out of his hearing, people said all kinds of things about Lusmore. They said no human being could be as deformed as he was, and that he must be a changeling. They said he warbled strange words to himself. They said he was a master of magic and medicine.

Lusmore seemed unaware of all this. His daily suffering had made him gentle and sweet. He was glad he was alive. He loved birds and butterflies. Every morning in summer, he tucked a foxglove through the band of his straw hat, sang as he worked, and eagerly greeted each and every passerby.

One day, Lusmore rode on the back of a cart into the town of Caher and sold his baskets and hats in the market there. He did a brisk trade and went off to drink a few beers afterward. But when he returned to the deserted marketplace, it was late, the light was failing, and the cart and its driver were nowhere to be seen. Poor Lusmore! He had no choice but to walk home.

The little hunchback trudged out of Caher down the road toward Cappagh, and by the time he reached the old moat at Knockgrafton it was already quite dark. Lusmore hauled his sad shape of a body off the road and over the molehills and tussocks and sat down on the edge of the old grassy ditch.

"And I'm not halfway home," said Lusmore, and he gave a great sigh — the kind he only permitted himself when no one else was nearby.

The hunchback sat cross-legged, his chin resting on one knee, and looked at the gibbous Moon. Lumpen clouds were swarming over it, and it seemed as if the Moon were running or rolling as fast as she could without getting anywhere.

"Like me!" said Lusmore, and he smiled ruefully. "Just like me! I'm a poor moon calf."

Lusmore pressed his chin against his knee and closed his eyes. He listened to the shushing of the light wind in the old lime trees down the road, and then he heard, rising above the wind and out of the grassy moat, a different sound, clearer and higher in pitch — a song without words. It was the sound of many voices, sweet voices, so mingling and

blending that they sounded like one voice. Then the voices began to sing words:

"Monday, Tuesday, Monday, Tuesday, Monday, Tuesday . . ." At this, they paused for a moment, and then they began the melody again.

Lusmore was spellbound by the singing. *Though to be sure,* he thought, *there's not much variety to it.* After a while, the hunchback began to hum the melody in tune with the voices, and then, when they paused, he sang out, *"Wednesday."*

"Monday, Tuesday . . ." sang the voices, and Lusmore sang with them. *"Monday, Tuesday, Monday, Tuesday."* And then, for a second time, *"Wednesday."*

When the little people heard Lusmore, they were delighted. They skipped and eddied up the bank and swirled him down to the bottom of the moat in a whirlwind of cries and laughter. The hunchback was twirled 'round and 'round, light as a piece of straw, and the fairy fiddlers played faster and faster.

When the world stopped spinning, Lusmore saw that he had been swept into a fine fairy pavilion. True, it had a rather low ceiling, but that didn't bother him! The whole place was lit with candles and packed with little people—little people chattering, eating, playing fiddles and pipes and harps, dancing . . .

Lusmore was made most welcome: he was given a low stool and provided with food and drink.

"Grand! I feel grand!" he said as one fairy after another inquired whether he had all he needed and praised his skill as a singer. "Just grand!" said Lusmore. "I might as well be the king of the whole land!"

Then the music faltered and stopped; the dancers stood still; the feasters put down their knives and forks. Lusmore watched as the

little people crowded together in the middle of the pavilion and began to whisper. Now the hunchback began to feel nervous. "For all your kindness and courtesy," he muttered, "you fairy folk, you're fickle and chancy."

As Lusmore watched, one little man left the huddle and walked up to him. He smiled at Lusmore, and solemnly he said:

"Lusmore! Lusmore!
That hump you wore,
That hump you bore
On your back is no more;
Look down on the floor!
There's your hump, Lusmore!"

As the hunchback looked down, his ugly hump fell from his shoulders and dropped to the ground. Little Lusmore felt so light; he felt so happy. Like the cow in the story of the cat and the fiddle, he could have jumped over the Moon.

But seeing the hump was scarcely enough! Lusmore raised his arms and clasped the back of his neck. Then, very slowly, for fear of bumping against the ceiling, Lusmore lifted his head. For the first time in his life, he stood upright.

Lusmore laughed, and then he cried. The fair pavilion, the little people crowding around him, they were all so beautiful. Lusmore began to feel dizzy; his eyesight became dim; he slipped gently to the ground and fell fast asleep.

When Lusmore woke, the Sun was already well up. The dewy grass . . . cows chewing the cud . . . the moat at Knockgrafton . . . Then he remembered! He crossed himself. And still lying on the grass, he reached out with one hand and felt behind his back.

When Lusmore was sure that the hump was not there, he leaped up. He got down on his knees and said his prayers. Then he saw that he was wearing a new suit of clothes and shook his head, grinning.

So Lusmore stepped out for Cappagh, feeling as light as a piece of thistledown. He had such a spring in his step that you might have thought he had been a dancing master all his life. His mother and father and all the people living in the village were astonished at the sight of him — indeed, at first glance, many of them did not even recognize him. And it wasn't long before the story of how Lusmore had lost his hump was taken to Caher and then spread for miles and miles around; it was soon the talk of everyone in the midlands of Ireland.

Lusmore had learned to live with his misfortune, and now he took his good fortune with a shrug and a smile. Free of his ugly load, he delighted in his dapper appearance, but he had no wish to run harum-scarum off to Dublin or climb Croagh Patrick or drink himself into an early grave. He was already in the place he loved, and he was among the friends and neighbors he had known since the day of his birth. He went on with his old job of braiding rushes and straw.

One morning, Lusmore was sitting in the sunlight outside his cottage door when a woman walked up to him.

"This is the road to Cappagh?" she asked.

"This is Cappagh," Lusmore replied. "Who are you looking for?"

"I've come from County Waterford," said the woman. "Over thirty miles. I'm looking for one Lusmore."

"I know him," said Lusmore.

"He had the hump taken off him by the fairies," said the woman. "Is that right?"

"It is," said Lusmore, smiling.

"Well, the son of a neighbor of mine — Jack, Jack Madden the cobbler — he's got a devil of a hump on him that'll soon be the death of him."

"I am Lusmore," said the little man.

"You?" exclaimed the woman. "Well! There's an omen!"

Lusmore was quite happy to tell the woman what had happened at the old moat at Knockgrafton. He explained about the tune the fairies had sung, and how he had joined in and added to it, and about the fair pavilion, the whispering fairies . . .

The woman thanked Lusmore. She hurried back down the long lanes to her own county. She went straight to her neighbor, and it wasn't more than a couple of days before the two of them arranged for a horse and cart to take them and Jack Madden all the way back to Knockgrafton.

On the way there, Jack's mouth was full of complaints. "This jolting," he said. "That'll be the death of me! It's all right for you!" He complained that his mother would make him work twice as hard to pay for the cost of the cart. He complained about the taste of the ale they had brought with them. What with his peevishness and the noise of the cart, Jack's mother and her neighbor were worn out by the time they reached the moat at Knockgrafton.

"Don't forget what we've told you," they said. "We'll be back at sunrise." Then the cart rolled away down the road to Caher, and Jack Madden was left on his own in the darkness under the rising Moon.

Jack hauled his sad shape of a body off the road and over the molehills and tussocks and sat down on the edge of the old grassy ditch. The stillness of the place wrapped itself 'round him: the clucking of a bird, settling down for the night; a far barking; acres of silence.

And then, out of this silence, from somewhere down in the moat,

rose sweet singing, high-pitched clear singing that made Jack Madden catch his breath and listen intently. The fairies were singing their song just as Lusmore had shaped it for them.

"Monday, Tuesday," they sang, *"Monday, Tuesday, Monday, Tuesday, Wednesday."* There was no pause in their singing now; the melody and words were continuous.

Jack Madden's spirit was as shapeless as his body. He had no grace about him, and little sense of the fitting. He listened to the little people sing their song seven times, and then, without regard for timing and without thought for pitch, he stood up and bawled out, "WEDNESDAY, THURSDAY."

If one day is good, thought Jack, *two days are better. I should get two suits of clothing!*

The fairies whirled up the grassy bank. They lifted Jack off his feet and swept him down to the bottom of the moat and into their pavilion. There they jostled around him, picking at his clothing and banging him with their tiny fists, screeching and screaming, "Who spoiled our tune? Who spoiled our tune?"

Then one little man raised his hand, and the crowd of angry fairies fell back. The little man narrowed his eyes at Jack and said:

"Jack Madden! Jack Madden!
Your words were all wrong
For our sweet lovely song.
You're caught in our throng
And your life we will sadden:
Here's two lumps for Jack Madden."

At this, a troop of twenty of the strongest fairies staggered into the pavilion carrying Lusmore's hump. They walked over to poor

Jack and at once slammed it down on his back, right over his own hump. And as soon as they had done so, it became firmly fixed there, as if it had been nailed down with six-inch nails by the best of carpenters. Then the little people screeched and screamed again and kicked Jack out of their pavilion into the dark night.

In the morning, Jack Madden's mother and her neighbor came back from Caher. They found Jack lying just outside the moat, with a double hump on his back; he was half-dead.

The two women looked at him; they looked at each other. For fear of the fairies, they said nothing. They lifted poor Jack and laid him moaning in the bottom of the cart and rode straight home to Waterford.

What with the terrible weight of his second hump, and the strain of the long, jolting journey, Jack Madden didn't live long. "My curse," he muttered just before he died, "my curse on any fool who listens to a fairy tune!"

THE CHANGELING

LAST WEEK THERE WAS A WONDER.

Up at Hawes's there was a birth, a son to follow four bonny daughters. Such a scowl of a night, but no one was paying any attention to that. There was singing and dancing, all the neighbors in:

> *"They swaddled him in a mesh of muslin,*
> *They swathed him in pure rainbow silk . . ."*

That was the Tuesday, and they arranged with me to baptize the baby on the Sabbath.

But Saturday morning there was a horrible yelling coming out of the cradle. And when Mrs. Hawes looked in, she saw her baby had turned yellow and ugly. His nose was a sort of snout, his milk skin had become leathery, and his teeth were already coming through.

Mrs. Hawes cried out, and the farmer and his neighbors, they all rubbed their eyes. It made no difference, of course. The little baby just lay there and squinted up at them and thrashed its legs and yelled.

Poor Mrs. Hawes, she's a fragile woman, and she was in a terrible state. When she tried to feed the baby, he tore at her poor breasts. He wrestled around, and groused and grizzled, and one way and another, the farmer and his family were unable to get a minute's sleep for the next three nights.

That was when they sent for my lass Janey and asked her to try her hand. She knows what's what, Janey, just like her mother. She won't stand any nonsense.

Out trooped the farmer and his family, off to the market. They were all heartily glad to see the back of the little baby, and to get the sound of that yammering out of their ears.

Janey promised Mrs. Hawes she would be patient. After all . . . the poor wee baby, it was so ugly and so sad, and seemed so unhappy with this bright world.

But what with all the weeping and wailing, Janey finally lost her temper. She yelled right back at the baby and told him that his mewling was stopping her from winnowing the corn and grinding the meal.

The baby looked up then and opened its eyes as wide as could be. "Well, Janey," he said, clear as clear, with a knowing look. "Well, Janey, loose the cradle band! Watch out for your neighbors and I'll work your work."

Then that wee devil climbed out of his cradle. He stretched and grinned and strolled out of the house. He cut the corn; he fed the livestock in the fields; then the wind got up and the mill began to turn. . . .

Janey's knees were knocking together. She wasn't going to show

it, though. She knew that would only turn bad into worse. So when the wee devil had finished the work and strolled back into the house again, she fed him and played with him until the farmer and his family came home.

As soon as she saw them out the window, Janey popped the baby back into the cradle. And at that, the caterwauling began all over again.

Then Janey took Mrs. Hawes down to the kitchen and told her straight out what had happened. Poor Mrs. Hawes! "What shall I do, Janey? Help me, Janey!"

"The wee devil!" said Janey. "Leave him to me! I'll cook some trouble for him."

At midnight, Janey asked Hawes if he would climb up onto the farmhouse roof and lay three bricks across part of the top of the chimney pot, and she told his wife to work the bellows until the fire was glowing — a bed of red-hot coals.

Then my lass, she stripped that wee scrap; she undressed him and threw him onto the burning coals.

The little wee fellow shrieked and he screamed.

At once there was a rustling sound, quickly growing, like wind before rain. And then a rattling at the windows and tapping, tapping at the chimney and banging at the farmhouse doors. That was the fairies, right enough.

"In the name of God," shouted Janey, "bring back the baby!"

Darkness and wind! The casement window screeched. They brought back the baby then; they laid him safely in his mother's lap.

And the wee devil? He flew up the chimney laughing.

THE FARMER AND THE BOGGART

TERRY WAS VERY PLEASED TO BE ABLE TO BUY FAR WALLOW. TRUE, it wasn't much more than an acre, and the bottom end, down toward the stream, was a bit sticky, but all the same it doubled his holding and meant he could cater to his family's needs all the year round.

"And there might be something left over at that," he told his wife. "Something to sell."

On the evening the purchase was completed, Terry lit his pipe and strolled down Far Wallow to the stream. He put one foot on the stump of an old willow tree; he listened to the mouthing of the stream; he rubbed the bridge of his nose and closed his eyes. He looked just what he was: a man at peace with the world, savoring the particular satisfaction of owning land.

When Terry opened his eyes again, he saw a little man advancing down Far Wallow toward him. And then he saw that his visitor was a

squat boggart; his whole face was covered in hair and his arms were almost as long as fishing poles.

"Clear off my land!" said the boggart.

"Your land!" exclaimed Terry. "I've just bought it."

"No," said the boggart. "That's mine."

"It's not," said Terry.

"That is," said the boggart.

"It's not," said Terry.

"That's mine. That's always been mine."

"I've just signed the papers," said Terry.

The boggart scratched his hairy chin, looking as much puzzled as threatening. "I'm sure that's mine," he said.

"I'll take you to court," said Terry.

"Court!" said the boggart, and he spat at Terry's feet. "I'll take half what you grow. That's what."

Terry didn't like the boggart's suggestion at all, but he didn't want to risk antagonizing him. One swipe from the boggart's hairy right arm and Terry would be down in the stream.

"Well?" said the boggart.

"All right," said Terry slowly. "Right. What do you want, tops or bottoms?"

The boggart scratched the back of his head. "Tops or bottoms?" he repeated.

"Above ground or beneath ground?"

"Tops," said the boggart.

"Right," said Terry again. "No backsies, mind!"

"Tops," said the boggart and he stumped away.

The year became glum. The silver leaves from the willow trees danced and spun; winter opened her white fan.

In the spring, Terry planted the whole of Far Wallow with

potatoes. And when it was late July and time to lift them, the boggart came stumping back to the field to claim his share.

"Right!" said Terry. "No backsies, mind!"

So of course Terry got the whole potato crop, and the boggart was left with nothing but stems and leaves.

"Blast!" shouted the boggart in frustration, as Terry loaded his crop onto a cart. "Blast! Next year . . ."

"Yes?" said Terry.

"What was it?"

"Tops?" said Terry.

"No!" said the boggart, looking worried.

"Bottoms," said Terry.

"That's it! Bottoms!"

"Right," said Terry. "No backsies, mind!"

First Terry plowed and harrowed Far Wallow; then he sowed it with wheat. So when the boggart came the following August to claim his share, he was left with nothing but stubble, and Terry got all the wheat and straw.

"Blast!" shouted the boggart. "Blast!" Then he turned on Terry. "Next year," he said, "you sow wheat, and we'll mow side by side. Each to take what he mows."

"Ah!" said Terry.

"I'll start down here and you start up there," said the boggart. "That's what!" he bellowed in Terry's right ear. And then he stumped away, muttering to himself.

Before long, Terry went to see the wise man. "I've outwitted him twice," said Terry. "But what am I to do this third time?"

"Sow the field with wheat," said the wise man, "and during the winter, have the blacksmith make you a hundred thin iron rods. Then, in the spring, when the wheat rises, plant the rods in Far Wallow. Plant

them all over the part where the boggart wants to mow. That'll soon wear down his strength and take the edge off his scythe."

Terry did as the wise man advised him. The days lengthened; the wheat strengthened and turned pale yellow, pale rose, tawny.

The boggart came back in the middle of August to claim his share.

"I'll start down here, and you start up there," said the boggart.

"I remember," said Terry.

So the boggart swung his scythe, and before long he hit one of the iron rods.

"Tough old stalks," grumbled the boggart. "Tough old stalks, aren't they?"

But Terry kept scything and pretending not to hear. So the boggart had to stop and sharpen his scythe. And no sooner had he put a new edge on it than he struck another iron rod.

"Blast!" shouted the boggart. "Far Wallow never was worth much."

Terry leaned on his scythe and listened.

"You can take the mucky old land and the crops on it," shouted the boggart. "I won't have no more to do with it." And with that the hairy creature plodded away, over the stile and out of sight, without so much as a backward look.

For months after that, the boggart hung around the dykes and drains that ran between the fields in the fen; sometimes he scared people walking home alone late at night, and if a farmer left his dinner or his tools in the corner of some far field, he sometimes sneaked up and made off with them. But the years passed and the boggart never came near Far Wallow again.

THE SHEPHERD'S TALE

THAT'S WHERE I SAW THEM! UP ON THAT GREEN PATCH THERE . . .

That's fifty years, see. I was missing one ewe and high up and calling. First there was such a winking and glittering. Then I saw them quite clearly — little men and women dancing in a ring.

I'll tell you, then. I hurried toward them, and first thing caught my eye: they were wearing scarlet or white, every one of them. Scarlet or white. A kind of uniform, see. The men had tripled caps on their heads, and the women, they wore white lacy kinds of things. Fantastical! They waved in the wind.

My! Those ladies were lovely! I've seen some beauties, mind, some rare beauties. The men, too, they were handsome.

There were three harpists there, sitting on flat stones and playing for the dancers. Plucking and rippling! The strange thing is I couldn't hear a note. I saw them playing but they didn't make a sound.

'Round and 'round whirled the dancers, smiling and laughing. And when they spied me, they nodded and smiled, and some of them threw up their arms and beckoned me. Then they all joined hands again. Faster and faster, leaning backward, almost falling! Laughing faces!

There were others, too, mind. Little men running races, sprinting and scurrying, and others clambering over the old stone tomb — up one side, along the top, and down the other. That's as old as Adam, that. Prehistorical! Not so long back, two men came all the way from Cardiff just to measure it.

Where was I, then? Yes, and horses. There were ladies riding 'round on dapper white horses. Sidesaddle, mind. Nothing wanton! Their dresses were white — white as misty sunlight and red as young blood.

Well then, I'll tell you. I came close and very close. I stuck out one foot, just into the ring. I heard it then, the fairy music. Harps — what a sound, yes! My heart started jigging. There's a sound a man could die for.

So I stepped right into the ring, see. At once I saw I was in some kind of palace. The walls were covered with gold and pearls.

One young woman walked up to me. "Come with me, Dai!" That's what she said. "We've been expecting you." Then she showed me 'round — all the shining rooms and the colored gardens. "You can go where you want, Dai," she said. "There's just one thing."

"What's that?" I said.

"You see this well?"

I looked into the well, and it was teeming with fish, see. Red and blue and black and green. And some of them were gold.

"You see this well?" she said. "Whatever you do, Dai, never drink a drop."

The young woman led me back through the palace to a feasting hall. There was venison and lamb and suckling pig, pheasant and grouse and pigeon. All of it carried in on silver platters, mind. And you know who carried it? Beautiful ladies! That was a place, all right!

And there was red wine and yellow wine, I remember that. I drank them both, see. I drank them from gold goblets covered with diamonds and rubies and emeralds. Strong wine and sweet wine! Before then, I'd only tasted water and milk and beer.

Whatever I wanted, they brought it to me. Food, drink, warm water to wash with, a comfortable bed. I wanted harpists, singers, acrobats! Then I wanted to talk to their little children. A whole troop came in, chattering and giggling. They were small as dandelions.

You know what I wanted most? It's always the same, mind. You want what you can't have. That's the old Adam.

After dark, I sneaked out into the garden, see. I ran down to the well. Then I plunged in this hand—and all the colored fishes, they disappeared. Then I cupped my hands and lowered them into the water....

Oh! What a shriek there was! Glassy and piercing, like the Moon in pain. A shriek right 'round the garden and the palace.

Never mind, I closed my eyes and sipped the water!

The garden and the palace and the little people inside it, they all dissolved. In front of my eyes they just dissolved. Mountain mist.

It was dark, hopeless dark, and I was standing alone on the side of the mountain. Up there, that green patch, see. Standing right in the place where I stepped into the ring.

FAIRY

OINTMENT

FEBRUARY AND FREEZING. IN SUNLIGHT AND STARLIGHT THE WIND blew from the east. It gripped the land. It poked its fingers under doors and through peepholes and along passageways.

Joan sat by the fire and saw faces in it, and journeys and destinations. Joan rubbed her dry lips against each other. Slowly she shook her head.

"An old woman," she said, "sitting in her bone house. I grow old dreaming of all the things that never happened."

The wind gave tongue to the elm and the oak, the creaking house, and the taciturn stones: the night was so full of voices that at first Joan did not hear the knocking at her door.

The noise grew sharper: bare knuckle against wood. Joan stirred. "Of all nights," she said.

She unbolted the door, and then the wind swung it wide open and

threw in her visitor. He was small and dark like most of the hill farmers, and he was cross-eyed.

"Well," said Joan, forcing the door back into its frame, "what's blown you in?"

"It's my wife," said the man. "She's gone into labor. Can you come up and help?"

"Up where?" said Joan.

"Up the back," said the man. "Up past the old fish pond. I've brought a horse."

"I see," said Joan.

"It's not her first, mind," said the man.

So Joan parceled herself inside warm wrappings: gloves and a hood and scarves and leggings and a cloak that was really an old blanket with two holes cut in it for the arms.

Then the little man mounted his black horse, and Joan mounted behind him. The sky's pane was incised with sparkling stars and a full Moon; Earth's locked doors were covered with patches of snow. Joan buried her face in her cloak, and they rode over the hill at the back, past the blind eye of the fish pond, and up toward the mountain.

No sooner had the little man and Joan galloped into the farm courtyard than a door was thrown open and a young girl ran out calling, "Father! It's a boy! It's a boy!"

Inside the house, Joan was surrounded by a swarm of children. They followed her out of the big friendly kitchen, chattering and laughing. They followed her down the cold passage and up the stone stairs.

"Shush!" said Joan, rounding on them and wagging her finger at them. "She can do without that."

The little man led Joan into a hushed bedroom, and all the children trooped in after her. The room was lit with candles, at least

twenty of them, and the man's wife was lying pale on the bed. Her tiny baby was tucked against her.

"He couldn't wait," said the woman, "the little imp!"

"Now then!" said Joan. Firm and friendly, she pressed her palm against the woman's brow, plumped her pillows, and then picked up the little baby. He was fast asleep. "Welcome!" said Joan. "Welcome to this wide world!"

The woman raised herself on one elbow and fished in the little cupboard beside her bed. "No need to wake him," she said. "But when he does wake up, will you smear this ointment on his eyelids?"

Joan took the ointment and nodded. "Whatever you say," she said.

"And be careful," said the little man, "not to get any on your own eyes."

"All right!" said Joan. "Do we need all these children in here?"

The little man shooed some of his children out of the room, but it didn't seem to do much good. It only made more space for those who were left to wrestle and skip and squabble, and before long, those that had gone out at the door came in at the window.

Joan washed the baby and still he slept; the little man busied himself downstairs; the woman dozed after her labor.

Then the baby opened his eyes, and Joan saw at once that he had a bit of a squint, just like his father. "Ah me!" she said, and she shook her head and sighed.

Then Joan picked up the little box of ointment. *Anyway,* she wondered, *what's it for?* She opened it, dabbed at it with her little finger, and smeared a little onto each of the baby's eyelids. Then Joan glanced quickly and sideways at the baby's mother and smeared a little of the ointment on her own right eyelid.

Joan blinked and opened her eyes. With her left she saw no different—the squinting baby on her lap, wound and wrapped in

an old white shawl; his sleeping mother in the sagging bedstead; the scruffy children; the simple and homely farm furniture. But with her right eye, Joan saw that she was sitting in an airy and elegant room, surrounded by precious antique furniture. The baby on her lap was wrapped and wound in gauze flecked with silver and looked more beautiful than before, and his sleeping mother was robed in white silk.

The children in the room, however, looked even less wholesome than they had before. They were imps with squashed noses and pointed ears. They made faces at one another, scratched their heads like monkeys, picked and plucked their mother's bed clothing with their hairy paws, and pulled her ears.

Joan looked and looked. She looked and said nothing.

Before dawn, Joan had finished all her midwife's work. She had washed the baby as clean as a cat's tongue; she had made his mother's bed; she had driven the children out of the room for the seventeenth time; she had put the baby to his mother's breast, where he had fed and promptly fallen asleep again. There was nothing more for her to do.

"Take me home now!" Joan said to the little man. She sounded confident enough, but she was shaking. She glanced 'round the beautiful room; she looked at the little man, dressed in velvet and squinting. "East, west," she said, "home is best."

Joan needn't have worried. The little man was delighted at the way the midwife had looked after his wife and their new baby. He brought his coal-black horse around to the door, and now Joan saw that its eyes were fiery red.

Away they went into the crystal night, through the burning icy wind. They galloped past the old fish pond and down to Joan's little cottage at the foot of the hill. There, the little man helped Joan dismount. He thanked her and gave her a gold coin for her night's work. Joan unbolted her door and, safely inside, tested the coin between her

teeth. Then she threw some wood on the fire and lay down in front of it. She closed one eye, she closed the other, and she fell asleep.

A few days later, Joan picked her way along icy lanes into the nearby town. It was market day, and she needed meat and vegetables; she wanted some company.

In the market, Joan was among friends. She had known most of the people there, buyers and sellers alike, for as long as she could remember. So the morning was taken up with a pleasant mixture of business and talk.

While she stood gossiping at one stall, Joan saw something out of the corner of her right eye: a little man, just a couple of feet away, had picked up an apple and, without paying for it, slipped it into his canvas bag.

Joan frowned and watched more carefully as the man sauntered down to the next stall. There, he took two leeks and quickly dropped them into his bag too.

"You!" called Joan. "What do you think you're doing?"

The little dark man whirled around to face her.

"It's you," said Joan, astonished and fearful.

"Good morning, Joan," said the little man.

What Joan had meant to say stayed inside her mouth.

"How's your wife?" she stammered. "The baby?"

"You can see me, then," said the little man.

Joan nodded.

"Which eye, Joan?" asked the little man, smiling.

Joan covered her left eye. She covered her right eye. "This one," she said.

The little dark man raised a hand, and lightning flashed in Joan's right eye — a searing dazzle and then shooting stars and then complete darkness.

"That's for meddling!" cried the little man. "That's for taking the ointment, Joan! You won't be seeing me again."

Joan never saw anyone again, not with her right eye. She was blind on that side until the day she died.

CHARGER

"I'LL JUST HAVE TO SELL OLD CHARGER," SAID THE FARMER.

"Not Charger!" exclaimed his wife.

"He's one too many," the farmer said. "The other two are yearlings now."

So the farmer set off for the autumn horse fair. He rode Charger up the rainswept dale, feeling rather glum at the prospect of losing his loyal horse, and none too pleased at the thought of having to walk ten miles to get home again from the fair.

In the high hills, the farmer met a peddler, a little man with a wrinkled face, dressed from top to toe in chestnut brown. He was struggling through the wind and rain, carrying a battered old suitcase.

"Would you sell your horse?" said the little man.

"That's just what I'm going to do," the farmer replied.

"How much?" asked the little man.

The farmer narrowed his eyes. "You could have him for eight pounds," he said.

"No!" said the little man. "Not eight! I'll give you seven." And he dropped a hand into his pocket.

Well now, thought the farmer, *which is better: seven pounds for Charger here and now, or eight at the fair — or seven, or six?* The farmer looked at the poor wet little man. He thought of the long walk home. "It's a deal," he said.

So the farmer dismounted and the little man counted the coins into the farmer's hand: "One, two, three, four, five, six, seven."

"That's it," said the farmer.

Then the little man picked up his battered suitcase. He raised one foot as high as his hip, wedged it into a stirrup, and swung up into the saddle.

And there and then, right in front of the round-eyed farmer, the little man and Charger sank into the ground.

DATHERA DAD

THE KITCHEN WAS A MAGIC BOX, FULL OF LIGHT AND DANCING shadows. Shafts of winter sunlight lanced the range and the dresser and the pail of milk, and the hawthorn tree shivered outside the window.

The kettle sang, and the farmer's wife hummed as she put the large saucepan of water on the range, then mixed the ingredients — flour, eggs, breadcrumbs, sugar, salt, and suet, then nutmeg, cinnamon, and spice.

"And now the brandy," she said, pouring a generous dollop into the mixture, and then a second dollop for good measure.

The farmer's wife put the mixture into a white bowl and covered it with muslin tied 'round the rim. Then she lowered it into the steaming water.

As soon as the pudding felt the heat of the water, it jumped out of

the saucepan. It rolled over the sunlit range and fell onto the floor, cracking the white bowl. It wheeled across the floor toward the farmer's wife.

At that moment there was a loud knock, and Tom the tramp put his head 'round the back door.

"Morning, missus," he said. "Can you spare a pair of shoes?"

"I can't, Tom," said the farmer's wife.

"Christmas, missus."

"Here! You can have this pudding, then," said the farmer's wife, bending down and picking up the pudding in the cracked white bowl. "Christmas pudding!"

Tom was only a few yards down the frosty road when he felt something rolling around in the sack slung over his back. He stopped and opened the sack.

Then the pudding rolled onto the road. The white bowl broke into pieces, and the pudding burst open . . . and out stepped a little fairy child who took one look at Tom the tramp and cried, "Take me home to my dathera dad! Take me home to my dathera dad!"

YALLERY BROWN

IT WAS A SUNDAY NIGHT IN JULY, AND TOM WAS IN NO hurry to get back to High Farm. He didn't like hard work, and nothing but hard work awaited him — another week of grooming the horses, mucking out the stables, doing odd jobs at all hours around the farm.

So Tom took the long way 'round from his parents' home. He wandered along the path that led across the west field and down to the dark copse some people said was haunted. Tom was happy to be out in the moonlight, out in the wide and silent fields and the smell of growing things. It was warm and still, and the air was full of little sounds, as though the trees and grass were whispering to themselves.

Then, all at once, Tom heard a kind of sobbing somewhere ahead

of him in the darkness. He stopped and listened and thought it was the saddest sound he had ever heard — like a little child scared and exhausted and almost heartbroken. The sobbing lapsed into a moan, and then it rose again into a long, whimpering wail.

Tom began to peer about in the darkness. He searched everywhere, but though he looked and looked, he could see nothing. The sound was so close, at his very ear, spent and sorrowful, that he called out over and again, "Whisht, child, whisht! I'll take you back to your mother if you'll only hush now."

Tom searched under the hedge that ran along the edge of the copse. Then he scrambled over it and searched along the other side. He searched among the trees in the copse itself. Then he waded through the long grass and weeds, but he only frightened some sleeping birds and stung his hands on a bunch of nettles.

Tom stopped and scratched his head, and felt like giving up. But then, in the quietness, the whimpering became louder and stronger, and Tom thought he could hear words of some sort. He strained his ears, and mixed up with the sobbing, he made out the words "Oh! Oh! The great big stone! Ooh! Ooh! The stone on top!"

Tom started to search again. In the dark, he peered here and peered there, and at last, down by the far end of the hedge, almost buried in the ground and hidden amid matted grass and weeds, he found a great, flat stone.

"A strangers' table," said Tom to himself, and he felt uneasy at the thought of meddling with it. He didn't want to cross the little people and bring ill luck on his head by disturbing their moonlight dancing floor. All the same, he did get down on his knees and put an ear to the stone.

At once he heard it clearer than ever, a weary little voice sobbing, "Ooh! Ooh! The stone, the stone on top!"

Uneasy as he was about touching the thing, Tom couldn't bear the sound of the little child trapped under it. He tore like mad at the stone until he felt it begin to shift and lift from the ground. Then, with a sigh, the great slab suddenly came away, out of the damp soil and tangled grass and growing things. And there in the hollow was a little creature lying on his back, blinking up at the Moon and at Tom.

He was no bigger than a year-old baby, but he had long tangled hair and a long beard wound 'round and 'round his body so that Tom couldn't even see his clothes. His hair, like a baby's hair, was all yellow and shining and silken, but one look at his face and you would have thought he had lived for hundreds and hundreds of years. It was just a heap of wrinkles with two shining black eyes surrounded by masses of shining yellow hair. The creature's skin was the color of freshly turned soil in the spring, as brown as brown could be; and his hands and feet were just as brown as his face.

He had stopped moaning now, but the tears still shone on his cheeks. He looked quite dazed by the moonlight and the night air.

While Tom wondered what to do, the creature suddenly scrambled out of the hollow and stood up and began to look around him. He didn't reach up to Tom's knee, and Tom thought he was the strangest thing he had ever set eyes on: brown and yellow all over, yellow and brown, with such a glint in his eyes, and such a wizened face, that Tom felt afraid of him even though he was so little and so old.

In a while, the creature got used to the moonlight. Then he looked up and boldly stared Tom in the eye. "Tom," he said, as cool as you like, "you're a good lad." His voice was soft and high and piping like a bird, and he said it a second time. "Tom, you're a good lad."

Tom pulled at his cap and wondered what to reply. But he was so scared that his jaw seemed locked; he couldn't open his mouth.

"Houts!" said the creature. "You needn't be afraid of me. You've done me a better turn than you know, my lad, and I'll do the same for you."

Tom was still too scared to reply, but he thought, *Lord, he's a bogle, and no mistake!*

"No," said the creature, quick as quick. "I'm not a bogle, and you'd do better not to ask me what I am. Anyway, I'm a good friend of yours."

Tom's knees knocked together when the creature said that. He knew no ordinary being could read thoughts. But still, the creature seemed so friendly and reasonable that, in a quavery voice, he managed to say, "May I be asking your honor's name?"

"Hmm," said the creature, and he pulled his beard. "As for that . . ." And he thought for a moment. "As for that, yes, Yallery Brown you can call me. Yallery Brown. That's what I am, and it'll do as well as any other name. Yallery Brown, Tom; Yallery Brown is your friend, my lad."

"Thank you, master," said Tom meekly.

"And now," said the creature, "I'm in a hurry tonight, but tell me quickly, what shall I do for you? Do you want a wife? I can give you as much gold as you can carry. Or do you want help with your work? Only say the word."

Tom scratched his head. "Well," he said, "as for a wife, I've no wish to get married — wives spell nothing but trouble. And I've got a mother and sister to mend my clothes, and as for gold, that's as may be. . . ." Tom grinned and thought that the creature was boasting and couldn't do as much as he had offered. "But work," said Tom. "There! I can't stand work, and if you'll give me a helping hand I'll thank —"

"Stop!" said the creature, quick as lightning. "I'll help you, and you're welcome. But if ever you say that word to me — if ever you

thank me — you'll never see me again. Beware! I want no thanks and I'll have no thanks, do you hear me?" Yallery Brown stamped one little foot on the ground and looked as wicked as a raging bull.

"Mind that, now, you great lump!" said Yallery Brown, calming down a bit. "And if ever you need help, or get into trouble, just call for me and say, 'Yallery Brown, come from the ground, Yallery Brown, I want you.' Just call for me, and I'll be at your side at once. And now," said Yallery Brown, picking a dandelion puff, "good night to you." And he blew the dandelion seed into Tom's eyes and ears. When Tom could see again, the little creature had disappeared, and but for the uprooted stone and hollow at his feet, Tom would have thought he had been dreaming.

Then Tom went back home instead of going up to High Farm, and he went to bed; in the morning he had almost forgotten about Yallery Brown. But when he did go up to work at the farm, there was nothing to do! It was all done already: the horses were groomed, the stables were mucked out, everything was neat and tidy, and Tom had nothing to do but sit around with his hands in his pockets.

It was just the same the next day and the day after. All Tom's work was done by Yallery Brown and done better than Tom could have done it himself. And if the farmer gave Tom more work, Tom simply sat down and watched the work get done by itself. The branding irons, the broom, and this, that, and the other all set to and got through their tasks in no time. For Tom never saw Yallery Brown out in the light of day; it was only in the darkness that he saw him hopping about, like a will-o'-the-wisp without his lantern.

To begin with, Tom couldn't have been happier. He had nothing to do and got well paid for it! But after a time, things began to go wrong. Not only was Tom's work done, but the work of the other farmhands

was undone: if his buckets were filled, theirs were upset; if his tools were sharpened, theirs were blunted and wrecked; if his horses were clean as daisies, theirs were splashed with muck. That's how things were, day in and day out, always the same.

The other farmhands saw Yallery Brown flitting around night after night; they saw things that worked without helping hands; and they saw that Tom's work was done for him, and their work was undone for them. Naturally they began to stay away from Tom. After a while, they wouldn't speak to him or even go near him. And, in the end, they all went to the farmer and told him what was happening.

Tom often thought he would be better off doing his own work after all, and he wished Yallery Brown would leave him and his old friends in peace. But he couldn't do a thing about it — brooms wouldn't so much as stay in his hand; the plow ran away from him; the hoe kept slipping out of his grip. He could only sit on his own while all the other lads gave him the cold shoulder and Yallery Brown worked for him and worked against all the others.

At last, things got so bad that the farmer gave Tom the sack; if he hadn't, all the other farmhands would probably have sacked the farmer, for they vowed they would no longer stay on the same farm with Tom.

Tom was angry and upset then. It was a very good farm, and he was well paid; he was hopping mad with Yallery Brown for getting him into such trouble. And, without thinking, he shook his fist and shouted as loud as he could, "Yallery Brown, come out of the ground; Yallery Brown, you scamp, I want you."

Tom had done no more than close his mouth when he felt something tweaking the back of his leg. It pinched him and he jumped, and when he looked down, Tom could scarcely believe his eyes — for

there already was the little creature with his shining hair and wrinkled face and wickedly glinting black eyes.

Tom was in a fine old rage, and he would have liked nothing so much as to give Yallery Brown a big kick, but the creature was so small he would only have slid off the side of his boot. Tom scowled and said, "Look here, master! I'll thank you to leave me alone from now on, do you hear me? I want none of your help, and I'll have nothing more to do with you. Understand?"

The horrid little creature gave a screech of a laugh and pointed a brown finger at Tom. "Ho, ho, Tom!" he said. "You've just thanked me, my lad, and I told you not to! I told you not to!"

"I don't want any of your help, I tell you," yelled Tom. "I only want never to see you again, and to have nothing more to do with you."

The more Tom said, the more Yallery Brown laughed and screeched and mocked. "Tom, my lad," he said with a devilish grin, "I'll tell you something, Tom. It's true enough I'll never help you again, and call on me as you will, you'll never see me again after today."

"Good," said Tom.

"But I never said I'd leave you alone, Tom, and I never will, my lad! I was nice and safe under that stone, Tom, and I could do no harm. But you let me out yourself, and you can't put me back again."

Tom grimaced and shook his head.

"I would have been your friend," said Yallery Brown, "and worked for you if you had been wise; but since you're a born fool, I'll give you nothing but fool's luck. When everything goes wrong and arsy-versy, you'll know it's Yallery Brown's doing, even if you can't see him. Mark my words, Tom!"

And Yallery Brown began to dance around Tom, looking like a little child with all his yellow hair, but looking older than ever with his grinning, wrinkled face. And as he danced, he sang:

> "*Work as you will,*
> *You'll never do well;*
> *Work as you may,*
> *You'll never make hay;*
> *For harm and bad luck and Yallery Brown*
> *You've let out yourself from under the stone.*"

The words rang in Tom's ears over and again. Then Yallery Brown just looked up, grinning at Tom and chuckling as wickedly as the devil himself.

Tom was terrified. He could only stand there, shaking all over, staring down at the horrible little creature.

Then Yallery Brown's shining yellow hair lifted and rippled in a gust of wind. It wound 'round and 'round him so that he looked for all the world like a great dandelion puff. And then the little creature floated away on the breeze, over the wall and out of sight; as he went, Tom could hear a last shrill insult and a sneering laugh.

Tom was scared to death, and after that day, his fortunes took a tumble. He worked here and worked there, he put his hand to this and that, but something always went wrong.

The years passed by and Tom married and had children. But his children died and his wife didn't. When she scolded him, people could hear her a mile off, and Tom did think now and then that he could have done without *her*! And although he tried his hand with cattle and sheep and pigs and goats and hens, none of them fattened as they should. Nothing ever worked for him.

No, Tom had no luck at all after meeting Yallery Brown. For the rest of his life, until he was dead and buried and maybe afterward, there was no end to Yallery Brown's spite toward him. And day after day as long as he lived, even as an old man when he sat trembling beside the fire, Tom heard a voice singing:

"Work as you will,
You'll never do well;
Work as you may,
You'll never make hay;
For harm and bad luck and Yallery Brown
You've let out yourself from under the stone."

MEN AND WOMEN

THE THREE BLOWS

THEIR STONE FARMHOUSE SEEMED TO GROW OUT OF THE gray-green skirt of the mountain. The walls were lichenous; one part of the roof was covered with slate and the other part with turf. The whole building was so low-slung it seemed to be crouching.

It wasn't alone. Megan could stand at their door (you had to stoop to get in or out) and see three other small farms within reach, almost within shouting distance. And no more than a mile away, along the track north and west, huddled and patient, was the little village of Llanddeusant.

But when the wind opened its throat and rain swept across the slopes, when the lean seasons came to Black Mountain, when wolves circled the pens and small birds left their Sanskrit in the snow, the farm seemed alone then, alone in the world — and all the more so to Megan since her husband had died, leaving her to bring

up their baby son, Gwyn, and run the farm on her own.

But Megan was a hardworking woman. As the years passed, her holding of cattle and sheep and goats so increased that they strayed far and wide over Black Mountain. And all the while her son grew and grew until he became a big-boned young man: rather awkward, very strong-willed, shy and affectionate. Yet sometimes, when she looked at him sitting by the fire, lost in his own sliding dreams, it seemed to Megan that she didn't really quite know her son. *He's like his father,* she thought. *Something hidden. What is he thinking?*

Gwyn spent most of his time up on Black Mountain, herding the cattle and sheep and goats. More often than not, he followed them up to a remote place in a fold of the mountain. It was a secret eye, a dark pupil that watched the Sun and the Moon and stars: the little lake of Llyn y Fan Fach.

One spring morning, Gwyn was poking along the edge of the lake, on his way to the flat rock where he sometimes sat and spread out his provisions — barley bread, maybe, and a chunk of cheese, a wooden bottle seething with ale. Gwyn clambered onto the rock and stared out across the lake, silver and obsidian. And there, on the glassy surface of the water, he saw a young woman combing her hair. She was using the water as a mirror, charming her hair into ringlets, arranging them so they covered her shoulders; and only when she had finished did she look up and see Gwyn, awkward on the rock, openmouthed, arms stretched out, offering her bread.

Slowly, so slowly she scarcely seemed to move at all, the young woman glided over the surface of the water toward Gwyn, and entranced, he stepped down to meet her.

And then Gwyn heard her voice. It was like a bell heard long ago and remembered: very sweet and very low. "Your bread's baked and hard," she said. "It's not easy to catch me."

Which is just what Gwyn tried to do. He lunged into the lake, and at once the girl sank from sight; she left her smile behind, playing on the smooth surface of the water.

For a while Gwyn stood and stared. A stray cloud passed in front of the Sun; the water shivered. Gwyn felt as if he had found the one thing in this world that mattered, only to lose it. And he resolved to come back, to find the girl and catch her, whatever the cost.

Gwyn turned away from the lake. He set off down the string-thin sheep runs, the network that covered the steep shoulders of the mountain. At first he walked slowly, but by the time he reached the doors of his farmhouse he was almost running, so eager was he to tell his mother about the bewitching girl he had seen up at Llyn y Fan Fach.

"Stuff!" said Megan. "You and your dreams." But as she listened to Gwyn, she did not doubt that he was telling the truth. Perhaps she saw in the young man at her hearth another young man at the same hearth long before, shining and stammering. But then she quailed as she thought of what might become of Gwyn if he was caught up with the fairy folk.

"I won't be put off," said Gwyn. "I won't be put off, if that's what you're thinking."

"Leave her alone, Gwyn," said Megan. "Take a girl from the valley."

"I won't be put off," said Gwyn.

"You won't catch her," Megan said, "not unless you listen to me."

"What do you mean?" said Gwyn.

"'Your bread's baked and hard.' Isn't that what she said?"

Gwyn nodded.

"Well, then. Take up some toes. Take up some toes. Stands to reason."

"Toes?" said Gwyn.

"Pieces of dough. Unbaked and just as they are."

Gwyn followed his mother's advice. As night began to lose its thickness, yet before you could say it was dawn, he filled one pocket with dough and quietly let himself out of the farmhouse without waking his mother. He sniffed the cool air and began to climb the gray and misty mountain.

She was not there. Shape-changing mist that plays tricks with the eyes dipped and rose and dipped over the dark water until the Sun came down from the peaks and burned it away. Birds arrived in boating parties, little fish made circles, and she was not there.

Not long before dusk, Gwyn saw that two of his cows were lumbering straight toward the top of the dangerous cliff on the far side of the lake. He stood up at once and began to run around the lake after them. "Stupids!" he bawled. "You'll lose your footing."

Then she was there. She was there, sitting on the shimmer of the water, smiling, just as she had done the day before.

Gwyn stopped. He reached out his arm, and as the beautiful young woman drifted toward him, he gazed at her: the blue-black sheen of her hair, her long fingers, the green watersilk of her dress, and her little ankles and sandals tied with thongs. Then Gwyn dug into his pockets and offered her the unbaked dough, and not only that but his hand, too, and his heart forever.

"Your bread is unbaked," said the young woman. "I will not have you." Then she raised her arms and sank under the surface of the water.

Gwyn cried out, and the rock face heard and answered him, all hollow and disembodied. But even as he looked at the lake and listened to the sounds, each as mournful as the other, Gwyn thought of the girl's smile and was half comforted. "I'll catch you," he said.

"You caught the cows," said Megan later that evening. "That's what matters."

Gwyn grinned.

"Anyhow," said Megan, "you're not going up there again, are you?"

"You know I am," said Gwyn.

"In that case," said his mother, "listen to me. I'd take some partly baked bread up with you."

Gwyn reached Llyn y Fan Fach again as day dawned. He kept a watch on the lake, and his whole face glowed—his cheeks and chin and ears and eyes, above all his eyes—as if he had just turned away from a leaping fire. He felt strong and he felt weak.

This time it was the sheep and goats that strayed toward the rock face and loose rocks at the far end of the lake. But Gwyn knew how nimble-footed they were. Even when they loosened and dislodged a rock that bumped and bundled down the cliff and splashed into the lake, they were in no danger.

All morning wayward April shook sheets of sunlight and rain over the lake, and then, in the afternoon, the clouds piling in from the west closed over the mountain. For hour after hour, Gwyn crouched on the smooth rock or padded around the rim of the lake. Now he was no longer so excited or fearful; the long waiting had dulled him.

In the early evening, the mood of the weather changed again. First Gwyn could see blue sky behind the gauze of cloud, and then the clouds left the mountain altogether. The lake and the ashen gravel were soothed by yellow sunlight.

This was the hour when Gwyn saw that three cows were walking on the water. They were out in the middle of Llyn y Fan Fach and ambling toward him.

Gwyn stood up. He swung off the rock platform and down to the

lakeside. And as he did so, the young woman appeared for the third time, as beautiful as before, passing over the mirror of water just behind the three cows.

Gwyn stepped into the lake, up to his shins, his thighs, his hips. Still the young woman came on, and she was smiling — an expression that lit up her whole face, and above all her violet eyes.

Gwyn reached out his hands and, wordless, offered her the partly baked bread.

The young woman took the bread, and Gwyn grasped her cool hand. He was nervous and breathless.

"Come with me," he said. "Come to the farm. . . . I'll show you. Come with me. . . . Marry me!"

The young woman looked at Gwyn.

"I'll not let you go," said Gwyn. He could hear his voice rising, as if someone else were speaking. "I've waited!" He tightened his grip on the girl's hand.

"Gwyn," said the young woman. "I will marry you," she said, "on one condition."

"Anything!" said Gwyn. "Anything you ask."

"I will marry you and live with you. But if you strike me —"

"Strike you!" cried Gwyn.

"Strike me three blows without reason, I'll return to this lake, and you'll never see me again."

"Never!" swore Gwyn. "Never!" He loosened his fierce grip, and at once she slid away, raised her arms, and disappeared under the surface of the water.

"Come back!" shouted Gwyn. "Come back!"

"Gon-ba!" said the mountain. "Gon-ba!"

Gwyn stood up to his waist in the chill water. The huge red Sun alighted on the western horizon and began to slip out of sight.

But now two young women, each as lovely as the other, rose out of the water, and a tall old white-headed man immediately after them. At once they came walking toward Gwyn.

"Greetings, Gwyn!" called the old man. "You mean to marry one of my daughters; you've asked her to marry you." He waved toward the two girls at his side. "And I agree to this. You can marry her if you can tell me which one you mean to marry."

Gwyn looked from one girl to the other: their curtains of black hair, their strange violet eyes, their long necks . . .

One of the girls tossed her charcoal hair; the other eased one foot forward, one inch, two inches, and into Gwyn's memory. The sandals . . . the thongs . . .

Gwyn reached out at once across the water and took her cool hand. "This is she," he said.

"You have made your choice?" asked the old man.

"I have," said Gwyn.

"You've chosen well," the man said. "And you can marry her. Be kind to her, and faithful."

"I will," said Gwyn, "and I will."

"This is her dowry," said the man. "She can have as many sheep and cattle and goats and horses as she can count without drawing breath."

No sooner had her father spoken than his daughter began to count for the sheep. She counted in fives, "One, two, three, four, five — one, two, three, four, five," over and over again until she'd run out of breath.

"Thirty-two times," said the man. "One hundred and sixty sheep." As soon as they had been named, the sheep appeared on the surface of the darkening water and ran across it to the bare mountain.

"Now the cattle," said the old man. Then his daughter began to count again, her voice soft and rippling. And so they went on until there were more than six hundred heads of sheep and cattle and goats and horses milling around on the lakeside.

"Go now," said the white-headed man gently. "And remember, Gwyn, if you strike her three blows without reason, she'll return to me and bring all her livestock back to this lake."

It was almost dark. The old man and his other daughter went down into the lake. Gwyn took his bride's hand and, followed by her livestock, led her down from the mountain.

So Gwyn and the girl from Llyn y Fan Fach were married. Gwyn left the house in which he had been born, and his mother in it, and went to a farm a few miles away, outside the village of Myddfai.

Gwyn and his wife were happy, and because of the generosity of the old man, they were rich. They had three sons, dark haired, dark eyed, lovely to look at.

Some years after Gwyn and his wife had moved to Myddfai, they were invited to a christening back in Llanddeusant. Gwyn was eager to go, but when the time came for them to set off, his wife was not.

"I don't know these people," she said.

"It's Gareth," said Gwyn. "I've known him all my life. And this is his first child."

"It's too far to walk," said his wife.

"Fetch a horse from the field, then," said Gwyn. "You can ride down."

"Will you go and find my gloves," said Gwyn's wife, "while I get the horse? I left them in the house."

When Gwyn came out of the farmhouse with the gloves, eager to

be off, his wife had made no move toward the paddock and the horse.

"What's wrong?" cried Gwyn, and he slapped his wife's shoulder with one of her gloves.

Gwyn's wife turned to face him. Her eyes darkened. "Gwyn!" she said. "Gwyn! Remember the condition on which I married you."

"I remember," said Gwyn.

"That you would never strike me without reason."

Gwyn nodded.

"Be careful! Be more careful from now on!"

Not long after this, Gwyn and his wife went to a fine wedding. The guests at the breakfast came not only from Llanddeusant and Myddfai but many of the surrounding farms and villages. The barn in which the reception was held was filled with the hum of contentment and the sweet sound of the triple harp.

As soon as she had kissed the bride, Gwyn's wife began to weep and then to sob. The guests around her stopped talking. A few tried to comfort her, but many backed away, superstitious of tears at a wedding.

Gwyn didn't know quite what to do. "What's wrong?" he whispered. "What's wrong?" But his wife sobbed as bitterly as a little child. Gwyn smiled apologetically and shook his head; then he pursed his lips and dropped a hand onto his wife's arm. "What's the matter?" he insisted. "You must stop!"

Gwyn's wife gazed at her husband with her flooded violet eyes. "These two people," she said, "are on the threshold of such trouble. I see it all. And Gwyn," she said, "I see your troubles are about to begin. You've struck me without reason for the second time."

Gwyn's wife loved her husband no less than he loved her, and neither had the least desire that their marriage should suddenly come

to an end. Knowing that her own behavior could surprise and upset Gwyn, she sometimes reminded her husband to be very careful not to strike her for a third time. "Otherwise," she said, "I must return to Llyn y Fan Fach. I have no choice in the matter."

But the years passed. The three boys became young men, all of them intelligent. And when he thought about it at all, Gwyn believed that he had learned his lesson on the way to the christening and at the wedding, and that he and his waterwife would live together happily for as long as they lived.

One day, Gwyn and his wife went to a funeral. Everyone around had come to pay their last respects to the dead woman: she had been the daughter of a rich farmer and wife to the priest, generous with her time and money, and still in the prime of her life.

After the funeral, a good number of the priest's friends went back to his house to eat funeral cakes with him and keep him company, and Gwyn and his wife were among them.

No sooner had they stepped inside the priest's house than Gwyn's wife began to laugh. Among the mourners with their black suits and sober faces, she giggled as if she were tipsy with ale or romping with young children.

Gwyn was shocked. "Shush!" he said. "Think where you are! Stop this laughing!" he said. And firmly he laid a restraining hand on his wife's forearm.

"I'm laughing," said Gwyn's wife, "because when a person dies, she passes out of this world of trouble. Ah! Gwyn," she cried, "you've struck me for the third time and the last time. Our marriage is at an end."

Gwyn's wife left the funeral feast alone and went straight back to their fine farm outside Myddfai. There she began to call in all her livestock.

"Brindled cow, come! White speckled cow, spotted cow, bold

freckled cow, come! Old white-faced cow, Gray Squinter, white bull from the court of the king, come and come home!"

Gwyn's wife knew each of her livestock by name. And she did not forget the calf her husband had slaughtered only the previous week. "Little black calf," she cried, "come down from the hook! Come home!"

The black calf leaped into life; it danced around the courtyard.

Then Gwyn's wife saw four of her oxen plowing a nearby field. "Gray oxen!" she cried. "Four oxen of the field, you too must come home!"

When they heard her, the oxen turned from their task and, for all the whistles of the plowboy, dragged the plow right across the newly turned furrows.

Gwyn's wife looked about her. She paused. Then she turned her back on the farmhouse and the farm. Those who saw her never forgot that sight: one woman, sad and steadfast, walking up onto Myddfai Mountain, and behind her, plodding and trudging and tripping and highstepping, a great concourse of creatures.

The woman crossed over onto the swept slopes of Black Mountain, just above the lonely farm where Gwyn had been born and where Megan still lived in her old age. Up she climbed, on and up to the dark eye.

The Lady of Llyn y Fan Fach walked over the surface of the water and disappeared into the lake, and all her hundreds of animals followed her. They left behind them sorrow; they left a wake of silence and the deep furrow made by the oxen as they dragged their plow up over the shoulder of the mountain and into the lake.

THE FINE FIELD OF FLAX

I WILL TELL YOU WHAT I KNOW.

I was born on this island. My mother was born on this island. And her mother and her father.

I am part of this place, no less than the green curve of the hill, the twisted tree, the ring of dawn water. We are all part of one another.

She was sixteen when I was born. "Bonny," she murmured, as I fed at her breast. "Bonny. Brave." She was brave and bonny.

The Northern Lights shook their curtains on the night I was born. Glean and cold and burning.

"And the father," they said. "Who is the father? Where is the father?"

She said, "I cannot tell."

"Tell me," whispered her mother.

"Tell me," ordered her father.

"Tell Mother Church," hissed the minister. "What have you to say?"

"There is no more to say," she said.

Wind sang in the shell; Sun danced in the scarlet cup; dew softened the ear.

Days and questions, questions and days. Her mother, her father, her friends, the minister, the elders.

"I know nothing you do not know," she said. "Why do you ask me if you don't believe me?"

"Out," they said. "Away. Out of our sight. You and your issue."

We lived in a cottage by the ocean. One room with no cow: it smelled of pine and tar and salt.

The sea schooled me. I know her changes, her whiplash and switchback and croon. I know the sea voices, the boom of the bittern, the curlew's cry and the redshank's warning, the shriek of the white-tailed sea eagle and all her sisters. Mine is a sea voice.

We scratched the sandy wasteland behind the dune, and there we sowed our seeds of corn. We picked sea peas. Sometimes we went hungry.

When we walked into town, they crossed the street to avoid us. "Slut," they said. "Strumpet. Sweet sixteen and a whore." They spat at us.

I wore rags. What else was there to wear? The sea was my mirror.

"One dress," said my mother. "For my daughter. I wish you had one dress."

I grew up. I grew old. Fourteen, fifteen . . .

Once I went walking along the cliffs all the way to the edge of the gloup, the opening in the ceiling of the sea cave. The black water sluiced and boomed and exploded in the chasm far below.

I waited for a long time. The water moaned and sucked in the long cave that leads out to the sea. Then the chasm was empty.

I wandered up to the high headland between the gloup and the sea. And there I found it. It was all around me, growing wild, and I grew wild at the sight of it. I swayed with it. I waved with it.

Blue flowers were born after I came. They died before I left.

I picked the flax. I carried an armful back to the cottage. The next day, my mother and I hurried back for more.

She soaked the flax; she beat and combed and spun the fibers; she wove the linen. She cut out my dress.

She culled plants from the green curve and crushed them and boiled them. She scraped bark from the twisted tree. She lit my dress with bright colors. It was so bonny.

"You're bonny," she told me. "It becomes you."

I wore it: my first dress. It sang in the sunlight and danced on the windy dune. Then the lord saw it. He saw the bright signal and rode up. He rode right past our cottage.

The next day it was the lord's son. He stopped and spoke to me. He smiled at me. He talked to my mother.

The lord's son came back with food for us, clothes, and gifts. My mother smiled. And when he had gone, she wept and hugged me.

He told me he loved me.

There was a fine wedding. My mother came to live with me in the big house. She lived there, and there she died.

I have made you this song:

On the ridges two three
between the gloup and the sea
grew a fine field of flax
for my mother and me

THE FINE FIELD OF FLAX

we picked the flax
on a brave bonny day
and we jumped in glee
my mother and me

the flax we spun
and wove and all
mother made me a gown
so bonny and brave

and the lord when he saw me
thought I would do
as a wife for his son
who was young and gay
so we both fell in love
and were married one day

and it's all because
of the ridges two three
where the flax grew so bonny
between the gloup and the sea

I bore him two sons
who traveled afar . . .
yet they never forgot
the ridges two three
where the flax grew so bonny
between the gloup and the sea

After my mother died, the people on the island began to remember

what she had said, and could not say, in the days after I was born. And they began to believe her. Each week they put white flowers on her grave.

There! The lights have started their dance in the north.

I have told you what I know. You are my children's children's children. All this was long ago.

SEA WOMAN

IT WAS AN EMPTY OYSTER-AND-PEARL AFTERNOON. THE water lipped at the sand and sorted the shingle and lapped 'round the rock where the girl was sitting.

Then she saw a seal, like a mass of seaweed almost, until she gazed into those eyes. It swam in quite close, just twenty or thirty water steps away.

She looked at the seal; the seal looked at her. Then it barked. It cried out in a loud voice.

She stood up on her rock. She called out to the seal: not a word but a sound, the music words are made of.

The seal swam in a little closer. It looked at the girl. Then it cried. Oh! The Moon's edge and a mother's ache were in that cry.

The girl jumped off the rock. Her eyes were sea eyes, wide and flint-gray. "Seal!" she cried. "Sea woman! What do you want?"

And what did the seal want but the girl's company? As she padded down the strand, it followed her, always keeping fifteen or twenty water steps away, out in the dark swell. The girl turned back toward her rock, and the seal turned with her. Sometimes it huffed and puffed; sometimes it cried; it wailed as if it were lost, all at sea.

The girl bent down and picked up a curious shell, opaline and milky and intricate.

"Listen, listen!" sang the wind in the shell's mouth.

Then the girl raised the shell and pressed it to her right ear.

"One afternoon," sang the shell, "oyster-and-pearl, a man came back from fishing. He was so weary. He peeled off his salt-stiff clothing. He washed. For an hour or two hours he closed his eyes. And then, when the Moon rose, he came strolling along this strand.

"He listened to the little waves kissing in the rocks. He smelled earth on the breeze and knew it would soon rain. This is where he walked, rocking slightly from side to side, in no hurry at all, for there was nowhere to go.

"Then he stopped. Down the beach, no more than the distance of a shout, he saw a group of sea people dancing. They were singing and swaying; they danced like the waves of the sea.

"Then the sea people saw him. At once they stopped singing and broke their bright ring. As the fisherman began to run toward them, they turned toward a pile of sealskins — in the moonlight they looked like a wet rock — and picked them up and pulled them on and plunged into the water.

"One young woman was not so quick, though. She was so caught up in the dance that the fisherman reached her skin before she did. He snatched it up and tucked it under one arm. Then he turned to

face the sea woman, and he was grinning.

"'Please,' she said. Her voice was high as a handbell and flecked with silver. 'Please.'

"The fisherman shook his head.

"'My skin,' said the sea woman. There she stood, dressed in moonlight, reaching out toward him with her white arms, and he stood between her and the sea.

"'I've landed some catches,' breathed the fisherman, 'but never anything like this. . . .'

"Then the young woman began to sob. 'I cannot,' she cried. 'I cannot go back without my skin.'

"*And this catch I'll keep,* thought the fisherman.

"'My home and my family and my friends,' said the sea woman.

"Now she wept and the Moon picked up her salt tears and turned them into pearls. How lovely she was, and lovely in more ways than one: a young woman lithe as young women are, a sea child, a sister of the Moon. For all her tears, the fisherman had not the least intention of giving her back her skin.

"'You'll come with me,' he said.

"The sea woman shuddered.

"Then the man stepped forward and took her by the wrist. 'Home with me,' he said.

"The sea woman neither moved toward the man nor pulled away from him. 'Please,' she said, her voice sweet and ringing. 'The sea is my home, the shouting waves, the green light and the darkening.'

"But the fisherman had set his heart against it. He led the sea woman along the strand and into the silent village and back to his home.

"Then the fisherman shut the door on the sea woman and went out into the night again to hide the skin. He ran up to the haystack

in the field behind his house, loosened one of the hay bricks, and hid the skin behind it. Within ten minutes, he was back on his own doorstep.

"The sea woman was still there; without her skin, there was nowhere for her to go. She looked at the man. With her flint-gray eyes, she looked at him."

For a moment the girl lowered the shell from her ear. She gazed at the emptiness around her, no one on the beach or on the hill slope leading down to it, no one between her and the north pole. The little waves were at their kissing, and the seal still kept her company, bobbing up and down in the welling water.

"Listen, listen!" sang the wind in the shell's mouth.

The girl raised the shell again and pressed it to her right ear.

"Time passed," sang the shell, "and the sea woman stayed with the fisherman. Without her skin, she was unable to go back to the sea, and the fisherman was no worse than the next man.

"For his part, the fisherman fell in love. He had spent half his life on the ocean. He knew all her moods and movements and colors, and he saw them in the sea woman.

"Before long, the man and the sea woman married, and they had one daughter and then two sons. The sea woman loved them dearly and was a good mother to them. They were no different from other children except in one way: there was a thin, half-transparent web between their fingers and their toes.

"Often the sea woman came walking along the strand where the fisherman had caught her. She sat on a rock; she sang sad songs about a happier time. At times a large seal came swimming in toward her, calling out to her. But what could she do? She talked to the seal in the language

they shared; she stayed there for hours. But always, in the end, she turned away and walked slowly back to the village.

"Late one summer afternoon, the sea woman's three children were playing around on the haystack behind their house. One of the little boys gave his sister a push from behind, and the girl grabbed wildly at the wall of the haystack.

"One hay brick came away. And the skin, the sealskin that the fisherman had hidden in one stack after another as the years passed, fell to the ground.

"The children stopped playing. They fingered the skin; they buried their faces in its softness; they took it back to show their mother.

"The sea woman scarcely dared to look at it and looked at it, scarcely dared to touch it and touched it.

"'Mother!' said the children, crowding around her. 'What is it?'

"The sea woman pulled her children to her. She dragged them to her and squeezed them. She hugged and kissed each of them. Then she turned and ran out of the house with her skin.

"The children were afraid. They followed her. They saw her pull on the skin, cry a great cry, and dive off a rock. Then a large seal rose to meet her, and the two seals leaped and dipped through the water.

"When their father came back from the fishing, his children were standing at the stone jetty.

"'You go home,' said the man. 'I'll come back in an hour.'

"Slowly the man waded in his salt-stiff clothing along this strand. He kept rubbing his pale-blue eyes and looking out across the dancing water.

"She rose out of the waves. She was no more than a few water steps away.

"'Husband!' she cried. 'Husband! Look after our children! Take care of our children!' Her voice carried over the water. 'You've loved

me and looked after me, and I've loved you. But for as long as I lived with you, I always loved my first husband better.'

"Then the sea woman, the seal woman, slipped under the sallow waves once more. One moment she was there; the next, she was not there. . . ."

The girl took the opaline shell away from her ear and set it down on the sand. For a long time she sat there. The seal had gone; it had deserted her, and the dark water shivered.

THE BLACK BULL OF NORWAY

AT ANOTHER TIME (AND THAT TIME WAS LONG AGO) AND IN another country (and the country was Norway), there was a poor mountain woman whose husband died while their three daughters were still small children.

The woman was determined her daughters should lack for nothing. She worked all day and half the night. The girls' dresses were simple and pretty; their food was nourishing; and the little cottage where they had always lived was as clean as a cat's tongue.

In the summer, the girls brought back wildflowers from the meadows every day, slipped one through the handle of each mug and jug on the dresser, tucked them through the collars of their three swishing cows, and arranged a bunch on the middle of the scoured table.

As the girls grew up, they saw their mother had paid a price for all

her hard work: her green youth and gaiety. They felt sorry and indignant for her, and like fledglings, they began to grow restless.

"I'll go down to the valley," said the eldest daughter, whose name was Betony. "Who knows whom I'll meet? Who knows where I'll go?"

The woman gave her daughter a barley cake and a good wedge of ham. Then Betony walked over the mountain slopes, through a pine forest, and down to a cottage far below — the home of the wise woman and her only daughter.

"Stay here today," said the wise woman. "Go and look out the back door and see what you can see."

"Nothing!" said Betony. "Nothing out of the way."

The eldest daughter saw nothing on the second day either. But on the third day, she saw six horses drawing a glassy coach toward the cottage.

"There's a coach-and-six coming," called Betony.

"Ah!" said the wise woman. "That's coming for you."

So one of the coachmen dismounted and opened the glass door for the eldest daughter, and they galloped away.

It wasn't very long before the second daughter, whose name was Bracken, wanted to follow in her elder sister's footsteps.

"Mother!" she said. "Make me a barley cake and a wedge of ham! I'll walk down to the valley. Who knows whom I'll meet? Who knows where I'll go?"

Bracken called at the wise woman's cottage, just as her sister had. She looked out the back door, and on the third day she saw four grays drawing a silver coach toward the cottage.

"There's a coach-and-four coming," called Bracken.

"Ah!" said the wise woman. "That's coming for you."

So the coachman dismounted and opened the silver door for the second daughter, and they galloped away.

"Mother!" said the youngest daughter, whose name was Flora.

"Make me a barley cake and a wedge of ham! I'll walk down to the valley."

"You too?" said her mother.

"Who knows whom I'll meet?" said Flora. "Who knows where I'll go?"

Flora took her leave of her mother and picked her way over the mountain and through the forest and down to the cottage of the wise woman.

"Go and look out the back door," said the wise woman, "and see what you can see."

"Nothing," said Flora. "Nothing out of the way."

The youngest daughter saw nothing on the second day either. But on the third day she saw a huge black bull bucking and bellowing its way down toward the cottage.

"There's a black bull coming," called Flora, "and it's a big one."

"Ah!" said the wise woman. "That's coming for you."

"For me?" cried the girl. And her eyes brimmed with tears.

But the bull waited outside the cottage, and the wise woman helped the youngest daughter up onto its back, and away they went.

The black bull was an ugly great beast. His shoulders were broad, his eyes were bloodshot, and his hair was matted and rough.

"Take hold of my horns, Flora," said the bull.

Flora leaned forward and gripped the bull's horns, and at once the bull began to charge over the slopes. He jumped across a stream; he kicked up stones that went bumping and leaping down the mountainside behind them.

After a while, Flora's fear gave way to curiosity. The black bull was traveling at a great pace and taking her into a remote and rocky area. For hour after hour he ran on without shortening his stride.

"I'm hungry," said Flora.

"There's food in my right ear," said the black bull.

"And thirsty," said Flora.

"And there's drink in my left ear. Eat and drink as much as you want."

So Flora ate and drank, and she felt wonderfully refreshed.

Quite late in the evening, as a chill, damp mountain mist began to rise and fall around them, Flora saw a castle that seemed to grow straight out of rock. It was all parapets and pinnacles and peephole windows.

"That's where we'll stay tonight," the bull said. "My eldest brother lives there."

"Who are you, then?" said Flora.

But the bull did not reply; he galloped up to the castle courtyard.

Servants helped poor Flora down from the bull's back and escorted her into the castle, and then they ushered the bull into a pasture flanked by mountain ash and sweet-smelling pine.

Flora ate well and slept well, and in the morning a servant conducted her into a small and shining room that led out of the great hall. A man was sitting at the head of a long chestnut table.

"You've been welcome here," said the man, and Flora saw he was holding a most beautiful apple. It glowed as if lit by its own inner light.

"This apple is for you," said the man. "And you must not break it or open it until you have great need of it."

Then the castle servants lifted Flora onto the bull's back. Away they went, and in the evening, after they had traveled many, many miles, they came to a castle alive with fluttering flags. There were flags surrounding it and flags on the keep and flags sticking out of almost every window.

"That's where we'll stay tonight," the bull said. "My elder brother lives there."

"Who are you, then?" said Flora.

But the bull did not reply; he galloped up to the castle courtyard.

Servants lifted Flora down from the bull's back and ushered the bull into a pasture for the night. Then, in the morning, a servant conducted Flora into a room hung with glinting tapestries. A man was sitting at the head of a long table, and Flora saw he was holding a marvelous pear.

"You've been welcome here," said the man. "And this pear is for you. You must not break it or open it until you have great need of it."

Again the castle servants lifted Flora onto the bull's back. Away they went, and they traveled many, many miles. Flora had never seen such a desolate place: one moment she was squinting up at a towering rock face, the next peering over the edge of a precipice. The bull hurried on, and in the evening they came to a third castle: it was made entirely of painted and decorated wood.

"That's where we'll stay tonight," the bull said. "My youngest brother lives there."

"Who are you, then?" said Flora.

But the bull did not reply; he galloped up to the castle courtyard.

Servants lifted Flora down from the bull's back and ushered the bull into a pasture for the night. Then, in the morning, a servant conducted Flora into a room with mirror walls. A man was sitting at the head of a table, and Flora saw he was holding a wonderful plum.

"You've been welcome here," said the man. "And this plum is for you. You must not open it or break it until you have great need of it."

Once again, the castle servants lifted Flora onto the bull's back. Away they went until they came to a dark and frightful valley. Soaring rock shoulders rose up on either side of a fast-running

stream, blocking out all but the midday Sun, and the stream itself was littered with boulders.

"This is the place," said the black bull. "Get down from my back."

Flora dismounted and looked up at the black bull, his broad shoulders, bloodshot eyes, and matted, rough hair.

"You must wait here," said the bull, "while I go on and fight the devil. You must sit on that rock."

Flora looked at the saucer-shaped rock lying half in and half out of the water.

"Sit on that rock and move neither hand nor foot until I come back! If you move even once, I'll never be able to find you. If everything around you turns blue, I'll have beaten the devil," said the bull. "But if everything turns red, he'll have beaten me."

Flora sat down on the saucer-shaped rock. She stared at the water; she dreamed of her mother and sisters, so far away; and she wondered about her traveling companion.

After a while, everything around Flora began to turn blue. The high rock shoulders turned indigo, and the rocks in the stream turned slate blue; the silver water turned aquamarine, and the clouds parted overhead.

Flora cried out in delight. She wanted to shout and to dance. She lifted her left foot and crossed it over her right foot.

When the black bull came back to the dark valley, he was unable to find Flora. She heard him and called out to him again and again. But he could neither see her nor hear her.

In the end Flora stood up. Without knowing where she was going, she walked on up the valley. Now and then she glimpsed a shining peak far ahead, and as she drew closer to it, Flora saw it was made entirely of glass.

"If I can climb this mountain," Flora said to herself, "I'll see how

the land lies. I need food and shelter. Unless I climb this mountain, I'll never find my way home."

But Flora wasn't able to climb the mountain. She couldn't get more than a few feet up its steep side before she slid down to the bottom again.

Flora began to sob. Slowly she picked her way across the rocks and around the foot of the glass mountain. And that evening, on the fringe of a pinewood, she came across a mountain hut. It was little more than a large shed, and at first Flora thought it was deserted. But then an old man got up and hobbled toward her.

The man saw that Flora was so tired she could scarcely speak or eat or drink. He gave her a bowl of soup and asked her no questions. "You can sleep here," he said, pointing to a piece of dirty sacking.

Flora slept, and in the morning she learned that the old man was a blacksmith and asked for his help. "Unless I can climb the glass mountain," she said, "I'll never find my way home."

"I'll help you if you help me," said the old man. "If you work for me for seven years, I'll make you a pair of iron shoes, and with those you'll be able to climb over the mountain."

After seven years, Flora got her iron shoes and climbed over the glass mountain. She could see around her a great spread of peaks and glaciers and high grazing pastures and forests and valleys. The whole country was at her feet. She looked and she looked, and at last she picked out her way home.

Flora walked for eight days. And on the ninth day she reached her own mountain slopes and stopped at the cottage of the wise woman.

"Ah! So you've come back," said the wise woman, "and maybe just in time. A young knight and his two hunting companions are taking shelter here for a few days. The knight has given me these blood-stained shirts to wash. 'And whoever washes these shirts clean,' that's what he said, 'whoever washes these shirts clean will be my wife.'"

"And you cannot wash them?" asked Flora.

"I cannot," said the woman. "And my daughter cannot."

"Then how can I?"

"I can read things that will happen," the wise woman said. "Try to wash them!"

So Flora warmed a bucket of water over the fire and washed the shirts. One by one, the stains disappeared.

"The shirts are spotless," said the wise woman.

"Then this knight and I will be married," said Flora.

But Flora was so tired after her adventures that, while she was waiting for the young knight to return that evening, she fell asleep. The wise woman welcomed the knight and told him that her own daughter had washed the shirts clean, and he agreed to marry her.

When Flora woke, she saw she was lying on the wise woman's bed. First she spied how handsome the knight was, with his bull neck and broad shoulders and black hair. "I know you," Flora whispered to herself. "I know who you are. And now I know why for seven years I have worked and walked and waited."

But then Flora heard him and the wise woman discussing plans for a wedding between the knight and the woman's own daughter — and it was to take place that very evening. She felt alone and very unhappy. She felt in great need.

"My apple," she whispered.

Flora broke open the apple and found it was full of gold and fine jewelry. Then she called out to the wise woman's daughter.

"You're awake, then," said the daughter.

"You see this?" said Flora.

The wise woman's daughter gazed at the jewelry and her mouth dropped open.

"And you're going to marry that knight?" said Flora.

"You can't stop me," said the daughter.

"I'll give you all this," said Flora, "if you put off the wedding until tomorrow and let me go into his room alone tonight."

The daughter agreed, but when the wise woman heard of the arrangement, she mixed a sleeping potion into the knight's ale. Then she and her daughter laid out the knight in their own bedroom and settled down to sleep beside the fire.

Flora crept in and stared at the sleeping knight, his bull neck and broad shoulders and black hair. "I know who you are," she said to herself. "I know who you are." Then she sat down beside him and softly began to sing:

"Seven long years I worked for you,
The glass mountain I climbed for you,
The bloodstained shirt I wrung for you,
And will you not wake and turn to me?"

But the knight did not wake; he did not even stir. Flora began to weep and to sing again, but the knight slept until daylight.

The next morning, Flora broke open the pear. It was full of jewelry even more precious than that in the apple. With these jewels she bargained for a second time with the wise woman's daughter. And that night, after the knight had returned with his two hunting companions, and they had all eaten together, Flora again crept into

the room where the knight was asleep. With the soft voice of a dove, she sang:

> "*Seven long years I worked for you,*
> *The glass mountain I climbed for you,*
> *The bloodstained shirt I wrung for you,*
> *And will you not wake and turn to me?*"

Again and again she sang; she sobbed and she sang. But the knight did not wake; he did not even stir. The wise woman had given him another sleeping potion.

In the morning, the knight and his companions went off hunting again, promising to return in time for the celebration of the wedding that evening.

"What was that noise?" asked one companion. "All last night, that cooing and moaning?"

"I heard nothing," the knight said.

"In your room," said the other companion. "Singing and sobbing."

"That's strange," said the knight. "I'll take no chances tonight. I want to keep awake and hear these sounds for myself."

Flora lived in hope and despair. She broke open the plum; it held by far the most valuable jewelry of all. Once more she bargained with the wise woman's daughter, and for a third time the wise woman mixed a sleeping potion into the knight's ale.

"To tell you the truth," said the knight, "I've a sweet tooth, and this ale's rather sour! Will you get me some honey to sweeten it?"

While the wise woman went out for some honey, the knight quickly poured the ale into the rushes in one corner of the room and refilled his wooden mug with water from the pitcher.

“There!” said the wise woman. “This will sweeten it.”

Then the knight retired to his bedroom, and his two companions and the wise woman and her daughter spread themselves out around the fire. Before long, Flora returned to the knight’s room for the third time. With the clear voice of a nightingale, she began to sing:

“Seven long years I worked for you,
The glass mountain I climbed for you,
The bloodstained shirt I wrung for you,
And will you not wake and turn to me?”

The young knight heard and he turned to Flora. She told him all that had befallen her then, and he told her all that had happened to him.

The knight did not wait until morning. He stood up and ordered his companions to truss the treacherous old woman and her daughter and burn them to death.

Day dawned. Flora led the knight up through the pine forest and over the slopes of the mountain. At the door of the cottage far above, her mother was standing and watching and waiting.

Before long, the knight and Flora were married. How happy they were! And for all I know, how happy they are!

MOSSYCOAT

THERE WAS ONCE A POOR OLD WIDOW WHO LIVED IN A LITTLE cottage. She had one daughter who was nineteen and very beautiful. Day after day, her mother busied herself spinning a coat for her.

A peddler came courting this girl. He called at the cottage regularly and kept bringing her this trinket and that trinket. He was in love with her and badly wanted her to marry him.

But the girl wasn't in love with him; things didn't work out as easily as that. She didn't know quite what to do for the best and asked her mother for advice.

"Let him come," said her mother. "Get what you can out of him while I finish this coat. After that, you won't need him or his pretty little presents. You tell him, girl," the mother said, "that you won't marry him unless he gets you a white satin dress embroidered with sprigs of gold as big as a man's hand, and mind you tell him it must be a perfect fit."

The next time the peddler came 'round and asked the daughter to marry him, she told him just this—the very same words her mother had used.

The peddler looked at the girl and took stock of her size and build. And within a week, he was back with the dress. It was made of white satin and embroidered with sprigs of gold, and when the girl went upstairs with her mother and tried it on, it was a perfect fit.

"What shall I do now, Mother?" asked the girl.

"Tell him," said her mother, "that you won't marry him unless he gets you a dress made of silk the color of all the birds of the air. And it must be a perfect fit."

The girl told the peddler this, and in two or three days he was back at the cottage with the colored silk dress. And since he knew her size from the first dress, of course it was a perfect fit.

"Now what shall I do?" asked the girl.

"Tell him," said her mother, "that you won't marry him unless he gets you a pair of silver slippers that are a perfect fit."

The girl told the peddler just this, and in a few days he called around with them. The girl's feet were only about three inches long but the slippers were a perfect fit. They were not too tight; neither were they too loose.

Once more the girl asked her mother what she should do.

"I can finish the coat tonight," said her mother, "and then you won't need the peddler. Tell him," she said, "that you'll marry him tomorrow. Tell him to be here at ten o'clock."

The girl told the peddler just this. "Ten o'clock in the morning," she said.

"I'll be there, my love," said the peddler. "By heaven, I will!"

That night the girl's mother worked on the coat until very late, but she finished it, all right. Green moss and gold thread, that's what it was made of: just those two things. "Mossycoat," the woman called it, and that's what she called the daughter she had made it for.

"It's a magic coat," she said. "A wishing coat! When you've got it on, you have only to wish to be somewhere, and you'll be there that very instant. And you've only to wish if you want to change yourself into something else, like a swan or a bee."

Next morning the widow was up at dawn. She called her daughter and told her that it was time for her to go out into the world and seek her fortune. "And a handsome fortune it must be," she said.

"What about the peddler?" asked the girl.

"I'll send him packing when he comes 'round," said the mother. "Don't give him another thought."

The old widow was a seer and knew what was going to happen. She gave her daughter the mossycoat and a gold crown. "Take the two dresses and silver slippers as well," she said. "But travel in your working clothes."

So Mossycoat was ready to set off, and she put on her coat of green moss and gold thread.

"Wish yourself a hundred miles away," her mother said. "Then keep walking until you come to a big hall, and ask for a job there. You won't have far to walk, my blessed. They're bound to find you work at the big hall."

Mossycoat did as her mother told her, and soon she found herself in front of a big house belonging to a gentleman. She knocked at the front door and said she was looking for work. Well, the long and the short of it was that the mistress of the house herself came down to see her, and her ladyship liked the look of her.

"What work can you do?" she asked.

"I can cook, your ladyship," said Mossycoat. "In fact, people say I'm a very good cook."

"I can't employ you as cook," the lady said. "I've got one already. But I'll engage you to help the cook, if that will satisfy you."

"Thank you, your ladyship," said Mossycoat. "I'll be really happy in this house."

So it was settled that Mossycoat was to be the undercook.

And after her ladyship had showed her up to her bedroom, she took her down to the kitchen and introduced her to the other servants.

"This is Mossycoat," she told them, "and I've engaged her," she said, "to be the undercook."

Then the mistress of the house left them, and Mossycoat went up to her bedroom again to unpack her belongings and hide away her gold crown and silver slippers, and her silk and satin dresses.

The other kitchen girls were beside themselves with jealousy, and it didn't help matters that the new girl was far more beautiful than any of them.

"Here's this vagrant in rags," one girl said, "and she's put above us."

"All she's fit for," said another, "is work in the scullery."

"Undercook!" cried a third girl. "If anyone's going to be undercook, it should be one of us."

"One of us," said the fourth girl. "Not a girl in rags and tatters picked up off the street."

"We'll put her in her place!" the girls said. "That we will!"

So they went on and on until Mossycoat came down again, ready to start work. Then they really set about her.

"Who on Earth do you think you are, setting yourself above us?"

"You're going to be the undercook, are you?"

"No fear!"

"What you're going to do is scour the pans."

"And polish the knives."

"And clean the grates."

"And that's all you're good for."

Then down came the milk skimmer on top of her head: *pop, pop, pop.*

"That's what you deserve," they told her. "And, my lady, that's what you'll get."

So that is how things were for Mossycoat. She was given all the dirtiest work, and soon she was up to her ears in grease, and her face was as black as soot. And every now and again one or another of the servants would pop, pop, pop her on top of her head with the skimmer, until Mossycoat's head was so sore she could scarcely stand it.

Days turned into weeks, weeks into months, and Mossycoat was still scouring the pans and polishing the knives and cleaning the grate. And the servants were still pop, pop, popping her on the head with the skimmer.

Now there was going to be a big dance in a grand house nearby. It was to last three nights, with hunting and other sports during the daytime. All the gentry from miles around were going to be there, and of course the master and mistress and their son — they only had one child — planned to be there.

This dance was all the talk among the servants.

"I wish I could go," said one girl.

"I'd like to dance with some of those young gentlemen," said a second.

"I'd like to see what dresses the ladies wear," said a third.

And so they all went on — all except Mossycoat.

"If only we'd the clothes," said one, "we'd be all right. We're just as good as their ladyships any day."

"And you, Mossycoat," said another. "Wouldn't you like to go?"

"You'd look just right in all your rags and dirt," they said.

And down came the skimmer on Mossycoat's head: *pop, pop, pop.* Then they all laughed at her. What crude people they were!

Now Mossycoat was very handsome, and no amount of rags and dirt could hide the fact. The other servants might think as they liked, but the young master had his eye on Mossycoat, and the master and mistress had always taken particular notice of her because of her fine looks.

On the first day of the big dance, they sent for her and asked her if she would like to come with them.

"Thank you," said Mossycoat, "but I'd never dream of such a thing. I know my place better than that. Besides," she said, "I'd cover one side of the coach with grease. And I'd sully the clothes of anyone I danced with."

The master and mistress made light of that, but no matter what they said, they were unable to change Mossycoat's mind.

When Mossycoat got back to the kitchen, she told the other servants why she had been sent for.

"What! You?" exclaimed one servant. "I don't believe it!"

"If it had been one of us, that would have been different."

"You'd grease all the gentlemen's clothes — if there are any who would dance with a scullery girl."

"And the ladies, they'd be forced to hold their noses when they walked past you."

"No," they said, "we don't believe the master and mistress ever asked you to go to the ball with them. You must be lying."

And down came the skimmer on top of her head: *pop, pop, pop.*

On the next evening, the master and the mistress and their son, too, asked Mossycoat to go to the dance.

"It was a grand affair last night," said the master.

"And it'll be even grander this evening," added the mistress.

"Do come with us," said their son. "Mossycoat, I beg you."

But Mossycoat said no. She said she couldn't go on account of her rags and her grease and her dirt. Even the young master was unable to persuade her, and it wasn't for want of trying.

The other servants refused to believe Mossycoat when she told them that she had been invited again to the dance and added that the young master had been very pressing.

"Listen to her!" they cried. "What next? What an upstart! And all lies!"

Then one of the servants snorted and grabbed the skimmer and down it came once again: *pop, pop, pop* on Mossycoat's head.

That night, Mossycoat decided to go to the dance, all dressed up, and all on her own, without anybody knowing about it.

The first thing she did was to put all the other servants under a spell. As she moved around, she just touched each of them, without being noticed, and each fell asleep as soon as she did so.

Next, Mossycoat had a really good wash, her first since she had come to the big house. She had never been allowed to before. The other servants had made her dirty and kept her dirty.

Then Mossycoat went up to her bedroom. She threw off her working clothes and shoes and put on her white satin dress embroidered with gold sprigs, her silver slippers, and her gold crown. And, of course, underneath the dress, she was wearing the mossycoat.

When she was ready, Mossycoat just wished herself at the dance, and as soon as she had spoken, there she was! She felt herself soaring

up and flying through the air, but only for a moment. Then she was standing in the ballroom.

The young master noticed Mossycoat standing on her own, and once he had seen her, he was unable to take his eyes off her. He had never seen anyone so handsome, nor so beautifully dressed, in his life.

"Who is she?" the young man asked his mother.

"I don't know," said the mistress. "I've never seen her before."

"Can't you find out, Mother?" he said. "Can't you go and talk to her?"

The young man's mother saw he would never rest until she did, so she walked up and introduced herself to the young lady, and asked her who she was and where she came from, and so on. But all she could get out of her was that she came from a place where they hit her on the head with a skimmer.

After a while, the young master went over and introduced himself, but Mossycoat didn't tell him her name; she gave nothing away.

"Well, will you dance with me?" asked the young master.

"Thank you," said Mossycoat, "but I'd rather not." But the young man stayed at Mossycoat's side. He kept asking her to dance, over and over again.

"All right!" said Mossycoat. "Just once."

The young man and Mossycoat danced once, up the length of the ballroom and back down again; then Mossycoat said she had to leave. The young man pressed her to stay, but it was a waste of breath; she was determined to go, there and then.

"All right," said the young man. "I'll come and see you off."

But Mossycoat just wished she were back in the big house, and there she was! So the young master wasn't able to see her off! She vanished from his side in the twinkling of an eye, leaving him gaping in astonishment.

Thinking she might be out in the entrance hall, or on the porch, waiting for her carriage, the young man went out to look for her; but there was no sign of her anywhere, inside or out, and no one he asked had seen her leave. The young man went back to the ballroom, but he was unable to think of anything or anyone but the mysterious girl, and took no further interest in the ball.

When Mossycoat got back to the big house, she made sure that all the other servants were still under her spell. Then she went up to her bedroom and changed into her working clothes; and when she had done that, she came down to the kitchen again and touched each of the servants.

That broke the spell and woke them. One by one they started up, wondering what time of day it was and how long they had been asleep.

"A long time!" said Mossycoat. "The whole evening, in fact! The mistress wouldn't like to know about this, would she?"

The servants begged Mossycoat not to let on and offered her bribes to keep quiet about it. They gave her a skirt, a pair of shoes, a pair of stockings, a corset; they were all old but they still had a bit of wear in them. So Mossycoat promised to say nothing about it.

And that night, they didn't hit her over the head with the skimmer.

All the next day, the young master was restless. He could think of nothing but the young lady he had seen the night before and fallen in love with at first sight. He kept wondering whether she would be at the dance again that evening, and how he could stop her from disappearing.

I must find out where she lives, he thought. *Otherwise, how will I be able to bear it when the dance is over?*

"I'll die," the young man told his mother, "if I'm not able to marry her." He was madly in love with her!

"Well," said his mother, "she seemed a nice, modest girl. But she wouldn't say who she was or who her family are. She wouldn't say where she came from, except that it was a place where they hit her on the head with a skimmer!"

"She's a mystery, I know," said the young man, "but that doesn't mean I want her any the less. I must marry her, Mother, whoever she is and whatever she is. That's God's truth, Mother, and strike me dead if it isn't!"

It wasn't long before the young master and this wonderful, handsome lady he had fallen in love with were all the talk in the kitchen.

"And fancy you, Mossycoat, thinking he especially wanted you to go to the dance," they said. And then they really set about her, making all kinds of sarcastic remarks and hitting her on the head with the skimmer — *pop, pop, pop* — for lying to them.

It was just the same later on, too, when Mossycoat returned to the kitchen after declining to go to the dance for the third time. "This is your last chance," said the servants. "You're such a liar, Mossycoat! We'll give you one more chance." And down came the skimmer on top of her head: *pop, pop, pop*.

Then Mossycoat put the whole devil's breed of them under a spell as she had done the night before, and got herself ready to go to the dance. The only difference was that this time she put on her other dress — the dress made of silk the color of all the birds of the air. And underneath the dress, she was wearing the mossycoat, of course.

When Mossycoat entered the ballroom, the young master was watching and waiting for her. His horse was ready, saddled and standing at the door. He went over to the young lady and asked her for a dance.

She said just the same as on the night before: no at first, and in

the end, yes. And as soon as they had danced up the length of the ballroom and back down again, she said she had to leave. This time, however, the young man kept his arm around the girl's waist until they got outside.

But Mossycoat wished she were back in the big house, and almost as soon as she had spoken, she was there! The young man felt her rise into the air, but he was unable to do anything about it. Maybe he did just touch her foot, though, because she dropped one slipper.

The young man picked up the slipper. But as for catching up with the girl, it would have been easier to catch up with the wind on a stormy night.

As soon as she got home, Mossycoat changed back into her old clothes. Then she released the servants from the spell. When they realized that they had fallen asleep again, one offered her a shilling and another half a crown — a third of a week's wages — not to let on; and once again Mossycoat promised to keep quiet about it.

The young master spent the next day in bed, dying for the love of the young lady who had dropped one of her silver slippers on the previous night. The doctors were unable to do anything for him at all, so the young man's parents decided to make his condition known. They said the only person able to save his life was the young lady whose foot fit the silver slipper — and that the slipper was only about three inches long. They promised that if she would come forward, the young master would marry her.

Ladies came from near and far, some with big feet and some with small, but none small enough for the silver slipper, however much they pinched and squeezed. Poor women came, too, but it was just the same for them. And of course, all the servants tried on the slipper, but that was out of the question altogether.

All this time, the young master lay dying.

"Is there no one else?" asked his mother. "No one else at all? No rich lady? No poor woman?"

"No one," they said. "No one at all. Everyone has tried it on except for Mossycoat."

"Tell her to come here at once," said the mistress.

So the other servants fetched Mossycoat.

"Mossycoat!" said the mistress. "Try this slipper on."

Mossycoat slipped her foot into it easily enough; it was a perfect fit. Then the young master jumped out of bed and opened his arms.

"Wait!" said Mossycoat, and she ran out of the room. Before long, though, she was back again, wearing her satin dress with gold sprigs, her gold crown, and both her silver slippers. Again the young master opened his arms.

"Wait!" said Mossycoat, and again she ran out of the room. This time she came back wearing her silk dress the color of all the birds of the air. Mossycoat didn't stop the young master this time, and he took her into his arms and kissed her.

After all this, when at last the master and the mistress and the young master and Mossycoat had time to talk to one another quietly, there were one or two questions they wanted to ask her.

"How did you get to the dance and back again in no time?" they said.

"Just wishing," said Mossycoat. And she told them about the magic coat her mother had made for her, and the powers it gave her when she cared to use them.

"That explains everything!" said the mistress.

"But what did you mean," asked the master, "when you said you came from a place where they hit you on the head with a skimmer?"

"I mean just what I said," replied Mossycoat. "The skimmer's always coming down on my head: *pop, pop, pop!*"

The master and mistress were furious when they heard that. All

the kitchen servants were told to leave, and the dogs were sent after them to drive them away from the place.

Then Mossycoat sent for her old mother, and the master and mistress made her welcome at the big house. Mossycoat and the young master got married on the first day possible, and Mossycoat had a coach-and-six to ride in; she could have had a coach-and-ten if she had wanted, for as you can imagine, her every wish was granted. The young man and Mossycoat were always happy together. Mossycoat's mother lived with them, and they had a basketful of children.

TAM LIN

OH! I FORBID YOU, MAIDENS ALL,
Who wear gold in your hair
To cross the plain of Carterhaugh,
For young Tam Lin lives there.

No girl passes Carterhaugh
But leaves him to the good:
They leave their rings or green gowns
Or else their maidenhood.

But then fair Janet, she spoke up,
The fairest girl that breathed:
"I'll cross the plain of Carterhaugh
Without asking his leave."

Then Janet tucked her green skirt
A little above her knee,
And she braided her yellow hair
A little above her eye.

She set off for Carterhaugh
And walked by the hem of the wood,
And there she saw Tam Lin asleep
In the shadow of his steed.

She picked broom flowers from the bush
And strewed them on his mane
As a sign that maiden she had come
And maiden she had gone.

"O, where were you, my milk-white horse
I used to love so dear,
That you did not watch or wake me
When a maid came walking here?"

"I stamped my hoof, dear master,
I made my bridle ring;
But nothing at all would wake you
Until she'd come and gone."

"Woe betide you, my great goshawk
I used to love so dear,
That you did not watch or wake me
When my love herself was here!"

"I clapped my wings, dear master,
And often rang my bell;
I often cried 'Wake up, master!'
But you slept all too well."

"Make haste and haste, my good white horse,
To catch her in our mesh,
Or all the birds in the good green wood
Will eat their fill of your flesh."

"You needn't burst your good white horse
By racing over the coombe;
No hare runs quicker through the grass
Than your love through the broom."

Fair Janet, in her green clothing still,
Came home next day at dawn
And greeted her father's brother there,
The Lord of Abercom.

"I'll wager, I'll wager gold with you —
Five hundred ounces to ten —
I'll maiden go to Carterhaugh
And maiden come home again."

She prinked herself and preened herself
By the light of the silver Moon,
And she set off for Carterhaugh;
She walked and then she ran.

When she came to Carterhaugh
She hurried to the well;
She found his horse was tethered there —
Tam Lin not there at all.

She had scarcely picked a red, red rose,
A rose or two or three,
When up sprang the little wee man
At Lady Janet's knee.

"Why are you picking roses, Janet?
Why are you hurting the tree?
And why have you come to Carterhaugh
Without permission from me?"

"Carterhaugh, it is my own,
My father gave it me.
I'll cross the plaint Carterhaugh
Without asking your leave."

He led her by the milk-white hand
And by the grass-green sleeve,
He brought her to the fairy ground
And took her without her leave.

When she came to her father's hall
She looked all pale and wan;
They thought she'd caught some illness
Or made love to some young man.

She didn't comb her yellow hair
Or bother with lip and eye;
Whatever cure that lady took,
She seemed likely to die.

Four and twenty ladies fair
Were in her father's hall
When in walked lovely Janet,
Once the flower of them all.

Four and twenty ladies fair
Were playing games of chess,
And out walked lovely Janet
Once as green as any grass.

An old gray knight then spoke up
And leaned on the castle wall:
"Alas for you, fair Janet!" he said.
"But the blame will stain us all."

"Now hold your tongue, you withered knight!
A vile death is your due!
I'll make my child with whom I will,
I'll make no child with you."

But then her father he spoke up,
And his tone was meek and mild:
"My sweet Janet, alas!" he said.
"Are you carrying a child?"

"If I'm carrying a child, father,
I must take the blame.
There's no man in your hall here
Can share the baby's name.

"If my love were for a man
And not an elfin gray,
I'd never give my own true love
To any lord in your pay."

"Have you given it to a fine man
Or to a man who is mean?
Or given it to young Tam Lin
Who's lost to the Fairy Queen?"

"Father, I went to Carterhaugh,
And walked close to the well;
I saw there a little wee man,
The littlest man of all.

"His legs were scarcely a hand's length,
Yet manly was his thigh;
Between his brows was one finger span,
And between his shoulders, three.

"He seized and flung a huge rock
As far as the eye could see;
Old Wallace himself, he would never
Have raised it up to his knee.

"'O little wee man, you are so strong!
Where do you eat and sleep?'
'It's near that pretty glade down there;
Fair lady, come and see.'

"We leaped up and away we rode
Through the gray and the green;
Then we dismounted to feed our horse
And saw the Fairy Queen.

"Twenty-four ladies stood with her,
All of them dressed in green;
Had the king of Scotland been there,
The worst would have made his queen.

"We leaped up and away we rode,
Down to a marvelous hall;
The roof was made of beaten gold
And the whole floor of crystal.

"And dancing on the crystal floor,
Were ladies slender and small,
But in the twinkling of an eye
They vanished one and all.

"And in the twinkling of an eye
The little wee man had gone;
He said that if I made love to him,
He'd love no other woman."

Janet put on her green, green dress,
Nine months were nearly gone,
And she set off for Carterhaugh
To talk with young Tam Lin.

When she came to Carterhaugh
She hurried to the well.
She found his horse was tethered there—
Tam Lin not there at all.

She had scarcely picked two roses,
Two roses and their thorns,
When up sprang the little wee man:
"Lady, you'll pick no more.

"Why are you picking roses, Janet,
In this bright-green glade?
Do you mean to kill the pretty child
We two together made?"

"O, you must tell me how, Tam Lin,
And not one word a lie:
Have you ever set foot in chapel?
And have you been baptized?"

"I'll tell you the truth, Janet,
And not one word a lie.
You're the child of a lady and knight,
And the same is true of me.

"My grandfather was Roxburgh;
I lived with him as a child.
This accident befell me then
As we rode home from the field:

"Roxburgh was a hunting man
And loved riding to his hounds,
And on a cold and frosty day,
I was thrown to the ground.

"The Queen of Fairies caught me up
And took me into that hill,
I'm a fairy head and toe,
Fair lady, look at me well.

"The fairy land is beautiful
But, terrible to tell,
At the end of each seventh year
We pay a tithe to hell;
And I'm so strong-bodied and fair
I fear it'll be myself.

"Tonight is Hallowe'en, lady,
Tomorrow is All Hallows.
Win me, win me, if you will.
You have no time to lose.

"In the dark, at the hour of midnight,
The fairy folk take horse,

And she who would win her true love
Must wait at Miles Cross."

"But how will I know you, Tam Lin?
How can I be quite sure
Among so many strange knights
I've never seen before?"

"When the first troop comes riding by,
Say nothing, let them pass.
When the next troop comes riding by,
Say nothing, let them pass.
Then a third troop will come riding by—
I'll be one of those.

"Oh! Let the black horse pass, lady,
And then ignore the brown,
But quickly grasp the milk-white horse
And pull his rider down.

"For I'll be riding the milk-white horse,
The rider nearest the town.
Because I was christened as a knight,
They granted me that boon.

"My right hand will be gloved, lady,
My left hand will be bare;
The peak of my cap will be turned up,
And I'll comb down my hair.

These are the signs I'll give to you;
Without fail I'll be there.

"Lady, they'll turn me in your arms,
Into a newt and adder;
But hold me fast, don't let me pass,
I am your baby's father.

"They'll turn me into a cruel bear
And then a mighty lion;
But hold me fast, don't let me pass,
As you love your own scion.

"And then they'll turn me in your arms
Into red-hot iron;
But hold me fast, don't let me pass,
I'll cause no hurt or harm.

"First dip me in a bowl of milk
And then a bowl of water;
But hold me fast, don't let me pass,
I'll be your baby's father.

"And next, they'll turn me in your arms
Into a toad and then an eel;
But hold me fast, don't let me pass,
If you but love me well.

"They'll turn me in your arms, Janet,
Into a dove and then a swan;

And last they'll turn me in your arms
Into a naked man.
Cover me then with your green cloak —
I'll be myself again."

Gloomy, gloomy was the night
And eerie the sheen on the grass,
As Janet donned her green cloak
And walked to Miles Cross.

About the dead hour of the night
She heard the bridles ring;
She was as glad to hear them
As any earthly thing.

First she let the black horse pass,
Then ignored the brown,
But quickly she grasped the milk-white horse
And pulled his rider down.

She pulled him from the milk-white horse
And let the bridle fall;
And there rose up a ghastly cry:
"He's stolen from us all!"

They turned him in fair Janet's arms
Into a newt and adder;
She held him fast in every shape
To be her baby's father.

They turned him in her arms at last
Into a naked man;
She wrapped him in her green cloak,
As blithe as a bird in spring.

Then the Queen of Fairies she spoke out
From within a bush of broom:
"Whoever wins young Tam Lin
Has won a noble groom."

Then the Queen of Fairies she spoke out,
From within a bush of rye:
"She's taken away the fairest knight
In my whole company.

"Had I but known, Tam Lin," she said,
"How the matter stood,
I'd have struck out your two gray eyes
And put in two of wood.

"Had I but known, Tam Lin," she said,
"Before you came from home
I'd have ripped out your heart of flesh
And put in one of stone.

"If yesterday I had but known
What I have learned today
I'd have paid my dues to hell seven times
Before you were taken away."

YELLOW LILY

THE SON OF THE KING OF IRELAND RELISHED TESTS OF STRENGTH and trials of wit. A love of chance beat in his bloodstream.

"Tomorrow," said the prince, "I'm going hunting. I'll bring you back a deer or a wild boar."

"Bring yourself back," said the king, "safe and sound."

"We worry about you," the queen said.

"You fuss over me," said the prince. "Let me be my own man."

At five the prince rose and breakfasted alone. At six he was gone, up through the beechwoods, over the stile where the cuckoo sat and sang, and away onto the desolate hills roamed by wild beasts and birds of prey.

All day the king's son hunted, morning and afternoon, and he caught nothing. As the April Sun set, pale as a primrose, the young man threw himself full length onto the wiry turf, tired with tramping and the place's emptiness.

After five minutes, the prince felt somewhat rested. He stood up and shouldered his bow; he strapped on his belt with its quiver of arrows. "Tomorrow, then," he said, and turned his back on the brooding hillside.

Just before the young man went down into the beechwoods, he heard a sharp whistle behind him. At once he looked around, and there was the giant of Loch Lein hurrying down the hillside after him. The prince stood his ground and waited for the giant to come down to him. That didn't take long. The giant was three times as tall as a normal man and covered the ground as fast as the young prince could have run it.

"Well!" said the giant. "Can you play cards?"

"Cards?" said the prince. "I certainly can."

"All right," said the giant. "Let's play a hand here and now."

"Whatever you say," replied the prince.

So the prince and the giant sat down, and the giant pulled out a large pack of cards. "What shall we play for?" said the giant.

"I'm the king's son," said the young man, "and I'll play you for two farms — the buildings and all the land surrounding them."

"That suits me," said the giant. "I own rather a lot of land up here."

The prince won the game and went home with a spring in his step.

"What did you catch?" asked the king.

"I caught two farms," said his son, "the buildings and all the land surrounding them." And he told his father how he had played cards with the giant of Loch Lein.

"Ah!" said the king, looking very thoughtful.

"We worry about you," said the queen.

Next morning the prince was up early. All day he hunted without

catching so much as a rabbit. In the evening the giant came up behind him for a second time.

"Well!" said the giant. "What shall we play for today?"

"I'll leave that to you," the prince replied. "I chose the wager yesterday."

"All right," said the giant. "I'm going to raise the stakes. I've got a herd of five hundred steers, and they all have golden horns and silver hooves. I'll wager them against the same number of your cattle — five hundred heads."

"Agreed," said the prince.

So they played for the second time, and again the giant lost the game. He gave a great bellow, and before long his precious herd of steers came charging over the hilltop and down to the fringe of the beechwoods.

"I'll get even with you," said the giant.

"You'll try to," said the prince.

Then the king's son went home, driving the beautiful herd of cattle before him. As they moved in the half darkness, their horns looked like soft sickle moons, and their hooves like a far field of broken ice.

When the king found out how his son had come by the steers, he called for his wise man, old and blind.

"Yesterday, two farms," said the king. "Today, five hundred steers."

"Better no tomorrow," the wise man said. "Stop your son from playing cards with the giant again."

But nothing the king or the queen said could dissuade their son. He was up and away even earlier than before. Once again, he hunted all day without success, and as the Sun set, he made his way off the hills. By the time the prince had reached the beechwoods, there was no sign of the giant, and so he sat down to wait for him.

The king's son sat there for a long while, and the giant did not come. So at last he stood up, stretched, and turned toward the beechwoods. At that moment, the prince heard a piercing whistle behind him, and down the hillside strode the giant of Loch Lein in rather a hurry.

"Well!" boomed the giant. "Are we going to play cards today?"

"That's what I've been asking myself," said the prince. "I thought you weren't coming."

The giant said nothing. His mouth tightened in a kind of smile.

"I'd like to play," said the prince, "but I've nothing I can wager."

"You have," said the giant.

"I haven't," said the prince.

"Haven't you got a head?" asked the giant.

"I have," said the prince.

"Well then," said the giant. "We'll play for each other's heads."

So the prince and the giant played cards for the third time. They played for their lives, and this time the giant won the game.

The prince sat and stared at the giant.

"I'll give you a little grace," said the giant. "A few days, a few months, more life. You must come to my castle in a year and a day and give yourself up to me."

The king and the queen saw their son walking slowly home. They ached, they felt old, and the wise man's warning rang in their ears.

As he entered the castle, the prince did not look up or say a single word. He walked straight past the king and queen, on and up to his own rooms. He ate no supper and summoned no servant. Nobody saw him again that evening.

The next day, the prince told the king and queen how he had played cards for the third time and forfeited his life to the giant of Loch Lein.

"We saw it in your step," said the king.

The prince lowered his eyes.

"There's nothing for it," the king said. "You'll have to go to his castle and take all your daring and your sharp wits with you. No game is finished until the last hand has been played."

The prospect of his journey preyed on the young man's mind. His old liking for tests of strength and his love of chance seemed foolish now. And then one morning, as the year was coming to an end, and without even telling the king and queen of his intentions, the prince simply disappeared.

He walked up through the green and easy beechwoods, and over the stile where the mournful cuckoo sang. All day he walked over the empty hills without seeing a man or a woman or a child, or even a shrew or a rabbit.

After dark, the prince dropped down into a lonely valley, and there he saw one light glowing. It came from a little cottage, and inside it he found a leathery old woman baking herself in front of the fire. Every tooth in her head was pointed and as long as a walking stick.

As the prince entered the cottage, the old woman stood up, stepped toward him, and took his right hand. "Son of the king of Ireland," she said, "you are welcome in this house."

Then the old woman brought the prince a bowl of warm water and washed his feet for him beside the winking fire.

When the prince woke the next morning, his breakfast was ready for him: steaming porridge and crusty bread and warm milk. The old woman watched while he ate and drank, and then she said, "You stayed with me last night, and tonight you'll be staying with my sister. Be sure to do whatever she tells you. Otherwise your head will be in danger."

"All right," said the young prince. "I will."

"Here's a gift for you — this ball of thread. Before you set off,

throw it on the ground in front of you. All day the ball will roll on ahead of you, and you must follow it and rewind it into another ball."

All day the prince walked uphill and downhill, rewinding the thread. In the evening, he came up to a high hill, and at the foot of it he found a little cottage with a light shining in it.

There was only one person within the four walls: an old woman with pointed teeth, each as long as a crutch.

"Ah!" said the old woman when the young man crossed her threshold. "Son of the king of Ireland, you're welcome in this house. Last night you stayed with my sister and tonight you'll stay with me, and I'm very glad to see you."

Then the old woman gave the prince meat and drink and a good bed to lie on. When he woke the next morning, his breakfast was ready for him. He ate and made ready to set off, and the old woman said, "You stayed with my younger sister the night before last, and you stayed with me last night, and tonight you'll be staying with my elder sister. You must do whatever she tells you, or you'll lose your head."

The old woman gave him a ball of thread. "Throw this ball in front of you," she said. "Follow this thread all day long."

For hour after hour the prince rewound the thread, and at nightfall he came to a third little cottage, a third light burning, and a third old woman.

"You're welcome," said the oldest sister, "and I'm glad to see you, son of the king." She washed him and fed him and made him a bed, just as her two younger sisters had done.

After the prince had eaten his breakfast, the old woman said, "I know where you're going; I know your sorrowful journey. You've lost your head to the giant of Loch Lein, and you're on your way to give yourself up."

"I'm taking my daring and my sharp wits with me," said the prince.

"The giant of Loch Lein has a huge castle, and it's surrounded by seven hundred iron spikes. Every spike — every spike but one — is topped with the head of a king, or a queen, or a king's son. The last spike is waiting, and nothing in the world can save you from it unless you take my advice."

"I'll take it," said the prince.

"Here's a ball of thread," said the old woman. "Follow this thread until at midday you come to a lake quite near the giant's castle. By then the whole ball will have unwound itself.

"Every day at noon, the giant's three daughters come down to the lake to bathe. You'll see that each has a lily fastened to her breast — the eldest a blue lily, the second a white, and the youngest a yellow lily. It's the daughter with the yellow lily you must watch.

"Don't take your eyes off her for one moment. When she undresses before entering the water, watch exactly where she puts her clothes. And then," said the old woman, "while the three daughters are swimming well out in the lake, pick up Yellow Lily's clothes and hide yourself nearby."

"I'm listening," said the prince.

"The three sisters will swim to the shore and step out of the lake. And when Yellow Lily discovers she has lost her clothes, her two elder sisters will laugh and tease her. Yellow Lily will crouch beside the water. She'll start to sob and say, 'How can I go home? Everyone will laugh at me.' She'll say, 'Let the man who took my clothes give them back to me. I swear I'll save him from whatever danger he is in; I'll save his head if I can.'"

The prince took leave of the eldest sister and followed the ball of thread. And at midday, while he was walking alongside a lake quite

near the giant's castle, the thread ran out; the whole ball had unraveled. The prince hid behind a rock at the water's edge and waited.

Before long, the giant's three daughters came down to the lake and threw off their clothes and dived into the water. Laughing and shouting, they swam out into the middle of the lake. Then the prince slipped out from his hiding place, quickly picked up Yellow Lily's clothes, and hid himself behind the rock again.

When Yellow Lily found her clothes had been taken, her sisters did nothing but laugh and poke fun at her. Her eyes filled with tears. "How can I go home now?" she said. "Even my own sisters are laughing at me. If I go home like this, everyone will see me and poke fun at me."

Yellow Lily's two elder sisters showed her no pity. They dressed and set off home, leaving their sister lying in the shallows and sobbing. The prince watched and listened, and after a while Yellow Lily drew up her knees under her chin and called out, "Let the man who took my clothes give them back to me. I swear I'll save him from whatever danger he is in."

When the prince heard this, he tossed the clothes into the air and over the rock so that they fell on the bank above Yellow Lily. She reached for them and dressed, and then she called out, "Whoever you are, come out from behind that rock."

Yellow Lily looked long at the young prince. "I know where you're going," she said. "The giant of Loch Lein is my father, and he's got a soft bed waiting for you — a deep tank of water for you to die in."

"We played cards," said the prince, "and when we played for the third time, we played for our heads."

"Go up to the castle before my father gets back this evening," said Yellow Lily, "and be sure to refuse whatever food he offers you. Go down into the tank, just as he tells you, and swim in it until I come to save you."

The way was short and the hours were long. The young man sat for a while beside the lake, and then he ambled along a rising track that led through a wood and straight up to the castle gates. Seven hundred spikes surrounded the castle, and they all had human heads impaled on them — all except one.

When the giant of Loch Lein got back to his castle that night, his very first words were "Is the son of the king of Ireland here?"

"I am," said the prince.

"Ah!" said the giant. "Card player! Come and take some meat."

"I won't eat tonight," said the prince. "I'm not hungry."

"All right!" said the giant. "Come with me then!"

The giant led the prince to a chilly room in which stood a huge metal tank. "This is your bed," he boomed. And he picked up the young man and dropped him into the tank.

The giant was tired. All day he had been out hunting on the hills and in the forests. He went to his bedroom, and five minutes later he was asleep.

At once, the giant's youngest daughter walked up to the tank, peered over the top, and helped pull the prince out. She gave him dry clothing and a fine meal and then showed him to a good bed.

Throughout the night, Yellow Lily kept watch, and as soon as she heard her father stop snoring and begin to stir, she roused the prince and put him back into the tank.

"You down there!" boomed the giant. "Son of the king of Ireland! Are you still alive?"

"I am," said the king's son.

"All right!" said the giant. "It's time you came out."

The giant of Loch Lein stooped and scooped the young man out of the pool. "I've a big task for you today. Next to this castle are my stables. They hold five hundred horses, and they haven't been cleaned for seven hundred years. When my great-grandmother was a young girl," said the giant, "she lost a hairpin somewhere in that stable. And often as she looked for it, she was never able to find it. You," said the giant, "will have that pin for me when I get home tonight. If you don't, I'll impale your head tomorrow on the seven-hundredth spike."

"Who can I have to help me?" asked the prince.

"No one," said the giant.

"What can I have to help me?" asked the prince.

"A shovel," said the giant, and he laughed a dark laugh.

One of the giant's servants brought in two shovels — an old one and a new one — and showed them to the prince.

"Choose one," said the giant.

"I'll take the new one," said the prince.

Then the young man was shown out to the stables, and at once he set to work. But for every shovelful of dung that the prince threw out the door, two flew in. Before long, the entrance was stopped from floor to ceiling with a huge bank of dung.

Yellow Lily walked up to the stable and called out, "How are you getting on, son of the king?"

"I'm not getting on at all," said a muffled voice. "However much I throw out, twice as much flies in. I can't even get out this door."

"Clear a way for me, and I'll help you," called Yellow Lily.

"How can I do that?" shouted the prince.

Yellow Lily smiled. With her bare hands she tore at the dung. She sent it flying like a leaf storm and stepped into the stable.

There she began again, and before long the stable was cleared and Yellow Lily spotted the pin that had once belonged to her great-great-grandmother.

"Can you see it?" she asked.

"Where?" said the prince.

"Over there," said Yellow Lily. "Winking in that corner."

The prince picked up the pin and fastened it to his shirt so that it would be safe until he gave it to the giant.

"Well?" boomed the giant when he got back that evening.

"There was nothing to it," said the prince.

The giant snorted. "Have you found the hairpin?"

"I have," said the prince. He unfastened the pin and dropped it into the giant's enormous palm.

"Ah!" said the giant. "Then you had the devil on your side — either the devil or my daughter. You didn't clear out all that dung alone."

"Neither the devil nor your daughter," said the prince. "I shoveled it out myself. I relied on my own strength."

"All right!" said the giant. "You've done the work, and you must have your meat."

"I won't eat today," said the prince. "I'm happy enough as I am."

The giant narrowed his eyes. "If you won't eat my meat," he said, "you'll have to sleep in the tank again."

And with that, the giant dropped the prince into the tank and retired to his own room. Before long, he was snoring, worn out with walking over Ireland and hunting all day.

At once the giant's youngest daughter hurried up to the tank, peered over the top, and helped pull the prince out. She gave him dry clothing and a fine meal and then showed him to a good bed.

Throughout the night, Yellow Lily kept watch, and as soon as

she heard her father stop snoring and begin to stir, she roused the prince and put him back into the tank.

"You down there!" boomed the giant. "Are you still alive?"

"I am," said the king's son.

"Well!" said the giant, scooping the prince out of the tank. "You've got a great task in front of you today. Those stables you cleaned out yesterday haven't been thatched for seven hundred years. Thatch them with birds' feathers — and no two feathers can be the same color or the same kind. If you haven't finished by the time I get home, I'll have your head tomorrow for that seven-hundredth spike."

"You won't let anyone help me?" said the young man.

"You can have a whistle," said the giant.

One of the giant's servants brought in two whistles — an old one and a new one — and showed them to the prince.

"Choose one," said the giant, "to summon the birds."

"I'll take the new one," said the prince, and at once he set off, hurrying over the hilltops, whistling as he went. But no matter how sweetly the king's son played, not a single bird came near him. The prince was hot; he was dusty and tired. He sat down on the hillside.

At this moment, Yellow Lily appeared at the prince's side. She knelt and smiled and spread out a cloth, and the cloth was covered with food and drink.

"You stay here," said Yellow Lily, "and I'll thatch the stables."

Before the prince had finished his meal, the stables were thatched with birds' feathers, and no two feathers were the same color or kind.

"Are the stables thatched?" shouted the giant of Loch Lein as he stumped into his castle that evening. "Have you finished the stables?"

"I have," said the prince.

"You have?" said the giant.

"There was nothing to it," the young man said.

"Ah!" said the giant. "Then you had the devil on your side — either the devil or my daughter."

"Neither the devil nor your daughter," said the prince. "I thatched it myself. I relied on my own skill."

The prince passed that night in the same way as the two previous nights, and when at daybreak the giant found him still alive in the tank, he said, "I've a very big task for you today, and unless you can do it, your head will be on that spike tomorrow. On the slopes beneath this castle, you'll find a tree nine hundred feet high. It has not a single branch except a little one right at the top, and that's where a crow has nested."

"I'm listening," said the prince.

"The trunk of the tree is covered with glass from the ground to the nest," said the giant. "There's an egg in that nest, and that's what I want for my supper tonight. Get me that egg or I'll have your head tomorrow for the seven-hundredth spike."

The giant went out hunting, and the prince picked his way down the steep slope to the tree. He put his arms around its trunk and tried to shake it; it didn't move. He put his arms around its trunk and tried to climb it; his hands and feet kept slipping.

"This time I'm finished," said the king's son. "This time I'll lose my head."

While the prince was standing and staring up at the shining tree, Yellow Lily came up behind him. "How are you getting on?" she asked.

"Not at all," said the young man. "I haven't even begun."

"Well," said Yellow Lily, "it's true enough! Cleaning and thatching the stables were nothing compared to this. We'd do

best to eat first. Let's eat together and then we'll talk."

Yellow Lily knelt down beside a little spring and smiled and spread out a cloth, and the cloth was covered with food and drink. When they had eaten, the giant's daughter took out a wicked knife from her pocket.

"What's that for?" asked the prince.

"For you to kill me with," said Yellow Lily. "You must kill me and strip the flesh from my bones, and use them as steps for climbing up this tree."

"I can't kill you," said the prince.

"As you climb the tree," Yellow Lily said, "my bones will stick to the glass as if they grew out of it. Then they'll support you as you come down again and drop into your hands when you touch them."

"Not after all you've done for me," cried the prince.

"When you come down, make sure you stand on each and every bone," said Yellow Lily. "Leave none untouched, otherwise it will get left behind."

Yellow Lily spread out a second cloth beside the little spring that watered the roots of the tree. "Put all my flesh on this cloth," she said. "And when you come down from the tree, arrange my bones on the cloth, and lay my flesh over them, and sprinkle it with water from this spring. And then I'll stand in front of you, alive and well. But don't forget — don't leave one bone behind on the tree. If you won't obey me," said the giant's daughter, "we are both finished. You'll only be able to climb this tree if you do as I say."

The king's son did as Yellow Lily said. He killed her, stripped the flesh from her bones, and unjointed her. Then the prince placed the bones one by one against the trunk; he used them as steps and climbed and climbed until, with the very last bone, he was within reach of the crow's nest.

The prince put up one arm and dipped his hand into the nest and took the crow's egg. Then at once he started down, carefully putting his foot on each and every bone, and taking the bones back from the tree as they dropped into his hands. When he was only a few feet from the ground, the prince jumped down from the tree; he didn't touch the very last bone.

Now the prince arranged all Yellow Lily's bones on the white cloth at the foot of the tree. He laid her flesh over them and sprinkled them with water from the spring.

Yellow Lily, the giant's youngest daughter, stood up in front of him alive and well, and the first thing she said was, "Didn't I tell you to stand on each and every bone? You left my little toe untouched on the tree. Now I've only got nine toes."

No sooner was the giant through the door of his castle than he bawled out, "Have you got that crow's egg for my supper?"

"I have," said the prince.

"If you have," the giant said, "then you had the devil on your side — either the devil or my daughter."

"I relied on my own skill," said the prince.

"Well," said the giant, "whoever it was, I have no choice but to forgive you. You've performed all three tasks. Your head is your own."

So the prince was free to leave the castle. Away he went, over the high hills and the green valleys of Ireland. He didn't stop to eat or sleep until he was home with his mother and father again. How the king and the queen welcomed their son! They welcomed him with kisses and questions; they welcomed him with feasting and dancing and song. They'd believed he was dead, and there he was, their own son, standing in front of them.

Several weeks after the prince had come back from the giant's

castle, the king turned to his wise man, old and blind. "How can I protect the life of my son?" he asked. "He's my heir. When I die, he will be king."

"Listen!" said the wise man. "Find him a wife. Then he won't go off on his own again. For all his liking for tests of strength and his love of chance, he'll stay at home."

The king liked his wise man's advice. He sent a messenger to the king of Denmark, asking for his daughter in marriage. And before long, the Danish king set sail for Ireland, bringing his daughter as a bride for the prince.

The king and queen of Ireland laid plans for a magnificent wedding, to be attended by guests from far and wide. The prince asked his father to invite the giant of Loch Lein and his youngest daughter, Yellow Lily, so the king sent a messenger over the hill country to the giant's castle, bidding them to come.

On the day before the marriage, the king held a lavish feast for all his guests. While everyone was eating and drinking and toasting and laughing, the giant of Loch Lein said, "I've never been to a gathering like this one without one man singing a song, another telling a story, and a third playing a trick."

So the king of Ireland sang a song, and the king of Denmark told a story.

"This was your idea," the king of Ireland told the giant, "and now it's your turn."

"Yellow Lily," said the giant. "She can take my place."

Yellow Lily stepped forward. On her left palm lay one grain of wheat and on her right palm another. The daughter of the giant tossed both grains high into the air, and down to the feasting table flew two pigeons. The cock pigeon began to peck the hen and bustle her and jostle her so that she fell off the table. Then the hen called

out to the cock with the voice of a young woman, "You wouldn't have done that to me on the day I cleaned the stables for you."

Now Yellow Lily put a couple of grains of wheat on the feasting table. The cock ate both grains and pecked the hen and jostled her so that she fell off the table and down to the floor. Then the hen said, "You wouldn't have done that to me on the day I thatched the stables for you — thatched them with birds' feathers, and no two feathers of the same color or the same kind."

Again Yellow Lily put a couple of grains of wheat on the feasting table. The cock ate them both again and pushed the hen down to the floor. Then the hen called out, "You wouldn't have done that to me on the day you killed me, and took my bones to make steps up the glass tree nine hundred feet high, so as to get the crow's egg for the supper of the giant of Loch Lein — the day you forgot my little toe on your way down and left me lame for life."

"Well!" said the prince. "I used to roam all over Ireland in search of tests of strength and trials of wit. Once, far from here, I lost the key to a casket I owned. After a time, I had a new key made, and then I found the old key again. Now, friends, can anyone here tell me which key I should keep and look after?"

"My advice," said the king of Denmark, "is to keep the old key. It already knows the lock, and you're more used to it."

"That is honest and wise advice," said the prince, "and I thank you for it. Here then is my bride: Yellow Lily, the daughter of the giant of Loch Lein! I'll have her if she'll have me. I'll have her and no other woman!"

"My daughter," said the king of Denmark.

"Your daughter," said the prince, "has lost little. She's been saved from a loveless marriage. And she will be my father's most honored guest."

So the king's son married Yellow Lily, the youngest daughter of the giant of Loch Lein. The wedding celebrations lasted for weeks. And the prince and Yellow Lily, the giant and the king and queen, the king of Denmark and his daughter, and the hundreds of guests: they were all happy.

THE GREEN MIST

"HAVE YOU CARRIED THE LIGHT?"

"I have," said the woman. "Every day at sundown. I've lit it and carried it around both rooms."

"What about the words?"

"I've spoken the words."

"And the blood?"

"I have," the woman said fiercely. "Every night I've smeared it on the doorstep to scare away the horrors."

But still the girl lay ill. One by one, each neighbor called with all the same questions; pretty and ramping as she was, caring as she was, they all loved her next to their own daughters. In the back room she lay, never feeling better and slowly getting worse. No medicine cured her, no kind words cheered her for long, and people said she must be in the power of the bogles.

"She's white and waffling," said the woman, "like a bag of bones. And it's almost spring waking."

The low house moaned. The wind rushed over the fen, leaped the bank, and wailed in the village.

Day followed day and the girl grew whiter and weaker. She was no more able to stand on her own feet than a baby. She could only lie at the window, watching winter creep away.

"It's creeping," said the woman.

"Oh, Mother," the girl kept saying over and over again, "if only I could wake the spring with you again. If only I could wake the spring, maybe the green mist would make me strong and well, like the trees and the flowers and the young corn."

"You'll come to the spring waking," said the woman. "You'll come and grow as straight and strong as ever."

"If only," said the girl, lying at the window.

But day after day, the girl grew whiter and more wan. She looked like a snowflake melting in the Sun. And day after day, winter crept past; it was almost spring.

Anxiously, the girl waited. But she felt so weak and so sick that she knew she would never be able to walk to the fields, crumble bread, and sprinkle salt on them with her mother and all her friends.

"I'll lift you over the doorstep," the woman said. "I swear I will, and you can toss out the bread with your own poor thin hands."

"If the green mist doesn't come in the morning, I won't be able to wait. Not any longer. The soil is calling me. The seeds swelling and bursting now will bloom over my head."

"No," said the woman.

"I know it," said the girl. "And yet, if I could see the spring wake

again . . ." Gravely she stared at the little garden that lay between the low house and the lane. "If only I could," she said urgently, "I swear I'd ask no more than to live as long as one of those cowslips that grow by our gate each year."

"Quiet!" cried the woman.

The girl looked at her, unblinking.

"Have you no sense? They're all around. You know they can hear you, the bogles."

But the dawn of the next day brought the green mist.

The mist grew out of the ground, and as the gathering light gave color to everything, the people of the village could see that it was green.

Silently, the mist lifted and fell and lifted, almost luminous. It swayed and reached out its long arms and wrapped itself around everything — low fen houses and the people living in them, trunks of trees and their topmost branches, the church spire. The green mist wove mysterious patterns over the fields and pressed itself against the side of the bank. It was as green as grass and as fragrant as spring flowers.

The villagers got ready and met to go down to the fields, every man and woman and child who could walk; they all held bread and salt. But not the girl; she could not walk. Her mother took her from her bed and, despite her own aching bones, carried her across the room and over the doorstep, as she had promised.

The girl leaned against a doorpost, looking into the green mist. She looked and looked and smiled. It was everything and nothing, and beckoning.

"Take this," said the woman, standing at her side. She gave the girl bread.

The girl crumbled the bread and cast it out a little way from the doorstep.

"This," said the woman.

The girl took the salt and cast that, too. Then she murmured the old words that were spoken each spring, the strange words that everyone said and no one understood.

The woman took a deep long breath and gave a grunt of satisfaction. The girl's eyes were brown with orange irises. She smiled and, unblinking, looked at the garden, wrapped in green. She looked at the gate where the cowslips grew.

Then her mother carried her back to her bed by the window. All morning the girl slept. Then, like a baby, she slept all afternoon. Her face was unlined and untroubled. She dreamed of warm summer days and gathering flowers, the laughter of friends.

Whether or not it was the green mist, the girl began to grow stronger and prettier from that day forward. When the Sun shone, she got up from her bed and soon left the low house. She flitted about like a will-o'-the-wisp. She danced and sang in the sunlight, as if its warmth were her life.

And the girl went visiting from house to house. All the people of the village loved her, opened their doors wide and welcome, and felt well to see her well.

When it was cold, or late in the evening, the girl still looked very white and wan. She crouched close to the fire, shaking. But after the spring sowing, she was able to walk with her friends along the lane, collect flat stones, and lay bread and salt on them to get a good harvest. And when there was not one cloud in the sky for the first week in April, she and her friends trooped down to the fields with buckets; the girl spilled water in the four corners of each field and asked for rain.

By the time the cowslips had opened early in May, the girl had become strangely beautiful; her friends looked at her and thought they could almost see through her. She laughed often enough, but often she was silent, and they wondered what she was thinking. They all knew each other like brother and sister, living as they did a few yards apart in the middle of the great empty marsh; but now they felt that they did not quite know her and were almost afraid of her.

Every morning, the girl knelt by the cowslips at the garden gate. She watered and tended them and danced beside them in the sunlight.

"Leave them alone!" the woman called.

The girl took no notice.

"Let them be!" ordered the woman, coming out of the low house, abrupt and anxious. "Leave them alone, or I'll pull them up."

Then the girl stopped dancing and looked at the woman strangely. "Mother," she said in a soft low voice, "don't even pick one of those flowers unless you're tired of me."

The woman pressed her lips together.

"They'll fade soon enough," said the girl, "soon enough, yes, as you know."

Early one evening, a boy from the village stopped by the gate to gossip with the girl and the woman. The Sun cast long shadows and a light, slight wind breathed around them: just the time for passing time!

The boy picked a flower and twirled it between his fingers as they talked — talked of the birth of a baby and a midsummer marriage, talked of the fen that was full of prying bogles and horrible boggarts, talked of the need to improve the bank. They had no

thought or knowledge of the world and its worries beyond.

Out across the marsh, the wind started forward. It sprang over the bank, tousled and interrupted them.

"That's blowing," said the boy, and he dropped the flower.

The girl suddenly tightened and trembled. "You," she said, staring at the boy's feet. "Did you pull that cowslip?" She looked strange and white, and pressed her right hand over her heart.

The boy glanced down; then he stooped and scooped it up. He looked at the girl, thinking he had never really noticed quite how lovely and different she was. "Here you are," he said, offering her the flower, grinning.

The girl took the cowslip. She stared at the flower and the boy and everything about her, at the green trees and the sprouting grass and the yellow blooms, and up at the golden shining Sun. Then, all at once, shrinking as if the sunlight that she loved so much were burning her, the girl turned and ran into the low house. She said nothing; she only gave a sort of cry, like a poor dumb beast in pain. And she caught the cowslip close against her heart.

The girl lay huddled on her bed. She did not move. She did not move at all. She stared at the flower in her hand as it faded, hour by hour.

"Come," said the woman, and offered her food, drink, and friendly talk.

But the girl said nothing, and night came on. She never spoke again.

At dawn, lying on the bed, there was only a white dead shrunken thing, with a shriveled cowslip in its hand. The woman covered it with a quilt and thought of the beautiful laughing girl, dancing like

a bird in the sunshine, down by the yellow nodding flowers. *Only yesterday,* she thought. "Yesterday," she whispered to herself.

The bogles had heard her and given the girl her wish. She had bloomed with the cowslips and faded with the first of them.

"It's all true," the woman whispered, "true as death."

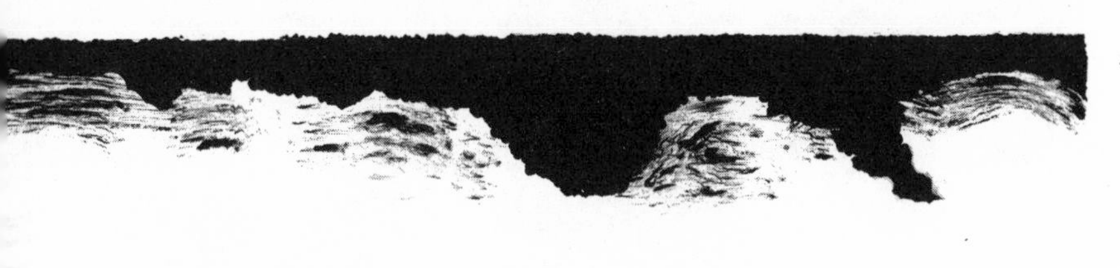

WITS, TRICKS, AND LAUGHTER

A VILLAGE OF FOOLS

"WHO ARE ALL THESE PEOPLE?" SHOUTED KING JOHN. "CLEAR them out of my way!"

But the crowd in front of him — all the men and women and children of Gotham — shouted back at the king. They yelled and waved their staves and cudgels. The last thing they meant to do was let the king pass through their village; they lived from their tolls, and wherever the king passed became by law a public road.

"Get out of my way, you fools!" roared King John. "I'm riding to Nottingham."

But the crowd stood firm and stood shoulder to shoulder. So at last the king and his train of followers turned back and, to the accompaniment of hoots and laughs and whistles, rode slowly away.

"I'll punish them for this," muttered King John. "I'll string them up by the thumbs and screw them down with corkscrews and chop them up for dog meat!"

Early next morning, one of King John's messengers rode to Gotham to find out why the villagers had stood in the king's way. But one old man saw him coming, and the word quickly went 'round from village pump to beer tap, from beer tap to shop, from shop to pump and 'round again.

The first villagers whom the king's messenger met were a group of old men standing up to their knees in the village pond.

"What are you doing?" he asked them.

"Trying to drown this eel," said one old man.

"And you," the messenger asked a number of able-bodied young women, some of them dragging carts, some upending them against the east side of a barn. "What are you doing?"

"The Sun's too hot," one girl replied. "We're guarding the walls of this barn against it."

"And you," called the messenger to a group of laughing children standing on the top of a knoll and cartwheeling whole cheeses down the side of it. "What are you doing?"

"What do you think?" they shouted. "We're sending our cheeses to market at Nottingham."

The messenger tapped his head. He squinted and looked at the end of his nose. All around him groups of villagers were hard at work.

"Dear! Oh dear!" he said. "A village of fools! King John would be wise to keep well clear of Gotham."

MARE'S EGGS

WHEN HE SAW THE GOURD, THE IRISHMAN'S EYES BRIGHTENED. There it lay, swollen and striped, among the carrots and onions and potatoes and radishes, and he had never seen anything like it before.

"No day's a good day unless you learn something new," the Irishman said to himself.

So he stepped into the shop and asked the greengrocer to tell him what the strange object was. "It's like a cannonball," he said. "Or a green-and-white football. And it's like a huge egg. So what is it?"

"Sure!" said the greengrocer. "That's exactly what it is. It's a mare's egg."

"A mare's egg," cried the Irishman. "Can I buy it?"

"It's yours for one pound," said the greengrocer.

So the Irishman bought the gourd and, to while away the time on his way home across the heath, tried to see how far ahead of him he

could roll it. The gourd ran into a bush, and a hare leaped out of the bush and galloped away as fast as his legs could carry him.

The Irishman gave chase. He ran as fast as he could. But long-legged as he was, he was not as quick as the leaping hare, and the hare escaped him.

Next day, the Irishman walked into town again and went back to the greengrocer's shop.

"You again," said the greengrocer, warily. "What can I do for you today?"

"That was a racehorse's egg," said the Irishman.

"Is that right?" said the greengrocer, grinning.

"The foal ran away from me. I couldn't catch up with him."

"Really?" said the greengrocer.

"So I've come straight back," the Irishman said. "Have you got any carthorse's eggs?"

THE COW THAT ATE THE PIPER

THE THREE HIRED MEN LEFT THE FARM ON A COLD NOVEMBER morning. They slung their sacks over their shoulders and set out on the long walk back home to Kerry.

That evening, the Moon shone, and the north wind pursed his blue lips and whistled. And the three men couldn't see so much as a haystack, let alone an old barn, to shelter and sleep in. They quickened their pace, they trotted, they sang, they swung their arms, and before long they fell into step with a laughing piper. He was barefooted and wearing no more than a tatter of clothing.

"I'll go along with you," said the piper.

The frost tightened his white fist. Bushes by the roadside hunched their shoulders; the road began to glitter.

"We're all dead men," said the piper, "if we don't keep moving."

The four of them kept walking, trotting, walking, and shortly

before midnight, they came across a dead man lying right across the road. He was wearing a brand-new pair of shoes.

"Faith!" said the piper. "Look at those shoes!"

The three men looked and the Moon polished the shining toe caps.

"And I haven't so much as a stitch on my feet," said the piper. "They're no use to him, are they now?"

"Not at all!" said one of the hired men.

"I'll take them off of him," said the piper. He got down on all fours and tugged at the dead man's shoes. But he could do no more than untie the laces.

"Death alive!" exclaimed the piper. "They're frozen to his feet!"

"Come on, now," said another of the hired laborers. "We're decent men."

"Give me your spade!" the piper said. "Let's see if I can't cut off his legs."

So the piper cut off the dead man's feet at the ankles. He picked them up and popped them into his sack. Then he and the hired men hurried on, and just after midnight, they came upon a little farm.

"Heaven be praised!" said the piper.

The men knocked; they waited, knocked again, and after rather a long time, a sleepy serving girl unbolted the door and let them into the kitchen — a low-slung smoky room with the fire at one end and three cows tied up at the other.

"You can sleep here," said the girl. "But keep clear of that gray cow. She's a devil. She'll eat the coats off of your backs." The girl latched the door at the foot of the stairs and padded up to her own room.

Before long, the three hired men curled up around the burning peats and fell asleep. The piper, though, still had work to do. He

opened his sack and took out the shoes with the two feet inside them and toasted them over the fire. The feet began to thaw, and he was soon able to pull off the shoes.

The piper smiled. He drummed his fingers on the shining toe caps and hummed a little tune. Then he put his own feet into the shoes! He stood up, he hopped and spun around, and he threw the dead man's feet down to the far end of the kitchen.

For a while, the piper dozed. Then at dawn, while the household and the hired men were still asleep, he got up, shouldered his pipes and his sack, and crept out of the house.

The serving girl was first to rise. She came downstairs and roused the huddle of sleepers. The three hired men groaned and rubbed their eyes and sat up.

"There were four of you at midnight," said the girl.

The men yawned and ran their hands through their hair.

"Where's the one with the pipes?"

"I don't know," said the first man.

"How should we know?" said the second man. And the third man just shrugged. The girl walked down to the far end of the kitchen, and there she stumbled right over the two feet.

"Holy mother!" she cried. "The cow has eaten him!"

The serving girl ran to the foot of the staircase. "The cow!" she yelled. "The gray cow! The cow has eaten the piper!"

"What's that?" shouted the farmer, and he stumped down the stairs, a great rumple and crease of a man.

"The cow's eaten the piper!" shouted the girl. "The poor cold piper! There's only his feet left."

The big pink farmer looked at the feet. He looked at the hired men, and the men advanced to the middle of the room.

"There were four last night, then?" he said.

"There were," said the first man.

"And our comrade," said the second, "he's been eaten by that gray cow."

The farmer looked around him, as if the walls themselves had ears. "Shush!" he said, and he put a stubby finger to his lips. "No need for any trouble now."

Then the farmer dipped into his clothing and fished out five gold coins. "Here's five guineas for you," he said, pressing the coins into the palm of the first hired man. "Now eat your breakfast and be off."

As soon as they had eaten breakfast, and it was not a small one, the three hired men shouldered their sacks and left the little farm.

Some way down the winding road, they caught up with a laughing man wearing no more than a tatter of clothing. The golden Sun polished his toe caps, and he was hopping and spinning and dancing a jig.

NOT SO LONG AGO, A WELSH MINER WAS WALKING SLOWLY ALONG the shady lane that led out of his village and down to the pit. Countless commas and colons of sunlight were dancing a jig on the road; a little wind sighed in the lime trees. And listening to it, the miner sighed too. The last place he wanted to go on such a day was the dark and dusty mine.

"Good morning!" said a voice.

The miner looked left. He looked right. He looked behind him. There was nobody there.

"Good morning!" said the same voice.

Again the miner looked to either side, in front of him, and behind him. There was still no one there.

Then the miner heard the voice for the third time, and it came from right above his head. He peered up and there, sitting on a gently swinging branch, was a gray parrot.

For a while the miner stared at it and frowned. *Most unusual,* he thought. *A most unusual kind of hawk.*

Then the parrot opened its beak again. "Good morning!" it said.

The miner, who was as polite as ever a man was, doffed his cap.

"Beg pardon, sir," he said. "I thought you was a bird!"

THE WISE MEN OF GOTHAM

— I —

TWO MEN FROM GOTHAM MET ON NOTTINGHAM BRIDGE. ONE of them was on his way to the market to buy sheep, and the other was on his way home.

"Good morning!" said the man coming from the village.

"Where are you going?" said the man coming from the market.

"Market!" said the first man. "I'm going to buy some sheep."

"Sheep!" said the other. "How will you get them home?"

"Over this bridge, of course," said the first man.

"By Robin Hood," said the second man, "you will not!"

"By Maid Marian," said the first, "I certainly will!"

"You will not," said the second man.

"I will," said the first.

Then the two men began to hammer the ground with their

cudgels. They pounded the cobbles and the bridge boomed.

"Keep your sheep back!" the first man shouted.

"Beware!" yelled the second. "Beware or mine will leap over the parapet!"

"My sheep will all come home this way," bawled the first man.

"They will not!" shouted the other.

While they were arguing, another wise man from Gotham rode up to the bridge on his way home from the market. He had a sack of meal up in the saddle behind him.

For a while this man listened to his neighbors arguing about their sheep, with not one sheep in sight. Then he jumped down from his horse. "You fools!" he called. "Will you never learn sense?"

The man's two neighbors turned and looked at him.

"Come on!" he said. "Help me get this sack up onto my shoulder."

When the man with the meal had shouldered his sack, he went over to the parapet, untied the sack's mouth, and shook out all the meal into the river. "How much meal is there in this sack?" he asked.

"None," said the first man.

"None," said the second man.

"There's just as much meal in this sack," said the wise man, "as you have wit in your two heads, arguing over sheep you don't even own."

So which of these three men was the wisest?

— 2 —

"That cuckoo," said the boys of Gotham. "Let's capture it and then we'll be able to hear it sing all year 'round."

So the boys made a circular hedge, and then they caught the cuckoo and put her into it.

"Here you are," said one.

"And here you'll stay," said another, "and sing all the year 'round."

"Otherwise," said a third, "you'll have nothing to eat or drink."

The cuckoo looked at the boys. She looked at the circuit of the hedge, spread her wings, and flew away.

"Curses!" shouted the boys. "We'll get her! We didn't make our hedge high enough."

— 3 —

Twelve men from Gotham made up a fishing party. Some of them fished from the bank of the stream; a few of them waded into the water — right up to their shins.

Before they left for home, one of the men said, "What an adventure we've had today, wading and all! I hope to God none of us have been drowned."

"Let's check before we leave," said another man. "There were twelve of us set out from home."

So each man counted his neighbors, and every one of them counted up to eleven.

"One of us is missing," they said. "One of us has been drowned." The men walked up and down the little stream where they had been fishing, looking for the missing man, wringing their hands and sighing and moaning.

At this moment, one of the king's courtiers rode up. "What's wrong?" he asked. "What are you looking for?"

"Oh!" cried the men. "We've been fishing here today. Twelve of us! One of us has been drowned."

"You count," said the courtier. "One of you count again and I'll check."

So one man walked around and counted his neighbors. But he did not count himself.

"Well!" said the courtier. "Well! Well! What will you give me if I can find the twelfth man?"

"All the money in my pocket!" said one man.

"All mine too!" cried another.

The wise men of Gotham promised to give the courtier every coin they had on them.

"All right!" said the courtier. "Give me the money!"

As the courtier walked around the group, collecting the money, he thwacked each man over the shoulders with his whip and began to count, "One, two, three . . ." When the courtier came to the last man, he thwacked him especially hard and called out, "Here he is! Here's the twelfth man!"

The wise men rubbed their shoulders. "God bless you!" they said. "You've found our friend and neighbor."

—— 4 ——

A man from Gotham was on his way to the market at Nottingham to sell his cheeses. On his way down the hill to Nottingham Bridge, one of the cheeses toppled out of his shoulder bag and ran down the hill.

"Ah!" said the man. "So you're able to run down the hill on your own." He looked at the cheese, rolling and cartwheeling down the slope, and it started him thinking. "In that case," he said, "I expect the other cheeses can run too. I'll get them all to run down the hill."

So the wise man swung the heavy bag off his shoulders, took out the cheeses, and sent them tumbling down the hill one after another. One disappeared into a thorn bush; one rolled into a rabbit

hole; one ran into a thicket. The man wagged a finger at the disappearing cheeses. "Make sure," he shouted, "that you all meet me in the marketplace."

The man stayed at Nottingham market until it was almost over. Then he made his way 'round, asking friends and strangers alike whether they had seen his cheeses.

"Why?" asked another man from Gotham. "Who is bringing them?"

"They are!" said the man. "They're bringing themselves."

"Bringing themselves!"

"And they know the way well enough, damn them!" exclaimed the man. "When I saw my cheeses running so fast, I was afraid that they would overrun this marketplace. I should think they're almost in York by now."

So the man spent what money he had with him on the loan of a horse. He rode after his cheeses. He galloped all the way to York.

But no one has been able to find out where the cheeses got to, not from that day to this.

— 5 —

A woman of Gotham was walking home from a neighbor's cottage late at night. In fact, it was after midnight.

As she passed the horse pond, she saw a whole green cheese floating just under the surface.

"My word!" she exclaimed. "This is worth some effort."

She ran back to her cottage, shouting as she went. Her husband heard her, and all her neighbors, lying in their beds, heard her too. They jumped up and opened their little windows.

"There's a green cheese in the pond," bawled the woman. "Come and help me rake it out!"

The woman's friends and neighbors hurried out of their little cottages in their nightshirts and nightcaps. They all brought their rakes and began to drag the surface of the pond.

Just then a passing cloud sank the cheese. The woman sighed a deep sigh, and all her neighbors went back to their beds, disappointed.

MAGPIES IN THE CRABTREE

UP IN THE CRABTREE THE MAGPIES WERE QUARRELING. THEN they began to fight. They thrust their beaks and clashed their beaks and struck sparks from them.

So the tree caught fire — the pinkish leaves and whiskered twigs, then the trunk itself.

Before long, well-cooked crabs started to clatter on to the ground. The village children shouted and dived after them. They scooped them up and popped them into their mouths. Then they picked the shells clean.

THE RIDDLER

A KNIGHT CAME RIDING IN FROM THE EAST,
O sing the hemp-banks, sing the bright broom
An ardent wooer at fireside and feast.
And you may beguile a young thing soon

He galloped up to a widow's door
O sing the hemp-banks, sing the bright broom
And asked where her three daughters were.
And you may beguile a young thing soon

"The oldest's gone out to wash clothes,
O sing the hemp-banks, sing the bright broom
The second's gone out to bake loaves.
And you may beguile a young thing soon

"The youngest's gone off to a wedding ball;
O sing the hemp-banks, sing the bright broom
Before she's home, it will be nightfall."
And you may beguile a young thing soon

The patient knight sat down on a stone
O sing the hemp-banks, sing the bright broom
Until these girls came tripping home.
And you may beguile a young thing soon

The oldest laid out their triple bed,
O sing the hemp-banks, sing the bright broom
And gave the second the sheet to spread.
And you may beguile a young thing soon

The youngest one was fresh and fair,
O sing the hemp-banks, sing the bright broom
And this strange knight had his eye on her.
And you may beguile a young thing soon

"Unless you answer one and ten,
O sing the hemp-banks, sing the bright broom
At first light I will make you my own.
And you may beguile a young thing soon

"O what is higher than a tree?
O sing the hemp-banks, sing the bright broom
And what is deeper than the sea?
And you may beguile a young thing soon

"And what is heavier than lead?
O sing the hemp-banks, sing the bright broom
And what is better than good bread?
And you may beguile a young thing soon

"O what is whiter than white milk?
O sing the hemp-banks, sing the bright broom
And what is softer than soft silk?
And you may beguile a young thing soon

"And what is sharper than a thorn?
O sing the hemp-banks, sing the bright broom
And what is louder than a horn?
And you may beguile a young thing soon

"And what is greener than the grass?
O sing the hemp-banks, sing the bright broom
And what's more sly than a woman is?"
And you may beguile a young thing soon

"O heaven is higher than a tree,
O sing the hemp-banks, sing the bright broom
And hell is deeper than the sea.
And you may beguile a young thing soon

"O sin is heavier than lead.
O sing the hemp-banks, sing the bright broom
A blessing's better than good bread.
And you may beguile a young thing soon

"Snow is whiter than white milk,
O sing the hemp-banks, sing the bright broom
And down is softer than soft silk.
And you may beguile a young thing soon

"Hunger is sharper than a thorn,
O sing the hemp-banks, sing the bright broom
And shame is louder than a horn.
And you may beguile a young thing soon

"Woodpeckers are greener than new grass,
O sing the hemp-banks, sing the bright broom
And Old Nick's more sly than a woman is."
And you may beguile a young thing soon

As soon as she gave the fiend his name,
O sing the hemp-banks, sing the bright broom
He flew away in a raging flame.
And you may beguile a young thing soon

GHOSTS

BOO!

SHE DIDN'T LIKE IT AT ALL WHEN HER FATHER HAD TO GO DOWN TO London and, for the first time, she had to sleep alone in the old house.

She went up to her bedroom early. She turned the key and locked the door. She latched the windows and drew the curtains. Then she peered inside her wardrobe and pulled open the bottom drawer of her dresser; she got down on her knees and looked under the bed.

She undressed; she put on her nightdress.

She pulled back the heavy linen cover and climbed into bed. Not to read but to try to sleep — she wanted to sleep as soon as she could. She reached out and turned off the lamp.

"That's good," said a little voice. "Now we're safely locked in for the night."

SAMUEL'S GHOST

POOR LITTLE SAMUEL! HE WAS ASLEEP WHEN HIS COTTAGE CAUGHT fire, and when he woke up it was too late. He was only a lad and he was burned to death; he got turned into ashes, and maybe cinders.

After a while, though, Samuel got up. The inside of him got up and gave itself a shake. He must have felt rather odd: he wasn't used to doing without a body, and he didn't know what to do next, and all around him there were boggarts and bogles and chancy things, and he was a bit scared.

Before long, Samuel heard a voice. "You must go to the graveyard," said whatever it was, "and tell the Big Worm you're dead."

"Must I?" said Samuel.

"And ask him to have you eaten up," said the something. "Otherwise you'll never rest in the ground."

"I'm willing," said Samuel.

So Samuel set off for the graveyard, asking the way, and rubbing shoulders with all the horrid things that glowered around him.

By and by, Samuel came to an empty dark space. Glimmering lights were crossing and recrossing it. It smelled earthy, as strong as the soil in spring, and here and there it gave off a ghastly stink, sickening and scary. Underfoot were creeping things, and all around were crawling, fluttering things, and the air was hot and tacky.

On the far side of this space was a horrid great worm, coiled up on a flat stone. Its slimy head was nodding and swinging from side to side, as if it were sniffing out its dinner.

Samuel was afraid when he heard something call out his name, and the worm shot its horrid head right into his face. "Samuel! Is that you, Samuel? So you're dead and buried and food for the worms, are you?"

"I am," said Samuel.

"Well!" said the worm. "Where's your body?"

"Please, your worship," said Samuel — he didn't want to anger the worm, naturally — "I'm all here!"

"No," said the worm. "How do you think we can eat you? You must fetch your corpse if you want to rest in the ground."

"But where is it?" said Samuel, scratching his head. "My corpse?"

"Where is it buried?" said the worm.

"It isn't buried," said Samuel. "That's just it. It's ashes. I got burned up."

"Ha!" said the worm. "That's bad. That's very bad. You'll not taste too good."

Samuel didn't know what to say.

"Don't fret," said the worm. "Go and fetch the ashes. Bring them here, and we'll do all we can."

So Samuel went back to his burned-out cottage. He looked and looked. He scooped up all the ashes he could find into a sack and took them off to the great worm.

Samuel opened the sack, and the worm crawled down off the flat stone. It sniffed the ashes and turned them over and over.

"Samuel," said the worm after a while. "Something's missing. You're not all here, Samuel. Where's the rest of you? You'll have to find the rest."

"I've brought all I could find," said Samuel.

"No," the worm said. "There's an arm missing."

"Ah!" said Samuel. "That's right! I lost an arm I had."

"Lost?" asked the worm.

"It was cut off," said Samuel.

"You must find it, Samuel."

Samuel frowned. "I don't know where the doctor put it," he said. "I can go and see."

So Samuel hurried off again. He hunted high and low, and after a while he found his arm.

Samuel went straight back to the worm. "Here's the arm," he said.

The worm slid off its flat stone and turned the arm over.

"No, Samuel," said the worm. "There's something still missing. Did you lose anything else?"

"Let's see," said Samuel. "Let's see . . . I lost a nail once, and that never grew again."

"That's it, I reckon!" said the worm. "You've got to find it, Samuel!"

"I don't think I'll ever find that, master," said Samuel. "Not one nail. I'll give it a try, though."

So Samuel hurried off for the third time. But a nail is just as hard to find as it's easy to lose. Although Samuel searched and searched,

he couldn't find anything, so at last he went back to the worm.

"I've searched and searched, and I've found nothing," said Samuel. "You must take me without my nail — it's no great loss, is it? Can't you make do without it?"

"No," said the worm. "I can't. And if you can't find it — are you quite certain you can't, Samuel?"

"Certain, worse luck!"

"Then you must walk! You must walk by day and walk by night. I'm very sorry for you, Samuel, but you'll have plenty of company!"

Then all the creeping things and crawling things swarmed 'round Samuel and turned him out. And unless he has found it, Samuel has been walking and hunting for his nail from that day to this.

SLAM AND THE GHOSTS

"NIGHT AFTER NIGHT," SAID SLAM'S MOTHER. "THE BOOR! THE great clodhopper!"

"You can't talk to him without getting angry," said Douglas. "You can't even talk about him without getting angry. I'll talk to him."

"I'll brain him! Bursting in at one o'clock night after night! Blundering about! Leaving his great hoof marks all over the house, the drunkard!"

"I'll talk to him," said Douglas again.

"I don't know," said his mother. "You're so alike — always loyal to each other, always wanting to avoid a scrap. You and Slam — you look the same too."

"I wonder why," said Douglas.

"And so unalike . . . You work; you bring home the bacon. And Slam . . ."

"I know," said Douglas quietly.

"It's the drink," said Douglas's mother. "It's wrecking him. Can't you get him off it?"

Secretly, Douglas agreed with his mother. *What Slam really needs,* he thought, *is a bit of a shock.*

Halfway between the pub and their cottage — and it was a couple of miles from one to the other, maybe a bit farther — the land passed under a very steep bank; and at the top of the bank was the old disused graveyard.

That same night, very late, Douglas pulled the white sheet off his bed. He let himself quietly out of the cottage and, under stars sharp as thorns, walked up to the graveyard. There, Douglas wrapped the sheet around him and sat down on a gravestone right on top of the bank, overlooking the lane.

"This will cure him," Douglas said to himself. "Kill him or cure him. Poor old Slam!"

At much the same time as usual, Slam came staggering up the lane. His shoes were made of lead, and he was singing a wordless song.

When his brother was right beneath him, Douglas stood up and whoo-hooed at him.

"I know!" said Slam, and he added a great hiccup. "You're the ghost! I know!"

Douglas whoo-hooed again, and Slam peered up at the graveyard and tottered sideways.

"Two ghosts!" exclaimed Slam. "There was only one ghost last night."

Slowly, Douglas turned around and stared straight into two furious, glaring eyes.

Douglas started back and fell headfirst over the steep bank.

He landed at his brother's feet and broke his neck. Poor old Douglas! That was the end of him.

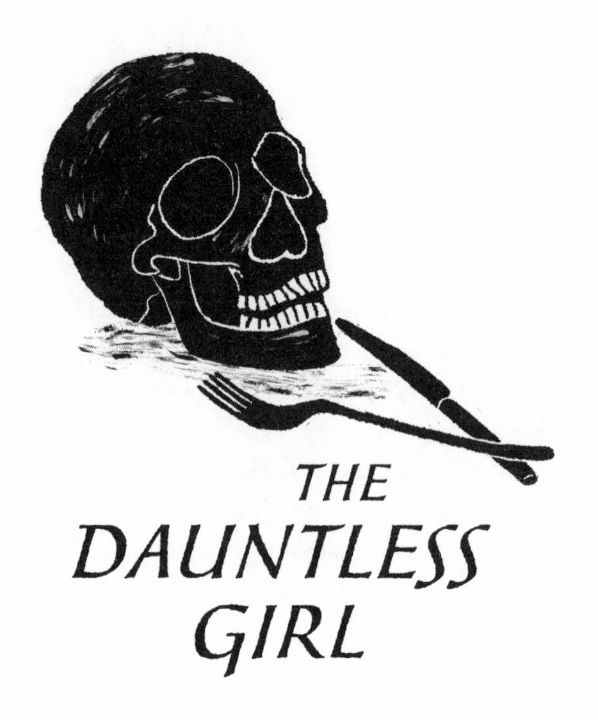

THE DAUNTLESS GIRL

"DANG IT!" SAID THE FARMER.

"Why?" said the miller.

"Not a drop left," the farmer said.

"Not one?" asked the blacksmith, raising his glass and inspecting it. His last inch of whiskey glowed like molten honey in the flickering firelight.

"Why not?" said the miller.

"You fool!" said the farmer. "Because the bottle's empty." He peered into the flames. "Never mind that, though," he said. "We'll send out my Mary. She'll go down to the inn and bring us another bottle."

"What?" said the blacksmith. "She'll be afraid to go out on such a dark night, all the way down to the village, and all on her own."

"Never!" said the farmer. "She's afraid of nothing — nothing live or dead. She's worth all my lads put together."

The farmer gave a shout, and Mary came out of the kitchen.

She stood and she listened. She went out into the dark night, and in a little time she returned with another bottle of whiskey.

The miller and the blacksmith were delighted. They drank to her health, but later the miller said, "That's a strange thing, though."

"What's that?" asked the farmer.

"That she should be so bold, your Mary."

"Bold as brass," said the blacksmith. "Out and alone and the night so dark."

"That's nothing at all," said the farmer. "She'd go anywhere, day or night. She's afraid of nothing — nothing live or dead."

"Words!" said the blacksmith. "But my, this whiskey tastes good."

"Words nothing," said the farmer. "I bet you a golden guinea that neither of you can name anything that girl will not do."

The miller scratched his head, and the blacksmith peered at the golden guinea of whiskey in his glass. "All right," said the blacksmith. "Let's meet here again at the same time next week. Then I'll name something Mary will not do."

Seven days later, the blacksmith went to see the priest and borrowed the key of the church door from him. Then he paid a visit to the sexton and showed him the key.

"What do you want with that?" asked the sexton.

"What I want with you," said the blacksmith, "is this. I want you to go into the church tonight, just before midnight, and hide yourself in the dead house."

"Never!" said the sexton.

"Not for half a guinea?" asked the blacksmith.

The old sexton's eyes popped out of his head. "Dang it!" he said. "What's that for, then?"

"To frighten that brazen farm girl, Mary," said the blacksmith, grinning. "When she comes to the dead house, just give a moan or a holler."

The old sexton's desire for the half guinea was even greater than his fear. He hemmed and hawed, and at last he agreed to do as the blacksmith asked. Then the blacksmith clumped the sexton on the back with his massive fist, and the old sexton coughed. "I'll see you tomorrow," said the blacksmith, "and settle the account. Just before midnight, then! Not a minute later!"

The sexton nodded, and the blacksmith strode up to the farm. Darkness was falling, and the farmer and the miller were already drinking and waiting for him.

"Well?" said the farmer.

The blacksmith grasped his glass, then raised it and rolled the whiskey around his mouth.

"Well," said the farmer. "Are you or aren't you?"

"This," said the blacksmith, "is what your Mary will not do. She won't go into the church alone at midnight . . ."

"No," said the miller.

"And go to the dead house," continued the blacksmith, "and bring back a skull bone. That's what she won't do."

"Never," said the miller.

The farmer gave a shout, and Mary came out of the kitchen. She stood and she listened, and later, at midnight, she went out into the darkness and walked down to the church.

Mary opened the church door. She held up her lamp and clattered down the steps to the dead house. She pushed open its creaking door and

saw skulls and thigh bones and bones of every kind gleaming in front of her. She stooped and picked up the nearest skull bone.

"Let that be!" moaned a muffled voice from behind the dead-house door. "That's my mother's skull bone."

So Mary put that skull down and picked up another.

"Let that be!" moaned a muffled voice from behind the dead-house door. "That's my father's skull bone."

So Mary put that skull bone down, too, and picked up yet another one. And, as she did so, she angrily called out, "Father or mother, sister or brother, I *must* have a skull bone, and that's my last word." Then she walked out of the dead house, latched the door, and hurried up the steps and back up to the farm.

Mary put the skull bone on the table in front of the farmer. "There's your skull bone, master," she said, and started off for the kitchen.

"Wait a minute!" said the blacksmith, and he was grinning and shivering. "Didn't you hear anything in the dead house, Mary?"

"Yes," she said. "Some fool of a ghost called out: 'Let that be! That's my mother's skull bone' and 'Let that be! That's my father's skull bone.' But I told him straight: 'Father or mother, sister or brother, I *must* have a skull bone.'"

The miller and the blacksmith stared at Mary and shook their heads.

"So I took one," said Mary, "and here it is." She looked down at the three faces flickering in the firelight. "After I had locked the door," she said, "and climbed the steps, I heard the old ghost hollering and shrieking like mad."

At once the blacksmith and the miller got to their feet.

"That'll do then, Mary," said the farmer.

The blacksmith knew the sexton must have been scared out of his

wits at being locked inside the dead house. He and his friends hurried down to the church and clattered down the steps into the dead house. They were too late. They found the old sexton lying stone dead on his face.

"That's what comes from trying to frighten a poor young girl," said the farmer.

So the blacksmith gave the farmer a golden guinea and the farmer gave it to his Mary.

Mary and her daring were known in every house. And after her visit to the dead house and the death of the old sexton, her fame spread for miles and miles around.

One day the squire, who lived three villages off, rode up to the farm and asked the farmer if he could talk to Mary.

"I've heard," said the squire, "that you're afraid of nothing."

Mary nodded.

"Nothing live or dead," said the farmer proudly.

"Listen, then!" said the squire. "Last year my old mother died and was buried. But she will not rest. She keeps coming back into the house, and especially at mealtimes."

Mary stood and listened.

"Sometimes you can see her; sometimes you can't. And when you can't, you can still see a knife and fork get up off the table and play about where her hands would be."

"That's a strange thing altogether," said the farmer.

"Strange and unnatural," said the squire. "And now my servants won't stay with me, not one of them. They're all afraid of her."

The farmer sighed and shook his head. "Hard to come by, good servants," he said.

"So," said the squire, "seeing as she's afraid of nothing, nothing live or dead, I'd like to ask your girl to come and work with me."

Mary was pleased at the prospect of such good employment, and sorry as he was to lose her, the farmer saw there was nothing for it but to let her go.

"I'll come," said the girl. "I'm not afraid of ghosts. But you ought to take account of that in my wages."

"I will," said the squire.

So Mary went back with the squire to be his servant. The first thing she always did was to lay a place for the ghost at the table, and she took great care not to let the knife and fork lie crisscross.

At meals, Mary passed the ghost the meat and vegetables and sauce and gravy. And then she said: "Pepper, madam?" and "Salt, madam?"

The ghost of the squire's mother was pleased enough. So things went on the same from day to day until the squire had to go up to London to settle some legal business.

The next morning, Mary was down on her knees, cleaning the parlor grate, when she noticed something thin and glimmering push in through the parlor door, which was just ajar. When it got inside the room, the shape began to swell and open out. It was the old ghost.

For the first time, the ghost spoke to the girl. "Mary," she said in a hollow voice, "are you afraid of me?"

"No, madam," said Mary. "I've no cause to be afraid of you, for you are dead and I'm alive."

For a while the ghost looked at the girl kneeling by the parlor grate. "Mary," she said, "will you come down into the cellar with me? You mustn't bring a light — but I'll shine enough to light the way for you."

So the two of them went down the cellar steps, and the ghost

shone like an old lantern. When they got to the bottom, they went along a passage, and took a right turn and a left, and then the ghost pointed to some loose tiles in one corner. "Pick up those tiles," she said.

Mary did as she was asked. And underneath the tiles were two bags of gold, a big one and a little one.

The ghost quivered. "Mary," she said, "that big bag is for your master. But that little bag is for you, for you are a dauntless girl and deserve it."

Before Mary could open the bag or even open her mouth, the old ghost drifted up the steps and out of sight. She was never seen again, and Mary had a devil of a time groping her way along the dark passage and up out of the cellar.

After three days, the squire came back from London.

"Good morning, Mary," he said. "Have you seen anything of my mother while I've been away?"

"Yes, sir," said Mary. "That I have." She opened her eyes wide. "And if you aren't afraid of coming down into the cellar with me, I'll show you something."

The squire laughed. "I'm not afraid if you're not afraid," he said, for the dauntless girl was a very pretty girl.

So Mary lit a candle and led the squire down into the cellar, walked along the passage, took a right turn and a left, and raised the loose tiles in the corner for a second time.

"Two bags," said the squire.

"Two bags of gold," said Mary. "The little one is for you and the big one is for me."

"Lor!" said the squire, and he said nothing else. He did think that his mother might have given him the big bag, as indeed she had, but all the same he took what he could.

After that, Mary always crossed the knives and forks at mealtimes to prevent the old ghost from telling what she had done.

The squire thought things over: the gold and the ghost and Mary's good looks. What with one thing and another, he proposed to Mary, and the dauntless girl, she accepted him. In a little while they married, and so the squire did get one hand on the big bag of gold after all.

BILLY WASN'T BORN CRIPPLED. HE FELL OUT OF THE APPLE TREE when he was four and broke both his legs. He broke them in several places.

There was no doctor within a day's ride of the village, so the two wise women laid poor Billy on a table, prepared splints, and set his legs as best they could. The legs set crooked, though, very crooked, and from that day forward, Billy was unable to walk.

While his friends played chase and turned cartwheels and flexed their lengthening limbs, all Billy could do was haul himself along on a pair of blackthorn sticks. Everyone liked him, though. They had no end of time for him, because he was cheerful and brave, and made the most of his life. His friends always carted him around to their games and gatherings.

When he grew up, Billy became a tailor. He sat cross-legged in his

cottage surrounded by bright rings of talk and laughter. And after supper, he used to swing along on his sticks in the direction of the village pub.

One Hallowe'en, while Billy and his friends were sitting in the pub, a band of children burst in with howls and shouts. The boys wore girls' clothing, the girls wore shirts and trousers, and all their faces were dirtied with soot. At once they blew out the two paraffin lamps that stood at each end of the bar, and then they swung their own turnip lanterns in front of the drinkers.

Billy and his friends stared at the swinging faces — their fiery eyes and rough-cut mouths, their glow and flicker. And later, when the hooligans had been given food and drink and gone on their way, leaving behind them an aftertow of quiet and emptiness, the owner said, "That's scared off the ghosts, then."

A log hissed and spat in the grate.

"There'll be ghosts in the churchyard, though," said a voice.

"That's no place to be tonight," another voice exclaimed.

"I'm not afraid!" said Billy quickly.

"The churchyard," said the owner. "That's alive tonight. . . ."

"I'm not afraid," said Billy again. "I'll go to the churchyard. I'll sit and sew there all night."

Laughing and alert, Billy's friends carried him back to his cottage to collect cloth and needle and thread; then they took one of the farmer's carts and rolled Billy up the hill to the graveyard.

"Come on, Billy!" said a voice.

In the moonlight, the tailor sat down on a flagstone and spread

out his cloth. It was so bright that he could see to sew. Billy sewed until eleven o'clock and sewed until twelve o'clock. "See you in the morning, Billy," said several voices.

Then Billy heard a rumble of a voice from the headstone right behind him. The grave began to open, and Billy was showered with fistfuls of sand. Out came a head, and the head thundered, "Do you see this head without flesh or blood?"

"Yes," said the tailor, "I see that, but I sew this."

"Do you see this arm without flesh or blood?"

"Yes," said the tailor, "I see that, but I sew this."

"Do you see this body without flesh or blood?"

"Yes," said the tailor, "I see that, but I sew this."

By now a huge man, eight feet tall, had come out of the grave. As he started to speak again, Billy finished his piece of sewing; he raised the cloth to his mouth and bit off the thread.

Then the thing reached out and clawed at Billy with its huge bone hand.

The little tailor leaped up. He ran across the churchyard and jumped right over the wall.

"Do you see this? Do you see this?" shouted the tailor. And he ran all the way home, laughing.

FEAR AND FLY

AT DUSK THE MIST CAME DOWN: NOT A SLOW THICKENING BUT cool white tides sliding across the sodden moor and lapping at the outcrops and canceling the paths and sheep pens and every other landmark.

When the old priest stood still, he could hear nothing but his own breathing and then, far off, the barking of a dog — so far away it seemed to come from another world or another time.

He knew he must press on. He knew he must get off the moor before darkness came. Prodding with his stick, and straining with his eyes until he could see nothing but writhing shapes, he worked his way down into the valley.

It was four hours before the poor priest came upon a little cottage, and that was entirely by chance. A dim light was shining in one upstairs window. With aching eyes and blistered feet, he made his way up to the door.

Over his head, the window opened. "Who's that?" said a cross voice.

"Father Ned," said the priest.

"Who?"

"Father Ned. I've gotten lost on the moor."

"Wait a minute," said the voice, and the window closed again.

A long minute it was! The voice talked to another voice; the voice got dressed and lit a candle and padded downstairs. It belonged to an old woman with eyes like apple pips and a face like sour milk.

"You had better come in," she said.

Father Ned felt much worse now that he had stopped walking. His old bones ached. His head hammered. He wanted to lie down.

"You'd better use our son's bed," said the old woman, leading the old priest upstairs. "He's away from home."

The priest mumbled his thanks.

"I can't promise you a quiet night, though," the old woman said. "This cottage is haunted."

The old priest lay down. He began to doze and then to dream. But then he was disturbed by the clinking of pots and the rattle of pans in the kitchen below.

The good old body, thought the priest. *She's not as sour as she looks . . . getting me a meal.*

Before long, Father Ned heard the sound of footsteps and then a voice calling up the stairs: "Armaleg! Armaleg! Come to your supper!"

"Armaleg!" said the old priest. "Father Ned! Armaleg! I don't know."

Slowly the priest sat up and put together his creaking bones. "I'll feel better," he said. "Yes, I'll feel better with something inside me."

Father Ned made his way downstairs. The kitchen was lit with

dozens of colored candles, and around the table laden with food, the priest saw in the soft light the faces of many beautiful men and women.

"Ali!" said Father Ned. He took the place that had been left for him and smiled at the faces surrounding him. "I always say grace before a meal," he said.

The old priest closed his eyes. "Lord, bless this board," he said:

"Lord, bless this board,
Apple, ale, and rye.
May your angels guard us!
May devils fear and fly!"

When Father Ned opened his eyes again, the company of beautiful men and women, and the table, and the supper on it — they had all vanished.

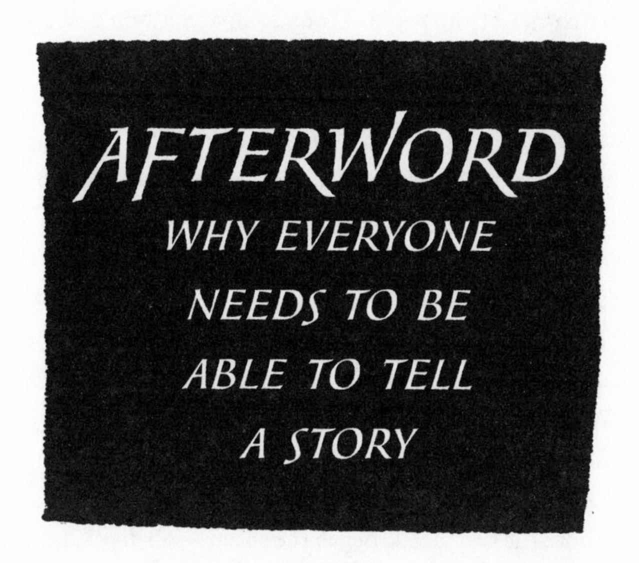

AFTERWORD

WHY EVERYONE NEEDS TO BE ABLE TO TELL A STORY

IT WAS COLD AND CLAMMY, AND I REALIZED I'D NEVER GET BACK to our holiday cottage before dark.

But as I walked along the riverbank, I saw a light coming toward me. No, the mist was playing tricks. The light wasn't moving. I was. It was a little stone cottage.

"I'm lost," I told the old man who opened the door. He had strange green eyes.

"I've only got one bed," the old man said in a light, lilting voice. "But I'll tell you what. You tell me a story and you can sleep by the fire."

Well, my head went empty. I couldn't think of a thing. You know how it is.

The old man's green eyes flickered. "Pity," he said. "I could have done with a story. Still, you can stay if you want." He waved toward

the far corner of the room. "Your companion won't be bothering you. Good night to you now."

My companion. He was a sheep! Dead as a dumpster.

I sat down by the fire, and soon as I closed my eyes I heard the cottage door creak. Then I saw two men creep into the room, cross to the far corner, and pick up the dead sheep.

Well, I followed them. Of course I did. I didn't want the poor old man thinking I'd rustled his dead sheep.

The two men hurried along the riverbank. Then one of them looked back over his shoulder.

"We're being followed!" he exclaimed.

"Come on!"

"Let's get him."

At once the two men dropped the sheep — *kerflup!* They ran back toward me, and me, I took off for the cottage. Fast as a hare.

You know what? I missed my footing and tripped into the water. Right down. Right under, and back up.

In the misty dark, I caught hold of a slimy tree root, and the two thieves stood on the bank and threw stones at me. As if I was a coconut.

"Come on," I heard one man say. "We're wasting our time."

And with that, they went back along the riverbank to the dead sheep.

I pulled on the root, but my feet slipped on the river mud.

I pulled again, but my hands slipped on the slimy root.

I pulled for a third time . . . and that's when I woke up.

Next morning, the first thing the old man said was, "Well, I fancy you've a story now."

"I have!" I exclaimed. "I have. The moment I closed my eyes —"

The old man waved his right hand, and his green eyes flickered. "I know," he said in his lilting voice. "That dream! I gave it to you. Everyone needs to be able to tell a story."

SOURCES AND NOTES

Each entry begins by identifying the source or sources (usually the earliest printed version) on which I have based my retelling. In the cases where I have changed the title of a tale, this identification also includes the original title of the tale.

MAGIC AND WONDER

— THE DARK HORSEMAN —

Ancient Legends, Mystic Charms, and Superstitions of Ireland by Jane F. "Speranza" Wilde (1887).

The town of Slane is a few miles west of Drogheda in County Meath, north of Dublin. My retelling of this tale has certainly been colored by a long affection for the magical paintings of Jack B. Yeats, teeming with country folk and horses, in which the everyday is fabulous and the fabulous everyday.

— THREE HEADS OF THE WELL —

Popular Rhymes and Nursery Tales: A Sequel to the Nursery Rhymes of England by James Orchard Halliwell-Phillipps (1849). Halliwell abridged the tale from a book of stories called *Three Kings of Colchester.*

It is, I fear, not easy to think of a benign stepmother in the canon of British folktales. A folktale stepmother is invariably the villain of the piece, although in this instance one might want to add that the king at Colchester was hasty, greedy, and stupid.

— THE SMALL-TOOTH DOG —

Household Tales with Other Traditional Remains by Sidney Oldall Addy (1895). Addy collected this tale in Norton in Derbyshire.

This is a jaunty variant of the tale known as "Beauty and the Beast." The earliest European version of the story comes from mid-sixteenth-century Italy, but it seems likely that the tale is very much older than that; indeed, tales about the interchangeability of human

and animal form (as also in werewolf tales) seem to hark back to prehistoric times, when humans were very much closer to the animal kingdom than they are today.

I have provided the tale with a completely new and modern setting.

— BUTTERFLY SOUL —

"The Soul as a Butterfly" in *Folktales of Ireland* edited by Sean O'Sullivan (1966); *Twenty Years A-Growing* by Maurice O'Sullivan (1933).

A number of religions (sometimes referred to as shamanistic religions) held that the soul or spirit could leave the body, converse with other beings in the spirit world, and perhaps acquire wisdom before returning to the body again. This is the belief underlying "Butterfly Soul," in which, as so often happens in folktale, a serious idea is borrowed from myth and treated with some charm and gaiety.

I do not think of the human characters in folktales as far removed from our world but, rather, as distillations of the people we meet every time we leave the house. And what the tales have to tell us is that there are wonders all around us every day and utter wonders if only we have the eyes to see them.

— KING OF THE CATS —

More English Fairy Tales by Joseph Jacobs (1894). Jacobs assembled the tale from five variants. The names Dildrum and Doldrum come from *Lancashire Legends, Traditions, Pageants, Sports, etc.* by J. Harland and T. T. Wilkinson (1873). I have chosen to retell this tale as a dramatic monologue, spoken by a grave digger.

— THE BAKER'S DAUGHTER —

"The Owl was a Baker's Daughter" in *Nursery Rhymes and Nursery Tales* by J. O. Halliwell-Phillipps (1843).

This tale survives in a number of variants, and this version comes from Herefordshire. At the heart of it is a tradition that has evidently been in circulation in England for at least four hundred years for it was known to William Shakespeare. In *Hamlet,* act 4, scene 5, Ophelia says, "They say the owl was a baker's daughter. Lord, we know what we are, but know not what we may be!"

—— *THE DEAD MOON* ——

"Legends of the Lincolnshire Cars" by Mrs. M. C. Balfour in *Folk-Lore, Vol. II* (1891).

Mrs. Balfour says that she heard the story from a girl of nine, who had heard it from her grandmother. "But I think," she writes, "it was tinged by her own fancy, which seemed to lean to eerie things, and she certainly reveled in the gruesome descriptions, fairly making my flesh creep with her words and gestures."

I have kept very close to the original but modified the heavy Lincolnshire dialect.

ADVENTURES AND LEGENDS

—— *THE SLUMBER KING* ——

"A Popular Tale in Glamorgan" in *Recollections and Anecdotes of Edward Williams* by Elijah Waring (1850); *Celtic Folklore, Welsh and Manx* by Sir John Rhys (1901). I have taken the verse quotation from

"The Prophecy of Britain" in *The Earliest Welsh Poetry* translated by Joseph P. Clancy (1970).

The tradition of the sleeping hero who will awake with his warriors and fight one last victorious battle is known throughout Europe. Charlemagne (Charles the Great, King of the Franks), Barbarossa (Frederick I of Germany), and the greatest of the Irish heroes, Fionn McCumhaill, are all said to be sleepers; and in Wales and England, slumber legends associate Arthur with Craig y Ddinas (Rock of the Fortress) eighteen miles northeast of Swansea, as well as with Sewingshields in Northumberland and Richmond in Yorkshire.

In Welsh lore, the eagle is a royal emblem and a herald of calamity. Here, the Golden Eagle represents Arthur and his warriors while the Black Eagle represents Arthur's enemies.

Of all British folk heroes, Arthur is the greatest. In folktale, legend, and literature he is *Rex quondam rexque futurus,* the once and future king who successfully led Celtic resistance to the Anglo-Saxon invaders and will one day return to "conquer the whole island of Britain." Never has there been a hero of such ubiquity: king of word and song and screen; king of singular and haunting places; king of time.

—— *THE GREEN CHILDREN* ——

Chronicon Anglicanum by Ralph of Coggeshall.

Ralph, who lived in the middle of the twelfth century, was abbot of the Cistercian monastery at Little Coggeshall near Colchester and a lively chronicler of English history. He heard about the green children directly from Sir Richard de Caine, who features in the story. Ralph says the green children were found at Woolpit, between Stowmarket and Bury St Edmunds.

As it stands, the story is a very strange and haunting mixture of

historical truth and much earlier vegetation myth (green coming up out of the ground). Quite how the two became combined, we cannot tell.

— THE LAST OF THE PICTS —

"The Pechs" in *Popular Rhymes of Scotland* by Robert Chambers (1826).

Chambers assembled this story from snatches he had heard from several sources. He noted that the tradition of the Picts as an extinct people was well known in the Scottish Lowlands but that recent scholarship had led him to suppose that "the Picts are far from extinct, being the ancestors of our modern Highlanders." The Picts flourished in Scotland until about 500 CE, after which they were driven into northeast Scotland and the Orkney Islands by the Scots (who came to Scotland from northern Ireland).

— THE OLDEST OF THEM ALL —

"The Long-Lived Ancestors" in *Welsh Fairy-Tales and Other Stories* by P. H. Emerson (1894).

The tale was collected by the author (perhaps better known as a very fine photographer) on the island of Anglesey.

Its cast of birds and animals comes from the great collection of Welsh hero tales known as *The Mabinogion.* In the tale that tells the story of Cawlwyd and Olwen, King Arthur's knights ask for the help of the blackbird, the stag, the owl, the eagle, and the salmon in their search for Mabon, the son of Modron, who was snatched from his mother when he was three nights old.

— FAIR GRUAGACH —

"The Fair Gruagach, Son of the King of Eirinn" in *Popular Tales of the West Highlands* by John Francis Campbell of Islay (1860–1862).

This tale, first told in Gaelic by Alexander McNeill, a fisherman on the Hebridean island of Barra, is one of the quite magnificent group of legendary folktales revolving around Finn and his Irish warriors collected by Campbell and his team of recorders in the northwest of Scotland. It is full of echoes of Celtic and Norse mythology and combines the world of the early heroic tribesmen with that of medieval romance — a story masculine and feminine, earthy, magical.

— *THE PEDDLER OF SWAFFHAM* —

The Diary of Abraham de la Pryme edited by Charles Jackson (1870); *The Norfolk Garland* by John Glyde (1872).

In 1462, a peddler paid for the new north aisle and contributed to the cost of the new spire of Swaffham Church in Norfolk. This is recorded in the fifteenth-century Black Book kept in Swaffham Church Library. The church additions were actually begun in 1452, but not completed until the mid-sixteenth century.

The motif of a dreamer who makes a journey only to be sent back home where some treasure or truth awaits him is common to many countries.

I see the tale as containing three truths: do not be too coldly rational but follow your dreams; persevere; and, thirdly, the greatest treasures are to be found on your doorstep — in other words, we must look to our own homes and communities to find real value in our lives.

— *THE WILDMAN* —

Chronicon Anglicanum by Ralph of Coggeshall.

Ralph of Coggeshall (see note to "The Green Children") tells us that a merman was caught by fishermen from Orford in Suffolk during the reign of Henry II (1154-1189). He was completely naked and

covered with hair. He was imprisoned in the newly built castle, did not recognize the cross, did not talk despite torture, returned voluntarily into captivity after having eluded three rows of nets, and then disappeared, never to be seen again.

— THE LAMBTON WORM —

More English Fairy Tales by Joseph Jacobs (1894); *Notes on the Folk-Lore of the Northern Counties of England and the Borders* by William Henderson (1866).

This is one of the finest of some seventy stories and songs associating worms (derived from the Anglo-Saxon *wyrm:* serpent) and dragons with places in the British Isles. It is also the subject of a racy nineteenth-century ballad from the north of England.

The Lambton Estate, near Chester-le-Street in County Durham, has belonged to the family for eight hundred years. Childe Lambton (later Sir John Lambton, Knight of Rhodes) lived in the mid-fifteenth century. The vow he made to the wise woman is sometimes called Jepthah's vow: in the book of Judges, Jepthah vows to the Lord that if He will give him victory, he will sacrifice "whoever comes forth from the doors of my house," and as a result has to sacrifice his own daughter. Of the nine generations succeeding Childe Lambton, we can account for six, and not one died in his own bed.

Where did this tale come from, and what does it mean? Maybe the childe brought it back with him from the Island of Rhodes: one fourteenth-century grand master of the Knights Hospitaller of St. John was reputed to have been a dragon slayer. In any event, the worm is both a powerful symbol of moral evil (a symbol of the profane life led by the childe before he mended his ways) and an enemy worth having. He proves the courage of his conqueror.

— SHONKS AND THE DRAGON —

The History of Hertfordshire by Nathaniel Salmon (1728); *The Folklore of Hertfordshire* by Doris Jones-Baker (1977); *Albion: A Guide to Legendary Britain* by Jennifer Westwood (1985).

The tombstone of Sir Piers Shonks lies in a recess in the north wall of the nave of Brent Pelham Church. And above it is a tablet with the inscription:

> *Nothing of Cadmus nor St George, those names*
> *Of great renown, survives them but their fames;*
> *Time was so sharp set as to make no Bones*
> *Of theirs, nor of their monumental Stones.*
> *But Shonks one serpent kills, t'other defies,*
> *And in this wall as in a fortress lies.*

These lines, telling us that Shonks first killed a dragon and then outwitted the devil by having himself buried inside a wall (a motif that occurs in several British folktales), were probably written in the late sixteenth century. The tombstone, however, dates from the thirteenth century, while Piers Shonks may well be one Peter Shank who lived in Brent Pelham in the fourteenth century. So we can say that the legend as we know it today, combining two elements (dragon slaying and tricking the devil), took shape between four and six hundred years ago.

To my ear, Shonks sounds a rather improbable name for a dragon slayer. So I've introduced a little humor into the story, and am also responsible for giving our hero a daughter and having her attend Sir Piers when he fights the dragon.

— SEA TONGUE —

"The Undersea Bells" in *Forgotten Folk-Tales of the English Counties* by Ruth Tongue (1970).

The tale was collected from Norfolk fishermen in 1905 and 1928 by the Reverend John Tongue, who was at one time Vicar of Mundesley. The tale of a church bell or bells pealing under the water is common to several places along the Norfolk and Suffolk coast, including Dunwich, as well as to Cardigan Bay and the Lancashire coast.

I see my "fractured narrative" as a kind of sound-story for different voices (or for one voice taking the different parts), and it owes something to the idea that everything in our universe, every stick and stone, has its own voice.

FAIRIES AND LITTLE PEOPLE

— THE PIPER AND THE POOKA —

"The Piper and the Puca" in *Fairy and Folk Tales of the Irish Peasantry* by W. B. Yeats (1888). This tale was translated for Yeats by Douglas Hyde from the Irish of his own *Leabhar Sgeulaigheachta.*

The pooka (also spelled *puca* and *pucca*) who overtakes the piper and trots him to the top of the holy mountain of Croagh Patrick is a supernatural animal. The weeping women for whom Patsy plays are Irish death spirits known as *banshees.* The *banshees* always have long unfastened hair, and they wear green dresses and gray cloaks. Their eyes are red as embers from their continual weeping.

Croagh Patrick (Patrick's mountain) in County Mayo has long been venerated as a holy mountain. Nowadays, it is climbed each year by a great gathering of pilgrims.

— *TOM TIT TOT* —

Ipswich Journal (1878). The tale was contributed to the journal by Mrs. A. Walter Thomas, who heard it as a girl from her old West Suffolk nurse.

This wonderful tale, so robust and witty, is the English counterpart to the Grimms' tale of "Rumpelstilzchen" in *Kinder- und Hausmärchen* (1812). The study of it still considered authoritative is Edward Clodd's *Tom Tit Tot: An Essay on Savage Philosophy in Folk-Tale* (1898).

The language of the original is so distinctive that I have done little more than transliterate it, trying always to keep the music of Suffolk speech.

— *MONDAY, TUESDAY* —

"The Legend of Knockgrafton" in *Fairy Legends and Traditions of the South of Ireland* by Thomas Crofton Croker (1825).

Throughout Europe, folktales have been *incidentally* recorded by historians, antiquarians, diarists, and others for many hundreds of years. But Thomas Crofton Croker was the first man in the British Isles to set out to record folktales in the field, straight from the mouths of people who had heard them from their parents or grandparents or other people living in the community. So "Monday, Tuesday" has a certain historical interest.

For me, however, this tale spells storytime in the little cottage in the Chilterns where I spent my childhood. I see now my father telling the tale to the accompaniment of his Welsh harp; I hear the drip of the rain from some overhead gutter onto the window ledge.

This is where my love of folktales began.

Lusmore (literally, the "large plant") is the Irish name for the foxglove, a plant with many fairy associations, used by the little people but also powerful against them.

— THE CHANGELING —

The Fairy Mythology by Thomas Keightley (1828).

The tale describes an incident at Caerlaverock in Nithsdale in Scotland. The tradition whereby the fairies exchange a human child for a child of their own is well known throughout the British Isles. The fairies stole children either because they admired their beauty, because they wanted them as future husbands and wives, or because they needed them to give as payment to the devil. It was customary for the fairies to steal a child before it was christened.

I have made my storyteller the village priest.

— THE FARMER AND THE BOGGART —

Tales and Rhymes in the Lindsey Folk-Speech by Mabel Peacock (1886).

Several versions of this tale were collected in the late nineteenth century. This one comes from Mumby near Alford in Lincolnshire.

About three feet tall, boggarts have weathered faces and shaggy hair, and they usually wear tattered brown clothes. They have sour tempers and are often nuisance makers, but they are not harmful; when the boggart in this tale has been thwarted, he does nothing worse than scaring people at night and stealing farm tools.

— THE SHEPHERD'S TALE —

Untitled story in *Cambrian Superstitions* by W. Howells (1831); *British Goblins* by William Wirt Sikes (1880).

Howells says that this event took place on Frennifawr (now usually spelled Frenifawr), a mountain about 1,300 feet high, eight miles south of Cardigan and eight miles southwest of Newcastle Emlyn.

The fairies show Dai the well and warn him not to drink a drop; before long, he drinks from it. Fairies invariably deal with humans on their own terms; and if a human breaks the prescribed rules, he or she (as in "Monday, Tuesday") may be punished, and contact between the two worlds is abruptly broken off.

—— FAIRY OINTMENT ——

Traditions, Legends, Superstitions, and Sketches of Devonshire, on the Borders of the Tamar and Tavy by Mrs. A. E. Bray (1838); *Popular Romances of the West of England* by Robert Hunt (1865); *English Fairy Tales* by Joseph Jacobs (1890).

I have known and loved this tale since I was a small child. I think of it as a kind of metaphor. We can all look at the world around us with, as it were, two eyes: we can look with the eye that is interested in the physical world, and in all that is factual and verifiable; and we can look with the eye of imagination.

But this is as far as the metaphor goes. Now the tale takes over again . . .

—— CHARGER ——

"The Fairy-Chapman" from *The Fairy Mythology* by Thomas Keightley (1828).

This tale comes from the Isle of Man. Manx fairies are said to have a fondness for riding, and riding "not on little steeds of their own," says Keightley, "or on the small breed of the country, but on the large English and Irish horses, which are brought over and kept by the gentry."

— DATHERA DAD —

Household Tales with Other Traditional Remains by Sidney Oldall Addy (1895).

Addy collected this snippet in the plague village of Eyam in Derbyshire. Its origin seems to be part of the fourth episode in *The History of Tom Thumbe* (1621). The meaning of *Dathera* is uncertain.

— YALLERY BROWN —

"Legends of the Lincolnshire Cars" by Mrs. M. C. Balfour in *Folk-Lore, Vol. II* (1891).

Under the general headings of "Legends of the Cars" and "Legends of the Lincolnshire Cars," Mabel Balfour — a niece of Robert Louis Stevenson — printed nine astonishing Lincolnshire folktales in the journal *Folk-Lore* during 1891. I have kept very close to the original but have modified the heavy Lincolnshire dialect.

MEN AND WOMEN

— THE THREE BLOWS —

The Physicians of Myddvai by Mr. Rees of Tonn (1861).

Rees collected the story in 1841 from the oral recitation of three natives of Myddfai and says the events described in the tale took place during the twelfth century. The tale goes on to tell how the three sons (the eldest was named Rhiwallon) were said to have met their mother on a number of occasions after she had returned to Llyn y Fan Fach.

This is another tale I have known for as long as I can remember. It is above all an elegy, and unusually for a folk tale, it is distinguished by gravitas and a sense of tragic inevitability.

— *THE FINE FIELD OF FLAX* —

"The Fine Field of Lint" in *The Folklore of Orkney and Shetland* by Ernest W. Marwick (1975).

This tale comes from the island of South Ronaldsay in Orkney. The gloup (or chasm) to which the girl walks is the Gloup of Root near Halcro Head.

There are certain folktales that seem to impress themselves forever on the mind. This innocent, tear-bright story is one of them, "The Wildman" (p. 101) another. In each, the pivot is the relationship between the outsider and a community that will not accept them, and in both retellings, it is the outsider who speaks.

— *SEA WOMAN* —

"The Mermaid Wife" in *The Fairy Mythology* by Thomas Keightley (1828).

This tale comes from the island of Unst in Shetland and is one of many that link the lives of humans and seals. I have chosen to retell this story as a tale within a tale in which, as I hope becomes clear, the voice in the shell is a kind of externalization of the girl's own memory and sense of loss. In writing it, I have drawn on firsthand experience of an afternoon spent in the company of a seal in the island of Rousay in Orkney.

— *THE BLACK BULL OF NORWAY* —

"The Black Bull of Norroway" in *Popular Rhymes of Scotland* by Robert Chambers (1826).

As it stands, this fine tale is certainly in corrupt form and almost

reads like two separate stories. I think it certain that, in some earlier version now lost, the knight would have turned out to be the black bull, released from some enchantment. This is just hinted at in the snatch of song Flora sings to the knight and in the words "And she telled him a' that had befa'en her, and he telled her a' that had happened to him." In my version, therefore, I have tried to supply the missing link and make the tale whole again.

—— MOSSYCOAT ——

Folktales of England edited by Katharine M. Briggs and Ruth L. Tongue (1965). This tale was collected by T. W. Thompson from the gypsy Taimie Boswell in Northumberland in 1915.

"Mossycoat" is one of the two best variants ("Rashin Coatie" is the other) of the tale of "Cinderella." The story of rags-to-riches Cinderella became very popular in England following the publication in 1729 of the translation of Charles Perrault's *Histoires ou contes du temps passé* (1697), but the bones of this folktale are more than one thousand years old.

Taimie Boswell was so strong and distinctive a storyteller that I have thought it inappropriate to impose new constituents or a new voice on this oral tale. I have confined myself to transcribing and translating his version from dialect; for example, "If only dey'd de clo'es, dey'd be al right, dey thought, as dey considered deirselves . . ." into standard English, and here and there clarifying and abridging the text.

—— TAM LIN ——

Minstrelsy of the Scottish Border by Sir Walter Scott (1802–1803).

Scott collated this magnificent ballad from several printed versions and oral recitations that he had himself collected. It contains a number of motifs familiar in folktale: the summoning of a spirit by

breaking the branch, the fairy ride, the rescue from Fairyland, and the essential ill will of the Fairy Queen.

I have followed Scott but here and there added a line or a quatrain from some other source.

— *YELLOW LILY* —

"The Son of the King of Erin and the Giant of Loch Lein" in *Myths and Folk-Lore of Ireland* by Jeremiah Curtin (1890).

The episode in which Yellow Lily instructs the prince to kill her and lay her flesh on the cloth echoes the Norse myth in which Thor allows one of his goats to be eaten and then brings it back to life again.

— *THE GREEN MIST* —

"Legends of the Lincolnshire Cars" by Mrs. M. C. Balfour in *Folk-Lore, Vol. II* (1891).

I have introduced into the story itself some of the folk customs alluded to in the source's preamble. I have also converted some of the reported action into direct action with the use of dialogue and have attempted a description of the green mist itself.

WITS, TRICKS, AND LAUGHTER

— *A VILLAGE OF FOOLS* —

The Book of Noodles by W. A. Clouston (1888). Clouston says he took his version from Robert Thoroton's *A History of Nottinghamshire*

(1797). The detail of the cheeses comes from the version of the tale in *English Fairy and Other Folk Tales* edited by E. S. Hartland (1890).

The idea of a village peopled entirely by simpletons is not peculiar to Gotham in Nottinghamshire. No less than forty-five villages in England are the butt of similar stories.

King John here makes an appearance in his traditional folk role of a Bad King, as he was described in *1066 and All That* by W. C. Sellar and R. J. Yeatman (1930). His very presence threatens the livelihoods of the villagers.

— MARE'S EGGS —

A Dictionary of British Folk-Tales in the English Language by Katharine M. Briggs (1970). The story comes from the *Thompson Notebooks* and was collected from Gus Gray, Cleethorpes, in 1914.

— THE COW THAT ATE THE PIPER —

Folktales of Ireland edited and translated by Sean O'Sullivan (1966). Collected in 1940 by Seosamh Ó Dála from Seán Bruic, an eighty-four-year-old fisherman in County Kerry.

Forty versions of this tale have been collected in Ireland.

— POLL —

"The Miner and the Parrot" in *A Dictionary of British Folk-Tales* by Katharine M. Briggs (1970). This anecdote was contributed by M. E. Nash-Williams in about 1940.

— THE WISE MEN OF GOTHAM —

The Book of Noodles by W. A. Clouston (1888). I have also taken one or two details from other sources.

— MAGPIES IN THE CRABTREE —

"The Pynots in the Crabtree" in *Household Tales with Other Traditional Remains* by Sidney Oldall Addy (1895).

Addy collected this surreal mouthful in Norton in Derbyshire.

— THE RIDDLER —

The English and Scottish Popular Ballads edited by Francis James Child (1882–1898).

The riddle contest for high stakes is common to myth and folktale. In this ballad, the last question is something of a trick. But the youngest daughter is able to answer it, and so innocence worsts evil.

Hempseed and broom are both plants highly valued by the lover.

GHOSTS

— BOO! —

A Dictionary of British Folk-Tales by Katharine M. Briggs (1970).

The original version of this tale is sometimes held to be the shortest of all short stories. This is wrong! How about this one, all of seventeen words long:

"He woke up frightened, and reached for the matches; and the matches were put in his hand."

— SAMUEL'S GHOST —

"Sammle's Ghost" in "Legends of the Cars" by Mrs. M. C. Balfour in *Folk-Lore, Vol. II* (1891).

After she came to live in the Ancholme Valley of Lincolnshire, Mrs. Balfour collected an earthy, gruesome, and haunting body of folktales. Among the well-known tales she wrote down (all of them in heavy dialect, just as she heard them) were "The Dead Moon" and "Yallery Brown."

Mrs. Balfour collected the story of Samuel's ghost from the youngest of her informants, a girl of nine called Fanny, who had heard this and other tales from her grandfather. "Sammle's Ghost" is so wonderfully well told that the best thing a reteller can do is "translate" the dialect into modern English and keep well out of the way.

— SLAM AND THE GHOSTS —

"The Two Ghosts" in *A Dictionary of British Folk-Tales* by Katharine M. Briggs (1970). The tale was told by Margaret McKay of Aberdeen to Kenneth S. Goldstein of the School of Scottish Studies.

And the lesson is: it is never safe to mock a ghost.

— THE DAUNTLESS GIRL —

The Recreations of a Norfolk Antiquary by Walter Rye (1920).

Although the squire thinks it "strange and unnatural" that his mother should walk, many folktales bear witness to the fact that whatever is concealed has intrinsic power, and may make the person who concealed it restless after death. Great wrong inflicted on another person, great wrong sustained, death before baptism, burial with a limb missing (see "Samuel's Ghost," p. 294), a promise made to a dying person and subsequently broken: these factors, too, may prompt a person to walk as a ghost.

— BILLY —

"The Wee Tailor" in *A Dictionary of British Folk-Tales* by Katharine M. Briggs (1970). Told by Andrew Stewart to Hamish Henderson of the School of Scottish Studies.

No more than a couple of hundred words long in the original, this tale contains a pair of familiar motifs — a fear test and a bloodthirsty ghost who tries to kill a person for food — and there are several Celtic folktales quite similar to it. I have left unchanged the exchange between the tailor and the ghost.

— FEAR AND FLY —

"The Minister and the Fairies" in *Household Tales, with other Traditional Remains* by Sidney Oldall Addy (1895).

This tale, one of fifty-two collected by Addy, comes from Calver in Derbyshire. Like "Slam and the Ghosts" and "Monday, Tuesday," it offers the reader a lesson in how to treat the supernatural.

ACKNOWLEDGMENTS

My sister Sally and I slept on bunk beds. I was on top because I was the older (and still am!). Often my father came in to our bedroom carrying his Welsh harp and said-and-sang folktales to us: stories from East Anglia and, above all, stories of the fairy folk from Wales and Ireland. These were the first tales I remember hearing and sharing, and so my first acknowledgments are properly to my father and my sister.

It has been such a privilege to see the many roughs drawn by Frances Castle, who has established a magical way of seeing entirely appropriate to these tales. I am so grateful to her.

At Walker Books, I want particularly to thank my editor, Denise Johnstone-Burt, with Daisy Jellicoe, Megan Middleton, Alice Primmer, Marina Rodrigues, and the art editor Ben Norland, not only for so skilfully shaping a book made to last but for their lovely enthusiasm in doing so.

On the home front, my thanks to my bright-eyed PA, Karen Clarke, and my loving wife, Linda, for reading, rereading, ordering, reordering, and typing.

My intention in retelling folktales is not to use them as springboards so much as to reclothe them in clean, bright, direct language. I'm always conscious of how they sound, and they stand, I suppose, somewhere between the oral and the literary. As a patron of the Society for Storytelling, I want to acknowledge the fine work of so many storytellers in keeping the oral tradition alive.

Et nova et vetera. I have grown old, almost without noticing it! And I have six eager young grandchildren who, with the help of stories (and parents who read to them), are all growing into their own stories. To them, I happily dedicate this book.

Kevin Crossley-Holland
Chalk Hill, June 2018

BIOGRAPHIES

KEVIN CROSSLEY-HOLLAND is a prizewinning writer for children, a well-known poet and translator from Anglo-Saxon, and the author of a memoir of childhood, *The Hidden Roads,* admired by Rowan Williams as "a lovely, poignant book, not wasting a word and evoking place in a deep way." His most recent books are *Heartsong* (2016), a novella with full-color illustrations by Jane Ray set in the Venice orphanage where Vivaldi was master of music, and *Norse Myths: Tales of Odin, Thor, and Loki* (2017).

His ghost story *Storm* was awarded the Carnegie Medal, while *The Seeing Stone* won the *Guardian* Children's Fiction Prize. The Arthur trilogy has won worldwide critical praise and has been translated into twenty-five languages, and its successor, *Gatty's Tale,* was short-listed for the Carnegie Medal.

He has worked with many well-known artists and composers, including Arthur Bliss, William Mathias, and Bob Chilcott. He collaborated with Nicola LeFanu on a widely performed opera for children, *The Green Children,* and with Cecilia McDowall on a cantata for the National Children's Choir, *The Girl from Aleppo* (2018).

He has a Minnesotan wife, Linda, two sons (Kieran and Dominic), and two daughters (Oenone and Eleanor). He is an honorary fellow of St. Edmund Hall, Oxford, a patron of the Society for Storytelling and the Story Museum, and a Fellow of the Royal Society of Literature. He has been awarded honorary doctorates by Anglia Ruskin University and the University of Worcester and was president of the School Library Association from 2012 until 2017.

FRANCES CASTLE is an award-winning illustrator who has worked across a variety of different mediums, from children's books to the BBC History website. Her art is inspired by comic books, vintage black-and-white book illustrations, and early-twentieth-century prints. Since 2011 she has been running her boutique record label, Clay Pipe Music, for which she creates beautifully illustrated limited-edition vinyl LPs. Frances Castle lives in North London.